the Stepsister's Tale

the Stepsister's Tale

TRACY BARRETT

HARLEQUIN® TEEN

Published in India 2014 by
Harlequin India Private Limited
R - Tech Park, 13th Floor,
Off Western Express Highway
Nirlon Complex Goregoan (E)
Mumbai - 400 063

ISBN 978-93-5106-652-1

Printed and bound by Thomson Press (India) Ltd.

For everyone who struggles with building a family
made up of new members, new configurations, and new relationships

prologue

The house—it was too small to be called a palace—sat at the top of a hill, overlooking thick woods and a river. At a distance, it appeared to be the same as when Mamma was a girl: stately, welcoming, a place of parties and balls, where visitors came to spend long weeks, where Mamma and Papa had danced until dawn the night of their wedding. But once a traveler drew near, changes appeared. Holes gaped in the roof; some of the windows lacked glass, and most were bare of the curtains that would have softened their black emptiness. The few remaining shutters dangled unevenly and banged when a high wind blew.

Inside, the grand stairway swept up in huge curves, gaps and broken boards making the going treacherous. Once upstairs, a curious visitor who tapped the breastplate of the suit of armor would raise twittering from the nests in the beams high above. The corridors were streaked with white bird droppings and were so dark that you never saw the faces in the portraits that hung crookedly on the walls, their frames riddled with wormholes, until you were almost upon them. And even then, they didn't look back. Within their grimy outlines the faces of beautiful ladies and handsome gentlemen stared out blindly but still proudly at the few who passed by in the dim halls.

And for many years, only two people had walked through those dark corridors: descendants of the proud women and men depicted in the portraits, the last of their line—Lady Margaret's daughters, Jane and Maude Montjoy.

1

Jane stopped at the gate, which was half-overgrown with shrubs and vines, and put down her basket. She balanced on one foot and scratched her calf with the toes of the other. She could tell that Mamma hadn't come back yet. The house looked dead, just a lot of wood and stone. It was only when Mamma was home that it looked alive.

She sighed and lifted her basket. It was light enough—berries were getting scarce, and the weather was too dry for mushrooms, except in the deepest part of the woods, where she didn't dare to venture. She had found only a handful of sticks suitable for firewood.

The drive curved around to the wide stone steps leading up to the massive front door. Jane took a shortcut across the brown grass, glad that Mamma wasn't there to see her. *Only stable boys tread paths,* she always scolded. Once, when Jane was particularly tired, she had reminded Mamma that there weren't stable boys at Halsey Hall anymore. Mamma's look of bewildered hurt and betrayal had stabbed like an icicle at

Jane's heart, and she never again mentioned the lack of stable boys—or of a proper stable—and never again walked across the grass while Mamma was home.

She climbed the uneven steps and leaned her weight into the door, which opened reluctantly. "Maudie?" she called. She heard scuttling to her left, where the North Parlor and the ballroom lay abandoned. She sighed again. Her sister was no doubt hiding a new treasure—perhaps some small gift from Hugh or his mother, Hannah Herb-Woman, or a brightly colored stone or snakeskin. Jane waited a few minutes and then opened the door, a little too noisily, so that Maude would have a chance to pretend she had merely wandered into the vacant part of the house for no reason.

Jane crossed the North Parlor and looked through the doorway—empty now of its door—into the ballroom. Maude seemed small in that vast space, her footsteps echoing as she crossed the scuffed and dusty floor that Jane dimly remembered gleaming, long ago. Now the grand room was a home for bats and mice, whose smelly nests cluttered the corners. The musician's gallery above them was empty save for a few broken chairs where the black-coated cellists and flutists and trumpeters used to make music that moved dancers' feet around the floor.

Maude's shabby dress, so faded that it was impossible to tell its original color, was too tight on her. Her hair hung in lank strands; one of the reasons Mamma had gone to the city was to buy soap so they could wash more often. By the way her sister was studiously avoiding looking into a dark corner behind her, Jane guessed that this was where she had stashed her treasure.

"Mamma still isn't back," Maude said.

"I know." When Mamma went to the little village down the hill she would return the same evening, but several times a year she made the longer trip to the city to barter cheese and eggs for soap and flour and the other things they couldn't grow or make on their own, and she stayed overnight before returning home. But she had never been away this long before.

Ladies do not farm, Mamma always said when they asked why they couldn't grow wheat and barley. *If a lady wishes to have a pretty pastime, keeping chickens and making cheese are suitable. She may tend a flower bed, and she may gather berries and nuts. She may embroider and make lace. She may exchange what she does not need with other gentlewomen who have an excess of what they themselves produce. But that is all. We are ladies, and ladies do not do heavy work.*

Yes, Mamma, they always answered, and then they would go out to chop wood or shovel out the stable or do their best to repair the chicken coop. *Yes, Mamma,* as dutifully and politely as if they really were the ladies that Mamma said they were.

Jane and Maude went through the main hall with its magnificent staircase and into the South Parlor, now not only a parlor but their sitting room, kitchen, and dining room, as well. Jane surveyed the room with satisfaction. As soon as Mamma had left, the sisters fell to work, cleaning and straightening, taking rugs outside to beat dirt from them, pulling and shoving the heavy chairs into the sun to bake out the mildew in their cushions. Now, clean curtains hung over sparkling windows, a small stack of firewood lay on the hearth, finally emptied of ash and cinders, and scraps of cloth covered the worn spots on the chairs that they had carefully positioned over the worst holes and stains in the carpet.

When Mamma came back, she wouldn't say how nice everything looked. She always acted as though invisible servants took care of things and never acknowledged that her own daughters, the last of the Halsey line, blistered their hands and reddened their eyes by firelight to keep things decent.

They had watched her disappear down the long drive that summer day, sitting erect on old Saladin, who'd been loaded down with packs full of cheese and butter. It had been—how long ago? Jane counted on her fingers. Two days to clean the South Parlor, another to muck out the stable, a fourth when Maude hunted herbs while Jane worked on the heap of mending and darning in the work basket, and today. Five days. Jane tried to ignore the wiggle of fear in her belly.

To conceal her worry, she asked, "Did you find any eggs? I'm starving!"

"Four," Maude said. "We can have two each."

"And I found some wood. Let's make supper now, shall we?"

Soon, the water in the little pot hanging over the hearth was boiling, and Maude gently slipped the brown eggs into it.

Jane sat while her sister tended the fire. Once, supper had meant a roasted duck or the leg of a pig, with vegetables and soft bread, and if they had been good, a sweet afterward. But there were no more cooks in the house, and the kitchen, with its fireplace of a size to roast a whole boar and mixing bowls large enough to bathe a baby in, had long been cold. Jane barely remembered how it had looked with servants bustling about, their cheeks red from the fire, their faces shiny with sweat. Rich smells of roasting meats and yeasty breads and bubbling sauces would intoxicate her. Cook would find something sweet for Jane, always with a second helping to carry back up to Maude, who'd been too little to come down the stairs. Now, the heavy iron spoons and spits and ladles rusted under layers of cobwebs, and the bitter smell of old ashes hung in the damp air.

"Janie?" Maude was standing over her, holding out a bowl with two steaming eggs in it.

It didn't take long to eat their meal. Maude licked her bowl but Jane pretended not to see this lapse in manners; her sister had seemed even hungrier than usual lately, ever since she had starting outgrowing her clothes, seemingly overnight. But neither of them had been getting enough to eat for months, and what little they had was monotonously the same. Maybe Mamma would surprise them with bakery-made sweets when she came back, or a ham, or even something exotic, like grapes or oranges.

Jane left Maude to wash up with almost the last of the soap and went to do the evening milking. When she returned, Maude was squatting at the hearth, poking the fire with a long stick. She looked up as her sister came in, her brows drawn together in worry. "When is Mamma coming home, Janie?"

Jane was about to snap, "How should I know?" but she softened when she saw Maude's lower lip trembling. She forced herself to speak carelessly. "Soon. She must have had business in town."

"What business, Janie?"

Rather than answering, Jane said, "It's still light out. Do you want to go on an explore?"

Maude leaped to her feet. "Now?"

The last time they had ventured up the stairs, Jane had stepped on a board that split under her foot, and although she had clutched wildly at the banister, she'd crashed heavily to the stone floor. She had lain there, dazed, for a few moments, and when she'd raised her head, Maude was peering at her,

her eyes wide. Jane had forced herself to sit up and brush her dress off calmly. She'd said, "The step above it looks good—let's see if you can stretch your legs far enough to reach over the hole." They had made it to the second story safely, and Jane had carefully hidden the purple bruise on her hip and her sore shoulder from Mamma after she'd come home.

This time they arrived upstairs without incident, placing their feet carefully at the edges of the steps and holding tight to the banister. They walked hand in hand down the long corridor. When she was very small, Maude used to shrink from the portraits lining the walls. "It's only Great-Great-Grandmamma Esther," Jane would reassure her, speaking of the painting of the stiff-looking little girl clutching an equally stiff-looking kitten. "They say that her mother was descended from the fairy-folk." Or, "only Great-Grandpapa Edwin," of the strong-jawed young man in evening clothes, holding a book and staring down his long nose at his descendants standing in the dust. "He was the one who had our hunting lodge built."

Jane would recite each room's story to her sister, who always listened in solemn silence. "This was Grandmamma's chamber," Jane would say. "She was very particular about her bed and couldn't sleep without three pillows, stuffed with the down of white geese." Through the dim light they would look respectfully at the bed. They knew that if they touched the pillows, still heaped up as though waiting for Grandmamma, their hands would go through the rotten silk cases and they would find the famous goose down full of bugs.

"Her bed curtains were of the finest damask," Jane would continue. "Damask was the only cloth beautiful enough for her taste and still heavy enough to keep out light and sound." The weight of the heavy, dark red cloth had made most of it pull through the shiny curtain rings—brass, Jane said, although Maude insisted they were gold—and it dangled in uneven loops around the dark, deeply carved bedposts.

Mamma's room, with its delicate furniture and dingy wallpaper that had once been bright with rosebuds, was the best. The girls took turns choosing what to look at first. It might be the cupboard where the ball gowns still hung, holes in most of them, the musty odor making Maude sneeze. Jane had once suggested cutting up one of the dresses and re-piecing it to make a dress for herself or her sister; Mamma had been so shocked at the idea of using a silk gown for everyday use that Jane never mentioned it again. Or they might turn to one of the drawers where the delicate undergarments and stockings and handkerchiefs retained something of their satiny sheen, or the heavy jewelry box on the dresser.

Everything of value had been sold long ago, but the glass beads and rings and brooches that Mamma had worn to costume parties still glittered coldly on black velvet. The girls would take them out reverently, holding them up to their chests or ears or fingers, never daring to put them on, asking each other, "How do I look? Which one suits me best?"

Today it was the turn of Papa's bedchamber. Their bare feet did not tap on the stone floor, the way Mamma's shoes used to, and the boom of Papa's boots was hard to remember. Jane pushed open the oaken door, showing the faded carpet and the broken riding crop that Papa had flung down years ago.

Maude took a step inside, then halted. "Why don't we look at one of the guest rooms instead?"

"It's not their turn. We have to do things the right way. We're *Halseys.*" She imitated Mamma's tone, and Maude snickered, and they entered. Papa had sold almost everything, even his guns and the signet ring he had inherited from his own father. Jane had rarely entered the room in the old days, and even now she found it uncomfortable to venture past the door. What drew their eyes in that dim chamber was the portrait of Mamma as a young woman, above the fireplace. The fresh eagerness of her smile, the energy of her step as if the painter had called out to her to come to him, the way her hand clutched her hat with the long sweep of a feather curving up toward her face—these gave her an interest that was deeper than beauty.

"She was happy," Maude said, as she always did. It was a strange thought.

"She was about to marry the handsomest man in the kingdom."

"And welcome him into the oldest family and the finest house in the kingdom."

They fell silent, each wondering if anybody—much less the handsomest man in the kingdom—would ever want to marry them. Neither thought they looked pretty the way the dainty ladies in the portraits lining the hall, with their pursed lips, pale glossy ringlets, and glowing fair skin, were pretty. They both resembled Mamma, with their dark hair, determined chins, and long hands and feet. But in the portrait, Mamma's hair was smooth and shiny, and her slender fingers elegantly held up the skirt of a gown that gleamed clean and unmended, while their own hair twisted in an unruly fashion around their heads and their work-roughened hands rested on faded dresses that were patched and worn, and that always seemed too small.

Rose had resembled Papa, Mamma said once, surprising them

with this rare mention of Jane's twin. Rose had had Papa's big eyes and fine features. But Rose was dead, and baby Robert, too, so Papa's looks had been lost. Lost, along with the gold and jewels and parties whose music and gay laughter Jane vaguely remembered—everything that had gone away when Papa had gone away.

When word came that he had died, poor and alone in a miserable room in an inn, surrounded by empty bottles, they were surprised—not that he was dead, but that he had so recently been alive, because for a long time he had been dead to them.

Maude said that all she remembered of Papa was a large, noisy presence, strong arms that would lift her up and then a scratchy face rubbing against her cheek and neck until she screamed and he laughed and put her down, all accompanied by a strong smell that she later learned was liquor. Jane remembered a deep voice shouting late in the night and their mother crying, and their father disappearing for days at a time, until that last disappearance when he'd never returned at all. They both knew without ever saying it that they must behave well and do everything Mamma said, so that she would not cry again. Or—and the thought was so bitter that Jane tried to push it away—so that she would not leave them like Papa.

Jane led the way back down the corridor, the eyes in the portraits boring holes in her back. She always felt that they would be different on the way back—Great-Grandpapa Edwin would be smiling, or the kitten would have squirmed out of Great-Great-Grandmamma Esther's arms. And as she climbed down the stairs, holding her skirts up with one hand and grasping the rail with the other, she heard the ancestors whispering behind her.

You are a Halsey. You are the last of your line, you and your sis-

ter. You have much to live up to. Never disgrace the Halsey name. On and on they whispered as Jane hurried, risking a dangerous tumble, and the voices didn't cease until she stood once more in the South Parlor, surrounded by their own familiar clothes and furniture and cooking things, and Maude made rose hip tea, to help them recover from the climb.

2

Jane opened her eyes first to a dim and misty sunrise, then to bright hope, and finally to bitter disappointment. Mamma had not returned in the night.

She walked through the haze to the barn, where Baby and the goats waited impatiently. She milked them and took the pails to the dairy, where Maude was churning butter. It was pleasantly cool in the little stone house, which was perched over an underground spring that carried snow melt from the distant mountains. Yesterday's cheese was progressing nicely, so Jane broke up the curds. *Six days,* she thought. *It's been almost a week since Mamma left. Maybe I should—*

Betsy's sharp bark interrupted her thoughts, and her heart lightened. Maude ran to the door of the dairy and exclaimed, "It's not Mamma! It's a carriage!" Jane joined her, and they leaned out to see.

A shiny carriage, pulled by two chestnut horses, came up the drive. The fine animals looked strong, yet they were leaning hard into their traces. *The carriage must be carrying some-*

thing heavy, Jane realized. As it rounded the last curve, an enormous gray horse tied to the back came into sight, head down, hooves dragging. "It's Saladin!" she said.

Surely all the eggs and cheese and butter in the world weren't enough to trade for a carriage and two beautiful horses. Maybe someone who owed Papa a gambling debt had decided to ease his conscience by giving them to Mamma. Maybe Mamma had fallen sick and a kind stranger had brought her home. Or maybe—Jane felt a chill—maybe Mamma had died, and the owner of the carriage was returning Sal to them. She took Maude's hand to comfort her and was herself comforted by its warmth. Together they walked to the drive, where the carriage was making the final turn.

The driver pulled on the reins. The horses stood with their heads down, their sides heaving. The carriage door opened, and Jane, dreading to see a messenger who would deliver bad news, felt her heart skip a beat. But out stepped Mamma, road dust caking the folds of her dress, her face drawn with weariness, but smiling. She opened her arms wide. The girls ran to her, Jane weak-kneed with relief, Maude showing only joy.

"Hello, my chickens!" Mamma said. "Wait till you see the surprise I brought with me!"

"We can see it," Jane said.

"Where have you been for so long?" Maude demanded.

"Oh, the surprise isn't the carriage," Mamma said. "I mean, yes, that is our carriage now, but that's not the surprise. The surprise is what's in it."

"Visitors?" Maude squeaked. Jane shrank back. Why would Mamma do this to them? What would they say to visitors? How could they receive them in their ragged dresses and bare feet and uncombed hair? She licked her finger and rubbed at her face, trying to remove the smudges that she knew she must have gotten in the barn.

"Not visitors," Mamma said. "Something better. Something you have been wanting for a long time." What had they been wanting? Before they could guess, Mamma told them. "A new papa, and a new little sister."

"Oh!" breathed Maude. "A baby!" There hadn't been a baby in the house for so long, not since Robert.

"Not exactly a baby." Mamma looked toward the carriage. A tall, balding man stepped out of it and then turned and reached back inside, speaking in a low, coaxing tone. He was answered by a torrent of words that the girls couldn't make out, although their meaning was clear: whoever was in the carriage was unhappy.

Mamma laid her hand on the man's arm. "Let me try, Harry." The man stepped back, and Mamma reached in the open door. "Come, Isabella. Come see your new home." She stood for a moment and then moved away, helping someone out and then down the two steps.

Jane caught her breath. The small girl looked unlike anyone she had ever seen before. Her hair was of that pale brown called ash-blond, and it hung to her waist in shiny waves. Her oval face was a clear, delicate white, and she had pale pink cheeks and dainty red lips. Her sky-blue dress stopped just below her knees, showing snow-white stockings and tiny white shoes. Her hair was held back by a blue ribbon that had to be silk. She was the most beautiful thing Jane had ever seen, standing perfectly still in front of the dry stone fountain in the curve of the gravel drive. Maude whispered to Jane, "Is she real?"

"Of course she's real, silly," Jane whispered back. She had a sudden flash of a memory—of Papa's mother, Grandmother Montjoy, who had died when Jane was four. Grandmother's face had been white and wrinkled, her staring eyes unfocused, and she'd mumbled as she reached out a shriveled finger and gently stroked something—a porcelain fairy, Jane remembered, with dark gold curls and blue wings.

The man, whose thin hair was a duller version of the girl's and whose sweat-streaked skin might once have been as perfect as hers, bent over and whispered in her ear. She crossed her arms and turned her head away from him, her lower lip sticking out and trembling.

Mamma called, "Girls, come here." Maude looked at Jane, who could read her own reluctance mirrored in her sister's eyes. They didn't dare disobey, and after another moment's hesitation, Jane walked to the carriage. Maude followed a step behind.

"Harry," Mamma said, "these are your new daughters. This is Jane, the elder, and behind her is Maude."

"I am happy to meet you," the man said. He didn't sound happy.

"Where are your curtseys, girls?" Mamma asked sharply. Startled, Jane tucked one foot behind the other and made an awkward bob. Maude did the same. It had been so long since either of them had had to perform a curtsey—Jane couldn't remember, in fact, the last time they had met someone new—that she knew they looked ridiculous. Especially with dirty, bare feet and knots in their hair. Especially in front of that fairy princess.

The fairy princess burst out laughing, and Jane felt herself flush. "What was *that?*" the girl asked. "Is that how people curtsey in the country?" Maude looked as though the child had slapped her.

"Perhaps you could help them learn to do it better," Mamma suggested. "Would you like to show them how a curtsey is done in town?"

I don't want her to show me anything, Jane thought.

The girl picked up her skirt in the tips of her fingers, and placing her right foot behind her left, she sank down nearly to the ground, then rose smoothly, lining her two tiny feet up next to each other again. Jane suddenly felt too tall, and lumpy. Her dress had grown so tight over her chest that her breasts were flattened against her ribs, and she'd had to let out the skirt of her dress to accommodate suddenly round hips. This girl was so slender that even her small curves were graceful.

Maude reached out and touched a tawny curl that dangled past the girl's shoulder. "You're *beautiful,*" she breathed.

The girl didn't answer, and Maude, looking embarrassed, dropped her hand.

"Take the horses into the barn and wipe them down well," the man said to the coachman. "When I am satisfied that you have done your work properly, I will pay you." The man, who had unharnessed the horses, made a quick bow and led them around in a tight circle and down to the barn.

Mamma held out her hand to the girl. "Come, Isabella. Have some supper and then go to bed. You'll feel happier after you sleep. In the morning, Jane and Maude will show you all around. There might be some new puppies in the barn—are there, girls?"

"Yes, Mamma." Maude was eager to catch Mamma up on everything that had happened in her absence. "She had eight right after you left, and only one died. There are three boys and four girls, two brown, three brown and white, two—"

"Father," Isabella said.

"Yes, darling," he said promptly.

"I don't want to see puppies in the barn."

"Then you won't have to. There are rats in barns, anyway. Come in and have some supper now, and then I'll put you to bed."

"I can put her to bed," Mamma said. "I'm her mother now."

"*Step*mother," Isabella said. "And I want my father to put me to bed." She clung to the man's hand.

He looked down at her. "Of course, sweetheart. Of course." He picked her up and carried her over the broken front steps. He stumbled over a crack and muttered something, and then set the child down at the door, which he pushed open. They followed him as his booted footsteps rang in the front hall. The sound, so familiar yet almost forgotten, made Jane's stomach lurch.

The man came to an abrupt halt as two mice scurried into their hole in a door frame, disgust clear on his face. "My God, Margaret," he said. His daughter pressed against his side, and he put his arm around her.

Jane knew the front hall was big—Hannah Herb-Woman's entire hut could fit in it with room to spare—but to her it had always been just the place you had to go through to get to the living quarters. Its marble floor gleamed only when one of the girls polished an area to play a game on it, and now that these strangers were staring, she realized how dingy the stone was. The velvet drapes framing the tall doorways were tattered, and the gold tassels that fringed their edges were faded and dull. The decaying staircase loomed above them, the flaking gilt of the scrolls and curlicues along its sides glinting even in the dim light that came through the open door. The light also caught the strands of a spider web that stretched from a banister to the remains of the chandelier high on the ceiling. When Jane saw the girl wrinkling her nose, she, too, caught the odor of mold and rot.

The man glanced at Mamma. "I told you it was in need of some repair," she said. Jane detected an uneasy note in her voice.

"I know, but I had no idea...." He shook his head. "It hasn't been that long—only a few years."

"The decay had started even when I was a child. My parents managed to hide the extent of it."

"Father!" burst out the girl. "You said we were going to have supper!"

"Yes, darling." He instantly turned to her. "Yes, of course. Where...?" He looked around.

"Oh, we don't use much of the house," Mamma answered vaguely. She gestured at the South Parlor. "This is where we spend most of our time. I'm afraid it's not very presentable." Not presentable? But they had been so proud of how they had cleaned it.

They all followed her in. Harry wrinkled his nose as he looked around. "The first thing we'll do is get the kitchen back in working order. I won't be comfortable in a room with the smell of cooking in it."

"We haven't cooked a thing all day," Jane said indignantly. They had eaten nothing but cheese and some nuts that Maude had found.

"Girls—" Mamma began, and hearing the exhaustion in her voice, Jane leaped forward.

"Sit down, Mamma," she said. "I'll find something." Maude was already heading out to the dairy, so Jane went to the pantry. She glanced at the bare shelves, hoping against all logic that somehow more food would have appeared there. Of course it hadn't. The shelves were waiting for whatever Mamma had brought home from the market; that's why she had gone to town. *Or was it?* Jane wondered, suddenly suspicious. Had Mamma really gone to meet that man?

Nonsense. They were almost out of everything. Jane poked around in one nearly empty bin and then another. Turnips, onions—no, she didn't think Mamma wanted her to take the time to cook anything. Apples—yes, that would do for a quick supper. She filled her apron, choosing the reddest ones. Into her pocket pouch she put almost the last of the biscuits, the twice-cooked bread that lasted a long time in the cool pantry. She sat on the floor and rubbed the apples to wipe off the dust and to bring out their shine. When they were as rosy as Isabella's lips, she gathered them up and went back to the South Parlor, passing through the long-unused dining hall, where marks on the floor showed where the long table had once stood.

Isabella was sitting on her father's lap on the big chair, her feet on the armrest. She squirmed, and her shoes made streaks on the cloth. Jane looked at Mamma, but Mamma appeared not to notice, and Jane put the food down and went to join Maude outside.

The sun was low, and the evening noises were starting. Crickets and tree frogs screeched out their songs, and a light breeze rustled through the trees beyond the henhouse, lifting a little of the heat from the late-summer day.

Maude showed Jane six new-laid eggs in her basket. "One

for each of us and two for the man. He's big and probably eats a lot," Maude explained. She had placed them carefully in the basket, nestled in straw to keep them from breaking.

Jane picked the few remaining berries from a bush near the kitchen door. Walking carefully, she entered the South Parlor just as Maude was placing the egg basket on the scarred wooden table they used for everything from sewing to cooking to eating. Mamma had lit the lantern.

"Look what I have, Mamma," Jane said. "We can eat these after the eggs." She carefully pulled the berries out of her pockets, heaping them on the table.

"Lovely, dear," Mamma said. "Where—"

But Isabella interrupted her. "I can't eat those," she said to her father. "She touched them with her dirty hands!"

"So wash them," Jane said, as she would to Maude. Her fingers were a little grimy, she supposed, but none of it was nasty—just good, clean dirt from pushing branches aside and picking fallen berries up off the ground.

"There appears to be no water," Mamma said as though to no one.

Oh, for heaven's sake, Jane thought. *Of course there isn't. There are no servants to fetch it.*

The man spoke to Isabella. "Don't worry, darling. We'll wash the berries, won't we, Margaret?"

Mamma's lips were pressed together. Jane looked at the man. Didn't he know that this meant he should stop now, before Mamma got angry? But Mamma just said, "There is nothing wrong with the berries. Isabella may wash them if she really wants to, or she can have apples and a boiled egg. That should be sufficient. A light supper is all a lady requires."

"I want berries," Isabella said. Mamma pressed her lips

together even tighter, and Jane waited for the storm. But it didn't come. Instead, Mamma reached into the back of the cupboard and pulled out a small white bowl painted with tiny flowers, one of the few pieces that had been saved from her beautiful china. They had not been able to sell this one because of a tiny crack.

They needed water to cook the eggs, anyway, so Jane went outside to the pump. They had used up the rainwater stored in the cisterns weeks before. While she was working the pump handle she thought how ridiculous it was to pretend they were still the Halseys of long ago, with servants to fetch heavy pails of water and to wash things that didn't need it. When she came back, the man took the jug and hastily poured a little water into the bowl holding the berries, splashing some on the table. "She really isn't used to country ways, Margaret," he said apologetically. "In the city—"

"I understand, Harry," Mamma said.

Jane could tell by the way Maude was looking at her that her sister shared her shock. Mamma would never have allowed one of them to tell an adult what to do, and she would have sent her to bed without any supper if she wasn't satisfied with what there was to eat.

When the water in the pot hanging over the fire steamed, Jane placed the eggs in it. They knocked about pleasantly. When they were done, Maude scooped them out. Jane cracked her egg quickly, blowing on her fingers after each touch. Soon the soft white and golden yolk were spreading on her plate, to be eaten while hot and delicious.

Isabella made no attempt to peel hers. Instead, her father did it, his big hands clumsy. He sucked on a reddened forefinger while his daughter daintily spooned up her egg. Jane watched, fascinated, as the girl wiped her mouth after each bite. Isabella caught Jane staring at her and glowered. Jane dropped her gaze and crumbled some biscuit into the smear of yellow that remained on her plate, and then spooned it up.

"Father, look what she's doing," Isabella said with a giggle.

"Hush, darling," he said. "That's how they eat in the country."

"In the country?" Jane asked. "Don't they eat eggs where you come from?" The girl and the man exchanged a glance, but neither answered. Jane felt she was doing something wrong, but what?

They ate the apples, Harry peeling and slicing Isabella's and his own, and then Mamma took Harry to see the gardens. Isabella perched on the edge of the big chair, whose brown velvet was almost rubbed away. Her toes barely reached the floor as she sat silently, her hands crossed in her lap, her eyes fixed on a spot a few feet ahead of her. Maude asked her abruptly, "How old are you?"

"Thirteen." Isabella didn't look up.

"*What?*" Maude asked. "That's older than I am! You can't be thirteen."

Isabella raised those extraordinary eyes to her. They glittered like the green ice on top of the pond in the winter. "Why can't I?"

"Because…" Maude gestured at her. "Because you're so small!"

"I'm not small," Isabella said. "You're big."

"But…" Maude started, and then fell silent. She looked at Jane, indignation plain on her face.

"Maude *is* tall." Jane came to her sister's defense. "Tall like Mamma. So am I. And you're short. Your hands and feet look like they belong to a baby." Their mother said that their long fingers and toes were an aristocratic trait, and besides, they would grow into them, but Jane didn't believe her. Secretly, Jane admired the girl's small feet and hands and her slender limbs, unlike her own arms and legs, which were unladylike and muscular. The girl crossed her arms over her chest, tucking her hands into her armpits, and looked away. Jane shrugged.

They heard footsteps, and then outside the parlor, the man laughed and Mamma said, "Oh, of course I remember that party, Harry! That was the one where that fat girl—what was her name?" They came in together, still laughing.

"Alexandra," Harry said. "She fell in the pond—"

"And when she came out she said she had seen a water-sprite—"

"And nobody could stop Daniel from jumping in and looking for it—"

They broke off when they saw the girls staring at them. "Serve the berries, Maude," Mamma instructed. Maude spooned some into each bowl. Jane could tell that she was counting them and stifled a smile. Maude loved anything sweet and would make sure that no one got more than she did. Maude passed the painted bowl to Isabella, who daintily dug in her spoon and lifted it to her lips. She swallowed a mouthful and then took another. Jane relaxed enough to take a bite.

A high-pitched scream made everyone jump. Isabella was on her feet, her face purple-red and distorted.

"What is it? What happened?" Harry shouted, kneeling in front of his daughter. Isabella either could not or would not talk, but kept screaming, and then spat something on the floor. A dead bee.

"Oh, my Lord!" Harry gasped. Isabella's lower lip was already starting to swell.

"Is the stinger out?" Maude asked.

Harry repeated, "Oh, my Lord—my little sweetheart—Ella, Ella, my poor darling."

Maude pushed herself between them. "Let me make sure the stinger is out." She lifted Isabella's chin, but the girl's hand flew out and slapped Maude's away. Jane stood stunned as Isabella buried her face in her father's shirtfront, and his arms wrapped tightly around her. Harry gathered up his screaming child and sat down on the big chair, rocking and soothing her. The screams turned to sobs, and the sobs went on and on.

When the fox cub had bitten Maude's thumb almost through, she had not made nearly as much noise as this. When Jane had broken her collarbone, she had allowed Hannah Herb-Woman to set it without a single cry.

Mamma said quietly, "Eat, girls."

It was hard to swallow even the sweet berries with all that crying filling the room. But when Jane tried to put down her spoon, Mamma looked at her the way a herd dog looks at a sheep that is moving away from the flock, and she forced herself to finish.

The sobs finally dwindled into whimpers, and Harry stood up, cradling his daughter. "Margaret," he said, "where does Ella sleep?"

"The girls' room is through there." Mamma moved toward the door to the hallway. "Jane has a big bed and Isabella can share it with her."

"No, that's all right," Jane said hastily. "Isabella can have her own bed. Maude will share with me. Won't you, Maude?"

"Oh, yes," Maude said.

"No," Isabella said. They all looked at her.

"What is it, darling?" her father asked.

"I won't share a room." Her words were thick. "I have never shared a room, and I won't share one now with someone who deliberately—" and her voice became ragged "—who *deliberately* put a bee in my berries."

"What?" Maude said. "You think that I—"

"I *saw* you." Isabella started to cry again, sobs shaking her thin chest. "I saw you poking in the berries. You put that bee in there so it would sting me."

Jane half rose from her seat as Maude's mouth gaped open. "She didn't!" Jane almost shouted. "She wouldn't! You know she wouldn't, Mamma!"

"Of course she didn't," Mamma said. "Isabella is tired, and her mouth hurts. She doesn't mean it, do you, Isabella?" The girl didn't answer. Mamma squatted next to her. "Look at me," she instructed. Isabella didn't move.

"Young lady," Mamma said in the tone that neither Jane nor Maude had ever ignored, "in this house the children do as the adults say. And I am telling you to look at me."

"Margaret—" Harry started, but Mamma must have turned that herd-dog look on him, too, because he settled back. After a moment, Isabella raised her eyes to Mamma's.

"You will answer politely when you are spoken to," Mamma said. "We are making allowances tonight because you are tired and your mouth hurts. In the future, I expect you to behave like a young lady." She stood up. "Now, Harry, Isabella has the choice of sleeping in the girls' room with them, or in here by herself. She will tell us her decision when supper has been tidied up."

Maude and Jane put the dishes in water to soak, and then

Jane went out to coax the goats and Baby back into the barn. When she returned, Maude made tea and served it to Mamma and the man. Isabella didn't even look up when Maude offered her a cup, so Maude shrugged and drank it herself. When Jane hung the dishcloths near the fire she sneaked a peek at the big chair, where the man was still soothing the girl. She heard a murmur from Harry and a word or two from Isabella in a quavering voice, but she couldn't make out what they were saying.

Mamma wiped her hands on her apron and turned to Harry. "Well?"

"Isabella will sleep in here."

"Good," Jane said to Maude, and hoped that Mamma hadn't heard.

"Very well," Mamma answered. "Girls, take Isabella to the necessary room."

In silence, Jane and Maude left for the privy in the yard behind the kitchen. Isabella followed, keeping several paces behind. They went and returned without exchanging a word.

In their absence, the pillows from the big chair had been put on the floor and a cloth had been smoothed over them. "This is your bed," Mamma said.

Jane and Maude stood awkwardly. The last thing every day, they sat and talked, and Mamma told them tales of parties and young men, of hunts and horses, of balls at the palace in the days when the old king was a prince, of fairies and sprites and the people of the woods. Obviously that could not happen tonight. They kissed Mamma, then stood in front of Harry and hesitated. Did one kiss stepfathers? Fortunately he made no move to kiss them, merely saying, "Good night, girls. We'll get better acquainted tomorrow." They murmured

"Good night" and escaped to their room, closing the door behind them. They undressed in the dark, said hasty prayers, and slid into bed.

A half-moon shone through their window. Jane heard Maude moving restlessly. Finally, Maude whispered, "Jane?"

"What?"

"Can I come into bed with you?"

The bedclothes rustled as Jane made room, and Maude slid next to her sister. As she drifted into sleep, Jane heard singing in the distance. She listened as a new voice joined in and another fell silent.

"The fairy singers are back," she whispered to Maude, but her sister grunted without replying, so Jane lay still while the sounds faded, as they always did. She didn't believe what Mamma told her—that it was just the wind. She wished the haunting melody would continue all night, reassuring her that she was not the only thing awake in the world.

After what seemed like hours, Jane was sleeping as soundly as her sister.

3

Jane woke to the sound of someone moving in the South Parlor and stretched happily. Mamma was home—but then she bumped into the sleeping Maude, and the memories of last night flooded back.

Jane's dress lay crumpled on the floor. She pulled it on and stared down at herself. The dress was stained and wrinkled and a rip was starting under one armpit. She hadn't noticed before how grimy it was. She tried to comb her hair with her fingers, but they stuck in a knot, so she gave up.

In the South Parlor, Mamma was drinking a cup of tea. "Good morning," Jane said, and stepped around the sleeping Isabella, who looked even more angelic than when she was awake. Rummaging in the chest, Jane found her best dress, the blue one with dingy lace around the neck and cuffs. Normally, she wore it only when the priest came to St. Cuthbert's, the village church, on his irregular rounds. It was getting small, but at least it was clean and not too much mended.

"What are you doing with your Sunday dress?" Mamma

asked. Wordlessly, Jane pointed at the worn elbows on the one she was wearing. She poked her finger through a hole near the hem and waggled it at Mamma. "A true lady always looks well, no matter what she wears," Mamma said, as Jane had been afraid she would.

Jane sighed and put the blue dress back. It didn't really matter, she supposed. Her best dress would still look like rags next to Isabella's clothes. Even the girl's nightgown was fastened at the neck with a shiny pink ribbon. "In any case," Mamma went on, "we won't be going to church again until next spring. Father Albert is getting too old to come all the way out here in bad weather, and autumn storms will be starting before long." After the hot and dry summer, when the crops withered in the fields and rabbits and deer left their forest homes and appeared in the drive in search of water, the thought of a cool rain shower didn't seem like bad weather.

Jane picked up a basket of grain in the pantry and stepped outside. She strolled through the bare patch between the house and the barn, tossing the feed by handfuls to the chickens. The early-morning dust was cool and dry under her toes. She threw some grain in front of the hen with the sore foot, who pecked it up quickly before her swifter sisters could steal it. Mamma appeared in the doorway, looking off to the horizon—to prevent herself, Jane thought, from seeing her daughter working like a farm girl.

"Mamma?"

"What is it?"

"Who is that man?" She didn't know if Mamma would answer; Mamma so rarely talked about anything personal.

"Your stepfather, dear."

You know that's not what I'm asking, Jane thought, but what she said was, "I mean, how do you know him?"

"Harry was a friend of Papa's. His father was a wealthy trader. When Harry was a young man, he met Isabella's mother on a journey across the border. He married her and stayed in her country for several years. I met her once, when they came to the city for Harry's mother's funeral," she said in a low tone, as though talking to herself. Jane moved closer to hear. "She was a lovely thing. I never saw a man so besotted." She shook her head and paused. "Isabella was very young at that time, but already she resembled her mother greatly. Harry moved back here with Isabella after his wife died, and I've seen him several times in the city since then."

The hens scratched in the dirt, seeking the last kernels.

"Why did you marry him?" Tears stung Jane's eyes. "Things were fine until now, with just you and me and Maude."

"Jane! How dare you question me—how dare you?"

"Sorry," Jane muttered. She kicked at the dirt, revealing a bug that a chicken instantly pounced on. She knew she should stop, but she couldn't help herself. "Do you love him, Mamma? Do you love him the way you..." *The way you loved Papa,* she wanted to say, but she didn't dare.

Mamma didn't answer. She looked at Jane with an expression that was hard to read. Sorrow? Irritation? Finally, she said, "There are many ways to love, and no way to explain them to someone who hasn't felt them. There's one's first love, and there's the love you feel for your children. Wait until you have your own children, Jane, and you'll know why I would do anything—*anything* to keep you girls safe and happy."

"But—"

"No, let me finish. I will say this once, and then you will

never ask me again. Harry loves his daughter as I love you, and we love each other the way old friends do. He has no more family. He wants his daughter to have a respected name, and I want you girls to be out in society. He has…" She hesitated. *Say it, Mamma,* Jane thought. *Say he has money.* But money was one of the subjects that Mamma considered indelicate. They watched the hens gather the chicks under their wings as a hawk flew overhead. "We should have more help in the house—"

More help? Jane thought sourly.

"—and you should be going to parties and meeting young men and…" Mamma sighed.

"We don't need him, Mamma," Jane said. "You have Maude and me, and Hannah Herb-Woman." Still, the idea of meeting young men interested her more than she liked to admit. How could she ever meet someone, living far away from town and never going anywhere except church? She had never been invited to a party, and the thought of guests seeing their decayed ballroom was ridiculous. And even if she did meet someone, any man who lived up to Mamma's standards would never be interested in a tall, gawky girl with work-hardened arms and a face darkened by the sun, especially one with no dowry and no fortune to inherit. But of course she couldn't say that to Mamma.

"Hannah and her family are good and honest neighbors, but they are not our friends, Jane. They are not of our station. You know that."

It irritated Jane when Mamma talked about their "station" as though nothing had changed since her own girlhood. "We see the villagers every month in church." Sometimes it seemed like they knew too many people, not too few. In the summer, they saw someone almost every week. Jane couldn't imagine wanting more company than that.

Mamma shook her head. "Those are not the kind of people I grew up with, and not the kind of people I want *you* to grow up with."

"The people you grew up with aren't here anymore. They all moved to the city." It was an old argument, and one that Mamma always refused to answer. Jane went on stubbornly. "And if they *were* here, I wouldn't want to grow up with them. I like Hugh and Hannah and the people in the village." What had been so wonderful about the past, to make Mamma cling to it so?

"You should be going to parties and meeting young men and—" Mamma said again.

"And getting married," Jane finished for her. Mamma nodded. Of course she and Maude had to get married one day. Mamma said it was because that was what a lady did; Jane knew that they had no other way to live. Maude had begged to be allowed to learn healing and herb lore from Hannah. Hannah had been willing, as she no longer had a daughter to whom she could pass on her knowledge. Jane could sew better than any seamstress in the village—as well as some in the city, she thought, after seeing their work on city-made gowns that ladies wore to church. But Mamma would not hear of either one of them working for pay.

"And I want you to have a father. You and Maude did not have much luck with your real father, and Harry is so gentle. He does not drink, either." Mamma's voice was bitter.

Jane thought, *We don't need a father.*

"And you two must set an example—" Mamma ignored the

exasperated sound that Jane could not help making "—and be good, obedient girls."

"Yes, Mamma." Jane tried not to let her irritation show again. Wasn't she getting too old to need her mother to tell her to be a good, obedient girl? She had already turned fifteen; Mamma had been married at sixteen.

A few chickens followed them hopefully to the back door, where Isabella stood, her bare feet poking out from under her white nightdress. She looked no more than ten years old, with her golden hair loose about her shoulders. "Where is my father?"

"Good morning, Isabella," Mamma said, and she nudged Jane, who repeated reluctantly, "Good morning."

"Good morning," Isabella said, with an obvious effort, and then she asked again, "Where is my father?"

"Your father is still asleep," Mamma answered. "You may wake him, if you like."

It was late, and the cow and goats would be uncomfortably full of milk. Jane hurried to the barn, which was familiar and calming after the strange, awkward-feeling parlor with those two new people inside it. Even when the house had fallen into disrepair, they had kept the barn sound and dry. Here the wood was solid, and instead of odors of mold and decay, she was bathed in the warm, living smells of healthy animals and clean hay.

The big door was open to the fenced-in field, letting in the morning sunlight and the rapidly warming air. A few flies buzzed, and the spiders crouched in their webs, ready to run out and wrap up anything that flew into their traps.

Baby shifted her heavy weight from one foot to another and swished her tail against her rump. The two new horses poked their brown noses through the bars of their stall, and she gave each a rub. "At least *you're* friendly." She laughed when they tossed their heads as though nodding in agreement.

She always tended to Sal first. The old gray hunter didn't look like much now, but in his day he had been famous. "Like Lady Margaret taking a fence on Saladin," people in the village still said, when they meant that someone had done something in a particularly fine way. His back was swayed now, and his eyes were dim, but when the girls blew one of the rusted hunting horns that hung in the nearly empty tack room, his neck would arch and he would paw the ground, and they could see a shadow of what he had once been.

"Good boy." She rubbed Sal's hard forehead between the ears as he ate. An impatient moo broke in on her thoughts, and she pulled the milking stool and bucket over to Baby.

Betsy and her puppies must have just woken up, and the fat little bodies squirmed over one another to get their breakfast. Betsy saw Jane looking at her and thumped her tail. Jane poured a little milk in the bowl that one of the puppies was blindly trying to climb out of, and Betsy lapped it up. Jane milked the goats next and then fed all the livestock. While they ate she mucked out the stalls and scattered a handful of straw over the floor. She drove Baby and the goats out to the pasture.

She was about to go back to the house when she thought she saw something flicker in the woods. She stood still and shaded her eyes against the early-morning sun. Yes—there it was again. Something pale flashed behind the trees and then disappeared. Fairies? No, they wouldn't dare come so near the barn. Fairies and witches and all their kind were terrified of iron, and there were rivets and old horseshoes and nails all over the barn. Outlaws? She had heard of them living among the trees. She strained her ears and thought she heard a little ripple of laughter and then a few notes from farther off. The notes were repeated, and then echoed closer by. She turned and ran back to the house.

In the South Parlor Maude had put out their least-stained tablecloth and least-chipped dishes. A tall vase of bright blue flowers stood in the middle of the table. No one else was there.

"Maude!" Her sister looked up from the fire she was tending. Jane told her what she had seen and heard.

"It was probably just one of the people of the woods," Maude said, but Jane heard the uncertainty in her voice. There was nothing that would bring one of the wild folk close to their house—she and Maude had gleaned all the nuts and berries and most of the edible roots, as far into the forest as they dared to go.

"I heard singing," Jane said, but before she could continue, Harry came in, stretching and yawning.

He called back over his shoulder, "Come, Ella dear. Breakfast time."

After a moment, she appeared. This time she was wearing a yellow frock, with ribbons threaded through the lace at her neck and wrists. Her long pale hair was held back by a matching ribbon.

Without looking at Mamma or the girls, Isabella sat down at the table and placed her hands in her lap. Mamma took the eggs out of the water with a wooden spoon and placed them in a blue bowl on the table. Mamma looked at Harry.

He cleared his throat. "Ella, dear, what do you say to your mother?"

She looked up at him and then at Mamma. "I say to my

*step*mother that I had eggs for supper last night, and I would like something different for breakfast today."

Mamma crossed her arms. "There is nothing else yet. When we're finished with breakfast, we will all unpack the carriage and find what else there is."

The girl's eyes were shining with tears. She stood and flung herself on Harry. "Take me home, Father," she sobbed. "They hate me here."

"Darling," Harry soothed his daughter, stroking her hair. "This *is* your home now."

She raised her swollen eyes to him. "This is not my home. You can't make me stay here! You can't make me live with this—with this *wicked* stepmother, and these two *ugly* stepsisters."

4

Jane felt as if Isabella had kicked her. "Mamma is not wicked!" she said. "She's been kind to you. Kinder than you deserve!"

"Child—" Mamma began, but then she glanced at Harry and stopped. *Go on,* Jane thought. *Tell her not to talk about us like that.* But Mamma said only, "Breakfast is on the table," in an odd, tight voice.

"A lady doesn't show her feelings," one of Mamma's favorite sayings, rang in Jane's head. She had never seen the wisdom of it, but she couldn't risk upsetting her mother further. A thin white line ringed Mamma's mouth, and a vein beat visibly in her temple. "I'm not hungry," Jane said.

"Sit," Mamma snapped, and Jane sat down and picked up her spoon. Maude was already halfway through her egg.

The meal was silent, except for Harry's quiet coaxing of Isabella. While the sisters cleared the table, Mamma showed the man the rest of the house. Jane listened as their footsteps echoed, listened to their low murmurs. They were in the kitchen, then the pantry, then back out into the hallway, past the staircase and into the North Parlor and the ballroom. She hoped they would not go upstairs. It would violate that ghostly region if someone strode in and threw open the shutters to reveal the dust and decay or pulled down the bed curtains to expose the rottenness under their beauty.

When the adults came back, it appeared that they had not indeed gone that far. "I had no idea that it had gotten this bad," Harry was saying. "The staircase is nearly rotted through and should not be used. The North Parlor looks to be in fairly good shape, and the ballroom is still beautiful. I remember the hunt ball when we were fifteen, Margaret, the one where your parents announced your engagement to Daniel. The two of you stood together in the ballroom while the orchestra played above you. It was a lovely room."

"I remember," Mamma said softly, and shook her head. "The hopes we have when we're young, Harry…"

He nodded. "Things don't always turn out the way we think they will, do they?" He put his hand on hers and gave it a squeeze.

She smiled up at him. "So, you think that if we start on the roof—" They made plans the rest of the morning.

Maude had pulled out their mending basket, and Jane reached into it and took out a stocking. "What are you doing?" Isabella asked.

Jane shook out the stocking and showed her the hole in its heel. "Darning. It's hard to make it smooth, but if it's lumpy, it will raise a blister when you walk. Do you want to do one?"

Isabella looked at her, bewildered. "Why do you do that?"

It was Jane's turn to be bewildered. "If I don't, Mamma won't have a stocking to wear."

"Why don't you just throw it out and buy another one?" Isabella persisted.

"Buy another one?" Maude asked. "You don't *buy* stockings. You make them. Or Mamma does. She's teaching me how. She can teach you, too."

Isabella said, "I didn't know they were something you could make." Maude and Jane looked at each other and then bent over their work. Isabella spoke again. "When I was at the palace—"

"You were at the palace?" Jane asked, and Maude said, "I don't believe you!"

"Oh, yes, I was." Isabella smoothed her bright skirt over her knees. Jane once again became aware of her own too-short dress, patched and mended, with threads hanging off the frayed ends of the sleeves. "Father had business with the king, so we came to your country for a visit. While Father was in the throne room, my mother took me to visit her friend, who was a lady-in-waiting to the queen. I even saw the prince. He came to the stable as we were leaving, to find a manservant he suspected of stealing his horses' oats. He was beautiful."

"Was he?" Maude asked. "I mean, was the man stealing the oats?"

"I don't know. The prince didn't either, but he had the man taken out and whipped anyway, as a warning. I was wearing silk stockings, and when I curtseyed they tore on a splinter, and after we went home Mother threw them away and gave me new ones."

"Silk stockings!" Jane tried to keep the awe she felt from showing in her voice. She had heard of such things but didn't know that they really existed. It was as if Isabella had told them that she had ridden to the palace on a gryphon and had been presented with a pet dragon.

"I don't believe—" Maude started, but Jane cut her off.

"We have to take care of the milk," she reminded her sister, and they left, Maude muttering, "Liar" under her breath.

In the dairy, Maude poured the cream from that morning's milk into the butter churn and pumped the handle. Jane uncovered the bowl where she had mixed starter into milk two days before. She lined a sieve with cheesecloth, spooned in the soft white mixture, and placed it over a bucket to catch the cloudy whey. Later, the people of the woods would fetch the bucket, and at Christmas time, they would thank Mamma with the haunch of a fat pig, its flesh sweet with whey, to feast on. Jane's mouth watered at the thought of the crisp skin and juicy meat. Mamma said that when she was a girl it would be a whole pig for the servants to roast on a big spit, but that was when there had been a large household to feed.

Maude took the top off the butter churn and peered inside. She reached in a finger and pulled out a glob of butter, inspecting it with satisfaction. Then she popped it in her mouth and covered up the churn again. "Mmm." She closed her eyes in enjoyment, then opened them. "Janie, do you like having a new sister?"

"She doesn't feel like a sister. And it's strange having that man around."

"I know. I thought I would like to have a papa. I like when Mamma takes me to Hugh's cottage and his father is there. He always gives me a sweet." Maude churned a few more strokes. "I don't think this man will give me a sweet."

No, I don't think he will, Jane thought, wishing suddenly that her sister wouldn't talk like a baby. Maude inspected the cream again and held out her hand. Jane passed her the slotted spoon, and Maude fished out the pale gold lumps, setting them to drain on a cloth. Jane poured the buttermilk into another bucket and set it in the back of the dairy, near the cool stream. Jane looked at her cheese once more and saw that it was dripping nicely.

While Maude went to hunt for eggs, Jane returned to the house, but her path was blocked by a large cart in the drive. It was full of boxes and bundles; three men from the village were unloading them. "Where do you want this one, Mistress?" a big man asked Mamma. He shifted his weight as he balanced the edge of a large crate on the side of the dry fountain.

"Oh, I don't know—what's in it?" She peered at the label. Lately, Jane had noticed, Mamma was having difficulty threading needles and making out small print.

"Mamma?" Jane asked. "What are these boxes?"

"Oh, Jane," Mamma said. "I'm glad you're here. Look, can you read what this label says?"

The man tilted the box. "'Serafina's gowns,'" Jane read. "Who is Serafina, Mamma?"

Isabella appeared at the door, her eyes red and her face swollen. "Serafina was my mother, and those gowns are *mine.* Just like the jewelry that your mother stole. She can't have my gowns, too." A fat tear slid down her pink cheek.

"Isabella, I already explained it to you," Mamma said wearily. "I did not steal your jewels. I am merely keeping them for you until you are old enough to wear them. You might lose them if I were to give them to you now, and in any case they are not suitable for a girl your age."

"But they're *mine,*" Isabella sobbed. "You can't have them. You'll sell them. I know you will." Jane pressed her lips together. Maude might sound like a child, but at least she didn't sound like a *spoiled* child.

"We will discuss it later," Mamma said. "Poor Jacob is getting tired of holding that heavy box." And even though the man's shoulders were so broad that he would have a hard time squeezing into the South Parlor, the wooden crate was indeed sagging in his arms. Mamma pointed. "Through there, and into the bedroom on the right."

"On the right?" Jane asked as Jacob turned sideways and maneuvered his way in. "But that's *our* room."

"I'm sorry, darling," Mamma said, "but there is just no space anywhere else. We can't put them in the rest of the house with the—" She stopped. *With the mice and bugs,* Jane thought, but of course Mamma wouldn't admit that there was anything of the sort in their house. "They have to go in your room," Mamma finished.

"Margaret." Harry was standing in the doorway.

"Yes?"

"I must ask you to remember that Ella has been through a great deal lately. Her dear mother has died, she was uprooted from her home, and now she has two new stepsisters who dislike her. You must be patient with her."

"I know how to be patient with a child. My own two girls—"

"And that's another thing." Harry cut her off. "The way they act is disgraceful. They are filthy and shoeless. They must comb their hair, at least, and wash themselves."

Mamma said apologetically, "When I am away, they run a little wild—"

"They are too old to run wild," Harry said over his shoulder as he turned to go back in the house. "Please, be sure they clean themselves up before I see them again."

Mamma stood with her hands on her hips, her head on one side, looking at Jane. She considered Jane's ragged dress, her dirty knees, her bare feet. "Where's Maude?"

"In the dairy." Jane's heart sank. She knew what was coming next.

"I'll fetch her. I want you two to take a good bath and then comb all the tangles out of your hair. And find some shoes," Mamma called as Jane headed toward the kitchen, feet dragging, to put water on the stove. Heating the water bucket by bucket and then bathing and drying would take hours. At least it wasn't winter, when the water would cool long before they were through.

She had almost finished filling the great iron washtub when Maude came in, scowling. Yes, Jane could see that her sister would appear a little wild to a stranger, with her hair a brown tangle, her callused feet dirty, her knees scabbed, her fingernails blunt and filthy. She suddenly felt resentful at the way the newcomers were forcing her to see everything—her home, her clothes, her sister, even herself—in a new and unflattering light.

"Why do we have to get washed?" Maude complained. "It isn't church day."

"We need to get cleaned up a little. He says we're too old to run wild. He thinks we're living in the city, with dukes coming to visit." Maude giggled. "You can have first bath." Jane unhooked her sister's dress and let it drop to the floor. Maude eased into the hot water. When they finished, they left their clothes in the tub to soak and put on their Sunday dresses.

They sat in the late-summer sunshine of the courtyard and took turns teasing the tangles out of each other's hair. Jane worked on a particularly nasty knot at the top of Maude's head as Maude squirmed with pain. When Jane straightened to ease her back, she saw Isabella watching them.

"What are you staring at?" Jane asked.

Isabella didn't answer for a moment, and then she said, "You look—different."

"Different how?" Maude demanded, and Jane wondered whether "different" was good or bad. She didn't want to ask for fear of being ridiculed, so she bowed her head to her work again. Maude said, "Ow! Janie, *stop* it!"

"Wouldn't a comb with wider teeth be easier?" Isabella asked. Jane's hand halted, suspended above Maude's head. "I have one," Isabella said. "I'll go find it." She glided into the house.

Maude snapped her mouth shut audibly and looked up at Jane, but Jane just shook her head in bewilderment. "Maybe she's settling in, like Mamma said," she suggested. Maude looked skeptical.

Isabella reappeared holding a tortoiseshell comb, its handle covered in gleaming silver. "Here, let me." She gently worked the comb into the end of the tangle, smoothing and straightening Maude's hair. Her small hands were so deft, and the comb had such wide, even teeth, that Maude could have felt scarcely a twinge as Isabella worked. Jane saw her sister's shoulders drop as she relaxed. One smooth lock followed another as Isabella worked her way around Maude's head.

As Isabella continued and Maude smiled up at her, Jane, too, lost her tension. Maybe Harry was right. They had not been upset when their father died, but a mother was different, Jane thought, feeling a twinge of sympathy. Maybe Isabella had just needed some time to feel comfortable with them. Maybe tonight she would move into their room and the three girls would stay up late talking, and tomorrow they would show Isabella how to find eggs and tell her which trees were best for climbing, and Isabella would tell them about the boys she knew and would show them how to curtsey like the ladies in town and—

Her daydream was interrupted by a shriek from Maude. Isabella held a long damp strand of hair in one hand, and she appeared to be twisting the comb deeper into it. Jane leaped to her sister and slapped Isabella across the face.

Harry came running and shouted, "Stop!" He pulled Isabella to him, shoving Jane away so hard that she fell in the dust. "What do you think you're doing? You brat!"

Mamma came running. "Girls, what happened?"

Isabella was sobbing. She lifted her face from her father's vest, and the marks of Jane's fingers were clear on her cheek. "I was *helping.* I was combing that one's hair, and the comb got stuck. I was trying to pull it out and I think it hurt her and then she—" Isabella pointed to Jane, who quailed but stood her ground "—she hit me. And she broke—" her voice shook, and she swallowed before going on "—she broke my mother's comb. Her beautiful comb that came from Spai-ai-ain." She sobbed as she held it up. Two of the brown teeth were missing.

Mamma swung to Jane. Her eyes were hard. "Jane?"

"She was hurting Maude," Jane said loudly.

"She did it on purpose," Maude broke in. "Janie had to hit her to make her let go."

"She's lying!" Isabella cried, her pale skin flushed.

"I don't lie!" Maude shouted back. She ran at Isabella, but Jane managed to catch her.

"Stop it!" Jane hissed at her sister, who wriggled to get away. For answer, Maude pinched Jane in the tender spot inside her upper arm. Jane gasped and almost let go. She looked at her mother, begging for help with her eyes, but Mamma stood as if thunderstruck. She neither moved nor spoke.

"Be quiet, all of you!" Harry said. "Margaret, I expect you to punish these girls. Come, darling," he said to Isabella. "Come inside and let me put some cool water on your face." He shot a ferocious look at Jane and went into the house, carrying Isabella, her head pillowed on his shoulder.

With a sudden twist Maude managed to break away, sobbing loudly, but to Jane's relief she ran off toward the woods instead of into the house after Isabella. Jane hesitated, rubbing the sore spot on her arm. It was red, and she knew it would bruise. Mamma raised a hand to her mouth and turned away.

Jane's hurt and indignation drained away like whey from cheese. She was suddenly so tired that she could barely keep to her feet. Maude must have run to Hannah Herb-Woman's house, where she would be consoled and soothed, to be sent home with an apple or a slice of new bread to fill the empty hole in her heart.

And where do I go? Jane asked herself. *Who will comfort me?* Not Mamma, certainly. She knew that Mamma would never refer to the incident again, as though nothing had happened.

She went inside to start supper but didn't want to see Harry and Isabella. If Harry was going to wash Isabella's face, he must have taken her outside. Creeping through the dank kitchen, she heard the squeak-squeak-squeak of the outdoor pump as someone worked its handle. She peered through the crack of the door and saw the man kneeling before Isabella, wiping her face with a large handkerchief. Were there really tear tracks to remove? Jane wondered. Had the girl really cried?

Isabella suddenly gave a large hiccupping sob that must have startled the man, for he rocked back on his heels and stopped what he had been doing, the handkerchief dangling from his hand. "Ella?" he asked, almost fearfully. "Ella, darling—"

She had bent her head and stood twisting the hem of her gleaming dress in her fingertips. She murmured something.

"What is it, my own?"

She raised her head, and Jane was shocked at the misery in her pale face. "Father, please take me home."

"Ella—" he began, but she rushed on.

"They hate me. She only likes her own girls, and *they* don't like anyone but themselves. It smells bad in that house, and there are mice and bats and spiders. You said I would have servants and fine clothes and my own bedroom with my own fireplace…." She turned her head from her father, but Jane could tell by her shaking back and hunched shoulders that she was crying silently. After a moment, the girl said in a voice thick with tears, "I was trying to be nice. I tried to tell them how much prettier they were now that they were bathed, but they didn't want to talk to me. And Mother's comb truly was stuck in a knot. I didn't mean to hurt her—I was just trying to take the comb out without breaking it." Jane swallowed a lump of guilt. Had she misunderstood what had happened?

"Ella," the man said again, his voice shaking. "I'm sorry, I'm so sorry, my darling, but I had no idea. She told me that the house was in disrepair, but I thought she was so accustomed to fine things that a little mold or a broken stair rail would strike her as disrepair. I didn't know it was this bad."

Isabella took a deep breath and straightened. "There aren't any servants. They do all the work themselves, and they want me to do it, too. They act like I'm stupid because I don't know how." Jane stifled a cry of protest. *They* acted like *she* was stupid? But it was Isabella who treated *them* like ignorant country girls!

"They don't really work," the man answered, but Jane heard his uncertainty. "A little fine needlework, keeping poultry, making cheese—she told me that these were their occupations, and those are all suitable ways for a lady to keep herself amused."

"No, father," Isabella said. "No, it's not just a little fine needlework and keeping poultry. They make stockings, and they sew everything they wear. They cook and clean the house. They must also chop the wood and do the laundry, because who else is there?"

"Well, Ella." He stopped. Jane wondered if his face mirrored the discomfort in his voice. "Well, Ella, I'm having a bit of difficulty getting the bank to release my funds. They don't want to send gold over such a long distance until the king recovers from his illness and puts more guards on the road. I'm working on it," he said hastily, as she seemed about to speak again, "and soon we'll have maids and cooks and footmen. Won't that be nice?" He stood and took her hand. They started toward the door, and Jane fled back through the empty dining room to the South Parlor. She wiped the table and set out the bowls for the midday meal, trying to act as though she had been there ever since the incident with the comb.

The man and the girl passed through the parlor, still talking to each other, and took no notice of her. As soon as they were out of sight, Jane sat down in the big chair, her thoughts flying in and out of her head as she tried to sort them. Had Isabella really been trying to be friendly? And had she meant it when she said that she and Maude were pretty—or at least prettier—when they were clean and neat?

Clean and neat, perhaps, but hardly the ladies Mamma kept insisting they were. Jane winced at the recollection of Isabella's biting words, even though the girl had merely repeated what Jane herself had recognized long ago: she and Maude weren't ladies who were so bored with their lives of ease that they played at being dairymaid and hen girl and needlewoman. She and Maude *were* dairymaids and hen girls and needlewomen, and they were also wood choppers and floor sweepers and cooks. It was a triumph, in a way, that an outsider had seen so quickly what Jane had been aware of but that Mamma had been denying for years.

Jane didn't feel triumphant, though. She felt sick and so weary that she didn't ever want to get up.

She had to, though. She hoisted herself out of the chair and went to look out the big door. In the drive, the man was still holding his daughter's hand. "I'm taking Ella to the village," he was saying to Mamma. "She needs something to divert her."

Don't say anything, Jane pleaded silently. *Just let them go.*

Mamma lowered her gaze without answering him. Harry led his daughter into the barn, and in a few minutes he emerged, leading the chestnut horses, now harnessed to the carriage. They tossed their heads and lifted their legs high. He helped Isabella inside and climbed awkwardly into the driver's seat. The horses set out at a brisk pace as he sawed ineffectually at the reins. When the carriage was gone, Mamma said, "They'll be back this evening." Then she looked down the drive again.

Maude reappeared, scuffing her feet in the dust as she came up the drive. She didn't say where she had been, and Mamma didn't ask.

Harry and Isabella did not return in time for supper, and they still had not come when Jane lit the lamps in the South Parlor. They sat on the rug, one girl leaning on either side of Mamma, as she told them stories of parties she had gone to when she was young. The ladies all in silk, their dresses so long and their movements so graceful that they looked as if they were floating as they danced. The tall men in their elegant black clothes, their hair sleek, their hands sheathed in white gloves.

Jane allowed her mind to wander. Maybe she was wrong about never being able to meet a suitable man. If Harry's money restored the house, Mamma could give a party, the way she had said. Maybe some young man would see her and lead her into the dance, his warm hand holding hers, his arms around her as they joined the others. Maybe he would have so much money he wouldn't care that she had none, and he would carry her away from here, to a place where she wouldn't have to worry about feeding and clothing and caring for herself and her mother and sister, a place where she could relax and be happy.

Don't be stupid, she scolded herself. *That kind of thing doesn't happen in real life.*

Now that supper was over, they allowed the fire to die down. That big ember in the middle looked like the castle, as Jane imagined it, with its fantastic spires and towers stretching up to the sky. The other coals looked like the forest, where the rarely-seen people of the woods lived. That little lump could be the hut where Hannah Herb-Woman lived with her husband and their son, Hugh. The larger ember to the right could be their own house, glowing and shifting in the red-gold light of the dying fire.

Suddenly the ember flared into flame, and the little copy of their house crumbled into ash. Jane sat up. She was half asleep, and Maude was yawning. She knew that Mamma was about to tell them to go to bed, but she didn't want the cozy evening to end. Neither did Maude, apparently, because before Mamma could say anything, she asked, "Did you have a dance at the party that Harry talked about?"

"Which party was that?" Mamma looked puzzled.

Maude glanced at Jane, who suddenly realized what her sister was going to say. She shook her head, but Maude ignored her. "The one where he said your engagement to Papa was announced."

Mamma was silent for so long that Jane hoped she hadn't heard, but then she said quietly, "Yes, it was a lovely party." She smoothed the ragged skirt over her knees and stared into the flames. "We danced.... Papa was a wonderful dancer, and he was so handsome and he always made me laugh." A smile came and went fleetingly over her face, making her eyes look even sadder. Jane slipped her hand into Mamma's and squeezed. Mamma squeezed back. "We were very happy, and I thought it would last ever after."

She sighed and let go of Jane's hand, and then said, "I don't think they're coming back until tomorrow, after all. Go to sleep, girls."

"Aren't you going to bed, too, Mamma?" Maude's words were almost swallowed up in a giant yawn.

"In a little while," she answered. But when Jane got up a few hours later to visit the privy, she saw Mamma sitting in the big chair, wrapped in a shawl, her head turned toward the door.

They did not return that night.

5

Breakfast was silent. As soon as Mamma left the room, Maude said, "Maybe they went back where they came from and we'll never have to see them again." Jane didn't answer.

Shortly before noon, Betsy's bark drew them outside. They stood on the steps as the carriage drew into the drive, the horses pulling it more easily than they had that first day, when it had been loaded with heavy crates. A small copy of the carriage was tied behind. It was painted deep yellow and white, and harnessed to it was a little brown pony, her head bobbing up and down as she trotted to keep up. Seated on the driver's seat was Isabella, proudly clutching the reins, a coach whip in a holder next to her.

"She pulls your hair out, and he buys her a pony and carriage," Jane said.

"It's all right, Janie," Maude said quietly, and looked at the ground.

The two carriages pulled up in front of the house. Ella stood, still holding the reins, not looking at the girls. She wore a coral-colored dress, and on her feet were the most astonishing shoes Jane had ever seen. They were covered in a mosaic of tiny pieces of glass. They sparkled and shone so that Isabella seemed to be wearing diamonds on her dainty feet. Isabella saw the girls' stare and lifted one foot up, its toe pointed. "Papa had them specially made just for me." She turned her foot slowly. "There's not another pair like them in the entire kingdom. Isn't that right, Papa?"

"That's correct, Ella, dear." His voice was thick with love as he untied her miniature carriage. "As there is no other like you in the entire world." *Well, thank goodness for that, anyway,* Jane thought.

"Help your sister," Mamma said.

"She's not my sister," Jane said.

"Jane," Mamma said, and startled at the sadness of her tone, Jane went to hold the reins. Harry swung his daughter out of the carriage without acknowledging her. She grimaced at Maude, who giggled. Harry and Isabella went inside, leaving Jane and Maude to stable the pony and the big horse.

When they finally went in the house, Mamma was slicing cheese. She appeared calm, but Jane saw that her hands were trembling. The man, seated at the table with Isabella, rubbed his hands together. "Sorry we couldn't send word that we were delayed," he said to Mamma, as though nothing unpleasant had happened.

"Yes, I was concerned." She poured his tea. She, too, sounded calm. Why didn't she say something to Harry about his daughter's behavior? Why did she pretend that she wasn't angry? Jane thought she would explode from frustration.

"We had to wait for Ella's carriage to dry." He smiled fondly at the girl as she nibbled on the corner of her bread. "It was white when we bought it, and nothing would satisfy her but to have it painted the color of the pumpkins by the road—"

"Stop it, Father." Isabella flushed. "I keep telling you, it's not the color of a pumpkin. It's gold like the prince's carriage."

"All right, then, it's gold." Harry was still smiling at Isabella. "Have some cheese, darling." The girl ate her bread and cheese without looking at anyone, ignoring her father's attempts at conversation. When they had finished, he stood up. "I have business to do," he announced importantly. "Have to see about getting that roof fixed."

Mamma nodded. "Ask the priest first. He'll know who needs work."

Harry sighed heavily. "Margaret," he said, in a patient tone that made Jane wince, "running the household is your business. This is man's business." Mamma's face turned red. She didn't answer, and after kissing the top of Isabella's golden head, the man left. His daughter trailed after him. Jane peeked through the door and saw her, looking even smaller than she really was in the huge empty front hall, standing at the door and staring out at the empty drive.

Jane returned to the South Parlor and scrubbed the remains of their breakfast off the worn wooden table. "What did he mean, 'man's business'?" Maude asked. "This is *our* house, isn't it, Mamma?" Mamma didn't answer. Maude and Jane washed the dishes with the last of the soap. Maude opened her mouth to speak, and Jane knew that she was going to ask whether Mamma had brought any more back with her. She shot her sister a warning glance, and Maude subsided.

Isabella came back as Jane and Maude were getting ready for their morning chores. She didn't look at them, but a line on her cheek sparkled where a tear slid down it. Jane sat down to pull on her boots and heard Maude say, "You can't wear that dress or your new shoes to do chores." Jane couldn't resist looking up to see Isabella's reaction.

After what seemed like a long time, the girl squeaked, "Me? Do chores?"

"You can choose," Maude said. "You can help me find eggs or go to the barn with Jane and milk the cow and the goats."

"I'm not—" Isabella began.

"You have to," Jane interrupted. "We all have to work, or there's nothing to eat." Mamma acted as though she hadn't heard, but she pressed her lips together tightly. Isabella glanced at Mamma, but even she seemed to know that no help would be coming from there. With a frown that somehow made her look even prettier, she stalked out.

Jane was soon instructing Isabella in the art of milking. "First, you wash your hands." She worked the pump handle up and down. Isabella complied but didn't look at her. *Fine,* thought Jane. *You don't have to talk.* She rinsed her own hands and wrung out a cloth in the cool water before the stream from the pump subsided. She sat down on her milking stool and wiped Baby's pink udder. The cow, a wisp of straw hanging from her mouth, swung her huge head around to look at Isabella. The girl yelped and jumped back.

"Baby won't hurt you," Jane said. "See, you have to make sure everything is clean so the milk stays fresh."

"How do you know she won't hurt me?" Isabella asked. "And why do you call such a big cow 'Baby'?"

"She wasn't big when she was born," Jane said. "That's when Maude named her." Jane rhythmically wiped, wiped, wiped the udder, long past the need to clean and dry it, as she remembered that day. It was shortly after they had gotten word that Papa would never be coming home again. Mamma had taken to her bed, and as soon as she recovered, she'd dismissed the milkmaids and cowherds and sold all the horses but Saladin, and all the cows except Duchess. A few days later, Duchess had started having her calf. Somehow Jane had been able to tell something was wrong, so she'd run for Hannah Herb-Woman, who'd rolled up her sleeves and got down on her knees, and she and Jane had wrestled the little creature out. Despite careful doctoring by Hannah, Duchess had died, and Jane had raised Baby on a bottle.

And now look at the size of her, Jane thought, briefly resting her head against the familiar hard, warm flank. Mamma acted as though someone else had saved the calf's life on the bloody wet straw in the stable. Not Jane Montjoy, daughter of Lady Margaret Montjoy, mistress of Halsey Hall, the finest house in the kingdom.

Jane roused herself. "When everything's clean, you squeeze like this."

Isabella upset the cow so that she would hardly let down her milk, despite Jane's coaxing and gentle touch. She finally told the girl to go, and once the disturbing presence was no longer there, Baby relaxed. Jane would just have to stop trying to make Isabella do her share. *It isn't worth the effort,* she thought. She filled half a bucket with Betsy's warm milk and then moved on to the goats. When she finished, she left the buckets to cool in the dairy, and then looked for eggs in the grass. Maude was protective about the chicken coop, claiming that when anyone else but she went in there the chickens would get upset and not lay. Jane suspected that the real reason was that Maude hid some of her treasures in there. She found two eggs under a bush and added them to Maude's basket when she emerged from the coop, and they walked back to the house together.

A group of men from the village stood in the drive with a mule cart full of tools and lumber. The girls caught little snatches of their conversation with Harry—"Too far gone" and "We might put a support under here" and "The outer wood is sound, but what is underneath has rotted."

Among the men stood a few boys, awkwardly holding tools that looked too big for them. Jane nudged Maude and pointed at Hannah Herb-Woman's son, Hugh. His red hair made him visible even from where they stood. Maude waved at him, but he pretended not to notice. Some rough-looking men and boys wearing ragged clothes and heavy boots hung on the edge of the crowd, not mingling with the others. Several were familiar to Jane from the rare services at St. Cuthbert's Church. One man had a large wooden mallet hanging from his belt. Another, the tallest and broadest, rested a wood ax on his shoulder. He stood with his hand protectively on the shoulder of a boy who appeared to be about Jane's age, with curls so long that they almost covered his eyes. The boy's mouth was turned down at the corners, although whether this was some trick of his features or a scowl, Jane could not tell. He must have felt her eyes on him, because he turned and glared at her. Jane flinched. What was he so angry about?

"From the woods," Maude whispered, pointing at them. Jane snatched her sister's hand down. Maude leaned close to Jane. "What are they doing here?"

"They must be desperately hungry," Jane whispered back. "Mamma said that they only come out of the woods when they're starving." The hot, dry summer had made game scarce, and she knew herself how scarce berries and mushrooms were.

"Why?" Maude asked. "Aren't they *glad* to be working for us? Mamma says the servants were always so happy, when we had them."

"Hush!" Jane was in an agony that her sister would be overheard. She didn't know how the people of the woods felt about the Halseys, but she didn't believe they were like the happy maids and nannies and footmen and butlers that Mamma talked about. She even thought, uncomfortably, that perhaps those same servants hadn't been as contented as Mamma always said.

Maude tugged at her sleeve. "If they fix the house, do you think we'll give parties like the ones Mamma talks about?" Jane felt a ripple of excitement at the thought, followed by dread. They didn't even know how to curtsey, much less dance. How would they talk to people they didn't know?

The men swarmed up ladders and over the roof, and tiles crashed down to the ground. They shattered as they fell from the great height, leaving scraps of dark gray slate everywhere, so the girls retreated into the house. Isabella was sitting in the big chair, drumming her little fingers on its arm. Her father was seated opposite her, leaning forward and speaking in a low and pleading tone. "Just until tomorrow, darling. You can take the carriage out all day tomorrow, if you like. The pony's too tired."

"Please, Papa," Isabella wheedled. "I want to take it out *today*. It's so noisy here—I'm sure it's giving you a headache. I want to take my carriage to the river where it's quiet."

Mamma came into the room, wiping her hands on her apron. The smell of slightly soured milk accompanied her, as it always did when she had been in the dairy. Isabella wrinkled her nose. Jane could tell that Mamma had noticed the grimace, but she said nothing about it, instead addressing the man. "The work is progressing nicely. There must be a dozen men. At this rate, they will have a little money to spend in the village on Saturday."

"I won't pay them until they've finished," Harry said. "You must be firm with workmen. If you're not, they take advantage of you. Leave it to me, Margaret." And he added in a lower tone, "It's *my* money, after all." Mamma turned away.

Maude pulled Jane into the hallway. "Why does he care when they're paid?" she whispered. "They'll finish the roof. Mamma wouldn't have hired someone who would cheat us. Harry can buy Isabella a golden carriage and shoes made of glass. Why won't he pay the roofers?"

Jane shook her head, unable to respond. She knew that Hugh's father had not had work for a long time. He was a herdsman, and the hot, dry summer had dried out the fields so much that many farmers had been forced to slaughter animals that they couldn't feed. Still, Hannah often managed to trade herbs or doctoring for eggs or even an occasional chicken. Some of the other families were in even more want.

The roofing went on steadily, except that a day was lost when it rained hard all morning, filling the dry fountain with water that turned to greenish muck. More water poured in through the holes of the roof, and Jane and Maude tried to catch the worst of it with buckets and washtubs. At least the cisterns on the roof would be filling, and they wouldn't have to wear out their arms pumping water.

After the sky cleared that afternoon, the men were able to resume work, but less than an hour later, a young man slid off the wet tiles and crashed down into the courtyard. He groaned as he was carried away on a ladder.

"Make them some tea," Mamma said the next afternoon. "There's a chilly wind, and they should be ready to take a rest."

"*Must* I, Mamma?" Jane knew that her protest was merely a token one, and she was already untucking her legs from under her. Neither of the younger girls stirred. Whenever Mamma didn't say whether she or Maude should do something, Jane always wound up doing it.

"The ladies of the house look after the workmen," Mamma said. Jane turned her exasperated sigh into a cough as she stuck her needle carefully back into the tablecloth she was mending. She knew that Maude's repairs would be ragged lumps rather than her own almost invisible seams, but if Mamma wanted her to leave her work…

She stood awkwardly on the drive, holding the largest tray she could manage, with a large pot and a stack of cups. Nobody took any notice of her. *I knew this would happen,* she thought, and was about to go back in when one of the men glanced down and saw her. He turned and said something over his shoulder that Jane couldn't catch. One or two of the men laughed, and she felt herself flush. She forced herself to hold the heavy tray steady as they came down the ladders, and then one by one they came to help themselves. Each nodded as he poured himself a cup, and a few tugged at the brim of their caps. "Thank you, Miss," one of them said, startling her so that her reply froze in her chest before it made it to her lips.

The tray grew lighter with each cup poured and removed. The large man she had seen holding the wood ax was the last. After the man had taken a cup and nodded his thanks, he turned as though expecting to find someone with him. "Will?" he called. No answer. The man put his cup back on the tray and strode off, returning a moment later with the boy, who was scowling and dragging his feet. The man picked up his cup again, and the boy stopped short. The man pushed him forward with an impatient, "Go on."

The boy raised his eyes but didn't look Jane directly in the face. "Thank you for offering—" His father nudged him in the back, and he hastily added, "Miss. But I don't care for any." He looked at his father as though to say, "Satisfied?"

Jane knew that the boy was feeling terribly uncomfortable, and she tried to keep "Serves you right" out of her voice as she answered, "I don't either. My sister usually makes the tea, but I did it this time and I don't really know how. I'm afraid it isn't very good."

As though surprised at her friendly tone, the boy finally looked at her, and he broke into a reluctant grin, showing white teeth. He instantly quenched the smile, but for that moment he had appeared friendly, and Jane could see humor in his dark eyes. The man gulped down his tea. The two of them returned to work, and Jane returned to the house, thinking she would never understand the people of the woods.

6

Jane pushed aside wet leaves and poked among tree roots, hunting for mushrooms under the trees near the house. No luck. The berries, too, were long gone, and the few nuts that fell rotted quickly in the soggy ground. She turned back toward home, her empty basket dangling from her arm, and was met by Betsy on the drive. The puppies were old enough to allow her to leave them occasionally, and she frisked around Jane, clearly thrilled with her liberty.

Jane paused. Mamma always said not to go into the forest, where there were wolves and boars, as well as bandits and the people of the woods, who, Mamma said, were half-wild. And there was that strange flicker as of pale cloth or hair that she had seen in the trees that day, followed by the singing. No, she wouldn't risk it.

But if she brought Betsy with her, and if she stayed on the paths that surely continued through the trees, what harm could come to her? Betsy would give warning of any wild beasts, and while she was gentle, she was large, and anyone seeing her would keep their distance. And maybe Betsy could catch a rabbit—even a squirrel would be welcome. If Jane skinned it and cut up the meat, they could tell Mamma it was a rabbit, and she would never ask why the bones were so tiny, or why it tasted different. Jane couldn't remember when she had last eaten meat. She made up her mind and whistled to Betsy, who followed along willingly.

As they left the familiar band of trees nearest the house, Jane rested her hand on the big hound's head. The touch comforted her. The narrow path soon dwindled to the point where it was barely visible. Branches overhung it, shaking cold droplets into her face as she pushed through them. Jane swallowed. Surely she would be able to find her way back, but even if she couldn't, Betsy could. Dogs always knew where they were, didn't they? Especially mother dogs who had left their puppies behind?

She searched in the wet leaves, but found nothing. She ventured a few steps deeper into the woods, and then a few steps more. Now that she had disobeyed Mamma by coming this far, she might as well keep going until she found something or until the sun was near setting.

The forest was eerily silent, as though it was watching her. No birds sang; no small animals rustled in the sparse underbrush. *Birds don't sing in the rain,* she told herself, even though the rain had stopped. *The rabbits and squirrels aren't gone—they're just keeping still so Betsy won't notice them.*

As she pushed aside a branch, she realized that Betsy wasn't next to her. She looked around and saw the dog standing a few yards away, her head up, ears pricked, nostrils twitching.

Betsy gave a little whine. Jane started to ask, "What is it, girl?" when she heard it, too: a distant voice, high-pitched like that of a woman or a child, singing a few notes of a song. *It's not the wind,* she told herself. *That's a person—a person singing deep in the forest.* She felt the hairs on her arms rise. The same voice repeated the notes, a little louder. Betsy's head whipped around to the left, and from that direction there came a deeper voice singing a different tune. A low rumble arose from Betsy's throat.

And then a dark shape moved out from behind a tree. Bare branches between her and whatever it was kept Jane from seeing it clearly, but she didn't wait for it to get closer. All the tales that Mamma told them by the fire on winter nights—stories of witches who baked children in their ovens, and evil little men who danced around bonfires and stole babies, and giants who ate people as though they were chickens—flashed into her mind. She turned and fled back up the path, dropping her basket and not daring to stop to pick it up. She barely noticed where she was going, and just as the thought *I'm lost* popped into her mind, Betsy appeared next to her. The two of them sped down the path and finally burst into the pastureland behind the barn, where their own two goats swung their heads up to stare at them, and Baby mooed at her.

Betsy ran on to the barn and her puppies, but Jane's knees felt weak, and she sat down on a stump. If Betsy hadn't been with her, she would have thought she had imagined the singing. But she knew she hadn't imagined that shape, that dark thing that had moved slowly from behind the tree. Was it a person? A bear? Someone from the world of the fairies?

The cow ambled up and nudged at her pocket. Jane pushed the big head away. She had found no late apples, and even if she had, she would have kept them to give to Mamma instead of to the cow.

When her heart slowed and her legs stopped trembling, she stood and smoothed her dress. She took a deep breath and headed toward the house. Something about what happened tickled at her brain. Something had not been the way it was supposed to be—and not just the voices singing and the shadowy form. What was it?

Trying to puzzle it out—and wondering how she would explain the loss of the basket—she rounded the corner of the house and stopped short at the sight of Mamma, Harry and the roofers, gathered in the drive. Harry scowled at the crowd, his hands on his hips. He stood on a step, forcing the workmen to look up at him. Mamma, next to him, had laid her hand on Betsy's head to quiet her, but this was unnecessary; the big hound looked out calmly at the assembled roofers, clearly sensing no threat.

"It's not that we're not glad of the work," the man in front was saying, his cap in his hand, "it's just that we were promised our pay on Saturday, and today is Saturday. We've worked hard and done as we were told—"

"You have not," Harry said sharply. "You were to have finished repairing the roof and there are still holes."

"We would have finished this afternoon," said the man, equally sharply, "and we will come back after the Sabbath and work until it's done, but you know what happened. First the rain, and then there was that mishap. Young Jeremy is a good worker, and without him it was impossible to end on time. We lost several hours tending to him, Lady Margaret." His voice was respectful as he addressed Mamma.

"I know you did. I was remiss in not visiting him. How is he coming along?"

"His leg is broken," said another man, in a rougher tone

than the first. "It's doubtful whether he'll ever again be a useful wage-earner."

Mamma made a distressed sound, but Harry broke in. "When he chose to be a roofer, he chose to take certain risks. If he couldn't afford the risk, he should have found other work."

"What other work?" said the second man, raising his voice. "It's been near impossible to make a living here ever since the prince forbade us to hunt in our forest and fish in our streams."

"He won't even let us chop wood for sale," chimed in a new voice. Jane saw that it came from the curly-haired boy—Will. He stood with a hand on his wood ax and his head thrown back defiantly. He glanced in her direction, and she quickly dropped her eyes, but she was sure he had seen her looking at him. She felt flustered and didn't know why. Why *shouldn't* she look at him? She glanced back and saw that his gaze was still turned in her direction, so she looked away again hastily.

"*Your* forest? *Your* streams?" Harry laughed, but without humor. "You forget whose land you live on. The land you call 'yours' belongs to the king. It's his privilege to decide what is done with it."

"We've always been allowed—"

"That's beside the point. You did not finish the work you had agreed to do and I will not pay you tonight."

Feet shifted and grumbles arose. Hugh clutched a trowel, his eyes cast down. The rough-looking man with a gray beard who stood in front, still holding his hat, said, "Lady Margaret?" Mamma looked at him. "Lady Margaret, your father would never have treated us like this. Nor your grandfather."

Mamma lowered her eyes.

The man turned to his fellows. "Come along. We'll get no

pay this day." They left, dragging their tools, some silent, some grumbling. Hugh cast a glance over his shoulder at Maude as he followed them. Will glared at Harry, his eyes so full of resentment that Jane flinched again, even though the look hadn't been directed at her.

When only a few workers remained, the spokesman stepped forward and tugged on his cap. "Good night, Lady Margaret," he said, and then more quietly, "We all know it's not your fault, Mistress. We'll be back on Monday morning and finish the task. If he pays us, well and good. If not, we'll call the work a friendly act to an old neighbor."

Mamma raised her eyes. Jane saw tears shining in them. Mamma nodded her thanks to the man, who tugged his cap once more, then turned and followed the others. Betsy trotted after them, hoping for a friendly pat on the head, but they ignored her, and she turned aside into the barn.

"What did that man want?" Harry asked sharply.

"He was just remembering my father," Mamma said. "Come, girls, it's getting chilly. Let's go sit by the fire." They left Harry alone on the steps.

"Where have you been, Jane?" Maude asked as they trailed after Mamma.

"Mushroom hunting," she answered shortly.

"Did you find any?"

Jane shook her head.

Maude's face fell. "I found some chestnuts," she said glumly. "And I pulled up the last of the carrots."

"That's what we'll have for supper, then," Jane said. She wished Maude would stop talking and let her think. What was it that had happened in the woods that was nagging at her?

They ate in silence. Harry gave Isabella most of his supper. Jane realized that the man's clothes were hanging a bit loosely.

"What are you staring at?" he snapped.

She turned her gaze away hastily and didn't answer.

Cleaning up after supper was quick, since they had no cooking pots to wash. Mamma laid the chestnuts on the fire to roast for a treat before bed, and Jane went out for the day's second milking. She took the full bucket to the dairy and was about to turn back to the house when her eye caught sight of something on the stump where she had stopped after running out of the forest. Had she left her shawl there? No, she was still wearing it.

She looked around, hesitating to go just those few yards closer to the woods in the dim evening light. A chilly breeze rustled the branches of the dark trees and raised the hairs on the back of her neck. Was it *really* a breeze, though, and not some forest spirit? *Don't be silly,* she scolded herself, and forced herself to hold her head high as she crossed the field, the soggy leaves squelching unpleasantly underfoot.

She stopped short when she reached the stump. It was her basket—the empty basket that she had dropped in her flight from the strange voices. Only it wasn't empty now. Jane marveled at the plump, white mushrooms that filled it almost to the brim. Something darker lay under them; she lifted out enough mushrooms to see three red and green apples. They were small, but bright and smooth.

Jane glanced at the woods. Nothing moved and she heard no sound, but somehow she knew that she was being watched. She stood, clutching the handle of the basket, and called, "Thank you" to the dark trees. Still nothing, so she turned, feeling a prickle on her back. How was she going to explain the food to Mamma? She had already told her she had found no mushrooms.

She walked slowly, trying to think of something. "I found these earlier today but I lost the basket and was ashamed to tell you, and then I found it again"? Even Maude, much less Mamma, wouldn't be fooled by that. "These were growing in a place I forgot to look in earlier, but I remembered as soon as I got to the barn, and went looking in the dark"? That *might* explain the mushrooms, but what about the apples?

Struck by a thought, Jane ran to the dairy and picked out a large round cheese that had been curing. It wasn't quite ready, but it would do. She rinsed off some big leaves and wrapped them securely around the cheese. Glancing at the house, she ran back into the field. It was almost full dark now, and the trees somehow looked larger and closer than they had before. She placed the cheese on the stump and straightened. "This is for you," she called as loudly as she dared. "It's cheese." No answer. She felt foolish, talking to nobody.

As she let herself in the front door, still puzzling about what to say to Mamma, she realized what had been bothering her about those last minutes in the forest.

The branch she had pushed aside off the path just before hearing the fairy singers had not shed raindrops on her. That could mean only one thing. Someone had been there just before her and had shaken off the water in passing.

Someone in the woods had been watching her.

"And you traded a cheese for them?"

Jane couldn't decide whether Mamma sounded disbelieving or merely confused. She nodded. "You said that ladies could exchange what they had too much of with other ladies."

"True." Mamma looked at the basket. "What lady was this? Why was she out so late, and how did she come to have mushrooms and apples with her?"

"I…I don't know. She didn't say." Jane was so unaccustomed to lying to Mamma that her mind was empty.

Help came from an unexpected source. "She must have been going to a harvest ball," Isabella said from the big chair, where she sat with her legs tucked up under her. "In my country, ladies bring food to share, to celebrate the harvest. Perhaps she thought that cheese would be more welcome than mushrooms and apples."

Jane turned to stare at Isabella in astonishment. Was she trying to be an ally? The girl returned her look calmly.

"Well— But surely— Certainly if there were a ball in the neighborhood, I would have been invited," Mamma said.

Jane bit her tongue. Mamma was never invited to people's houses, not anymore. The last time Mamma had gone to a party, a year after baby Robert had died, she had returned early with red eyes and a shiny nose, and had burst into sobs as soon as she closed the door behind her. Maude had been so frightened that Jane had taken her sister to their room and then tried to soothe Mamma. Mamma had tried and failed to control herself, and through her sobs Jane could make out only enough to understand that the other ladies had snubbed her, and had said unkind things about her dress that was out of style and about her suntanned face and work-roughened hands. Mamma had never before acknowledged that she was no longer the equal of the people she had grown up with, and her anguish had so frightened Jane that she gave up trying to calm her and crept into bed with Maude, holding her until the crying from the parlor ceased and they heard Mamma enter her own room. The next day, Jane had seen that the rag bag was filled with scraps of peach-colored silk that had been torn into shreds.

"What did this lady look like?" Mamma asked now.

"Oh…" Jane tried to imagine a lady going to a ball. "It was dark, so I didn't see her well. She was going by in a… in a carriage, and when she saw me she called me over and said she'd heard about our cheese, and asked for one. I ran to the dairy to get it and when I came back she filled my basket with these things."

"Whose carriage was it?" Mamma asked. Jane looked at her blankly. "What coat of arms was painted on the door?"

"I didn't see."

"What does it matter?" Harry broke in, much to Jane's relief. "Just cook them and be done with it."

Mamma's face got that closed look it always had when someone acknowledged openly that they didn't have servants to do the cooking, but she didn't object when Jane took the basket and went outside to wash the mushrooms and apples while Maude rummaged in her pouch for herbs.

Despite her full belly, Jane spent a restless night. She woke over and over from dreams of creatures reaching out branchlike arms to grab her and drag her into the forest, of mushrooms that turned into cheeses and back again, of fairy choruses enticing her deeper and deeper into the woods until she joined them, singing wordless tunes while Maude and Mamma wandered lost among the trees, sobbing and calling her name, and not hearing her answer them.

7

Jane wrung out a bed sheet with aching fingers. Clothing and dishcloths weren't so bad, but her hands cramped with the effort of squeezing out water from the big linens. If she didn't wring them out well, they would take forever to dry. The autumn continued cold and damp, and although this meant that now they were finding mushrooms every day, it also meant that mud was everywhere, both inside and out, and laundry took on a musty smell from being wet too long. It also meant that the few vegetables that Maude had managed to grow in a patch hidden from Mamma rotted before they were ripe, save for a few pumpkins and some hard beans that Jane cooked in a stew.

Maybe now that the roof was fixed and the kitchen chimney was usable again, they could hang the linens in here and dry them by the fire. She considered. No, it would be easier to use the lines that were already strung behind the house, as long as the rain held off for a while. Besides, the kitchen was so huge that it would take all their store of firewood to make it warm and dry enough to be worth the trouble.

She wrung out the last sheet as well as she could and dropped it into the basket with the others. She pushed a lock of hair off her forehead with the back of her hand, which was wrinkled and white. She shoved the basket over to the huge wringer and fed a sheet into it with one hand, turning the crank with the other. The machine squeezed out more cold water as Jane poked the sheet through with a stick. She leaned into the crank, and it groaned and squeaked as it turned the big wooden rollers.

It would have been easier with one person to feed in the sheet and another to work the crank, but Maude was tending to the chickens, and Ella, of course, was absent. The man wouldn't risk Ella's fingers in the wringer. The two of them were in the South Parlor, reading, eating candied fruit that Harry had bought in the village—Jane hadn't even remembered that such luxuries existed—and complaining if they stirred to put a log on the fire that was keeping them warm. *The logs that I cut,* Jane thought, *and that Maude stacked.*

Harry still hadn't hired any house servants, three months after his arrival there. He wouldn't come into the kitchen to help with the laundry, either. He had been complaining of a headache and fever for a few days. *He always has something wrong with him when there's work to be done,* Jane thought, dropping the nearly dry sheet into the second basket and starting to feed another one between the rollers.

"Jane!" Mamma's urgent voice interrupted her thoughts.

"I'll be done in a minute," Jane said.

"No, that's not what I meant. Run to Hannah and tell her that Harry is ill. Give me one of the wet linens. I need to try to bring his fever down."

"What's the matter with him?" Jane handed her a sodden dishcloth.

"I don't know. He's feverish and says his head hurts so that he can't sit up. Hurry, child."

Jane ran to the front hall to get a shawl to protect herself from the coming rain. Maude was waiting for her there, clutching the egg basket. "What if it's measles?" she whispered. "Or smallpox?"

"I don't know." Jane tied the ends of the shawl under her chin. "If it is, I suppose he'll get very sick. He might even—"

She stopped, not wanting to frighten her sister, but Maude finished the sentence for her. "He might even die." Jane nodded. "Like Robert," Maude said, and Jane nodded again.

She let herself out the kitchen door and took off at a trot toward Hannah's cottage. She wasn't sure if Maude really remembered Robert, born too soon, right after Papa had left for the last time, and dead a few weeks later. They had lost first Jane's twin, Rose, who had gone to sleep one night in the cradle they shared and never woken up, and then Robert. Jane barely remembered little Robert, with his tiny hands and solemn face.

She ducked under a branch so its wet leaves wouldn't slap her in the face. Hannah's baby, little Clare with her red-gold curls and ready smile, had died, too. Hannah's own son, Hugh, had only been three, like Maude, and when it became clear that both of them were stricken with the illness, they had been put in the same bed so that the herb-woman and Mamma could take care of them more easily. The two little ones had almost died, as well. Jane had been sick, but not so sick that she didn't know it when baby Robert was taken away.

Jane shuddered as she pushed through the damp underbrush

that had grown high since their visits to Hannah's house had dwindled with Harry's arrival. It wasn't only the cold water that chilled her, but the memory of the priest's man carrying away the baby, a tiny package wrapped in a white cloth. She had crept out of her sickbed and watched him hurriedly place the bundle into a little grave on the hillside, next to where Rose already lay under her gray headstone. Jane shivered again and made the sign of the cross on her chest as she broke into the small clearing where Hannah and her family's hut stood.

Hannah dropped her pouch on the floor near Harry's bed and leaned closer, examining him. The man's face was red, and Jane could feel the heat rising from his skin when she put a damp cloth on his forehead, as Hannah instructed. She drew back, frightened, when he mumbled something she couldn't make out. "Maude," Hannah said, and Maude took her sister's place, wiping the sweat off Harry's face, holding a cup of water to his unresponsive lips.

"Shall I brew some catnip tea?" Maude asked. Hannah grunted a distracted affirmative, and Maude rooted in the herb-woman's pouch and pulled out a bunch of dried leaves. She smelled them and then dropped them in the water that had been heating on the hearth.

"Take the child away, Jane," Hannah said. "Maude, you stay here and help." Isabella, frozen, kept her eyes on her father.

"Jane," Mamma said sharply, "take Isabella outside."

"Come with me." Jane took the younger girl's hand.

"I want to stay here," Isabella said, but Jane pulled her out the door.

The barn was warm with the animals' heat and blessedly sweet-smelling after the stench of the sickroom. A farmer had left them a big load of hay in exchange for his pick of Betsy's puppies when they were weaned, and Jane tossed some straw to each of the animals, who were soon munching contentedly. "You can look for eggs in here, and Maude will hunt them in the coop later," Jane offered. Isabella didn't answer. She leaned over the box that held the remaining puppies. Betsy watched the girl closely. "Be careful," Jane said. "She doesn't like people to touch them."

"They look like rats." Isabella poked a fat belly. She seemed to have recovered, but then Jane saw that her lips were pressed tightly together, and her eyes, when she glanced over her shoulder to address Jane, looked hard and bright.

"They do not!" Jane was stung. "They're beautiful puppies. Everyone always wants one of Betsy's litter. They're the best hunters in the county."

Isabella picked up a puppy. It squealed, and Betsy rose to her feet, her eyes glued on the girl, her upper lip curling. "Isabella." Jane tried to imitate Mamma's stern tone. "Put him down. Betsy doesn't like what you're doing."

Isabella started to lower the puppy into the box, but it wiggled to get free and let out a piercing yelp. Jane saw a brown flash and a snarl, and Isabella dropped the puppy and leaped back. "She bit me!" she cried. Clutching her wrist, she ran from the barn. Betsy settled down and licked her puppy, knocking it over with her tongue. Jane wanted to run after Isabella, but Baby's milk finally started coming down and she couldn't leave. She worked quickly, stripping each teat, and then dealt with the goats and left the pails in the dairy. She hurried back to the house and let herself into the parlor.

Isabella stood motionless by the bed, her face ashen. Hannah was gently closing the man's eyes as Maude wiped a trace of foam from his mouth. Still Isabella did not move, but when Hannah started winding a long strip of cloth under his chin and over the top of his head, the girl seized her arm. "No!" she howled, trying to yank the cloth out of the woman's hand. "No! He can't eat if you close his mouth! He can't talk if you tie that thing on him!"

"Child, child." Hannah unclenched Isabella's small fist from the bandage. "Your father can't talk anymore, he's—"

"He is *not,*" Isabella said. Mamma came up behind her and held the girl's shoulders, trying to turn her around. Isabella twisted free and lunged toward the still figure.

Mamma grabbed her. "Isabella, we don't know what illness he had." Her voice caught a little. "We can't risk your catching it. Think how much more he would suffer if he knew he had given it to you."

"Father!" called Isabella. "Father! Father!"

But there was no answer, save the distant howl of a dog and Saladin's answering whinny.

8

Hannah said she would remain with them for a few days, helping to take care of the house and of Isabella, who seemed to have forgotten how to eat, dress herself, even sleep. The herb-woman also had to stay long enough to be sure that she herself had not been infected before she returned to her own home. Her husband and son were accustomed to her remaining several days at a sickbed and wouldn't worry at her absence.

The morning after Harry died was cold and windy. Hannah and Jane went out to the small graveyard down the hill behind the house to bury Harry as decently as they could manage. Maude trailed behind. Mamma stayed indoors with Isabella, who had not said a syllable since her outburst at her father's deathbed and had hardly even moved from where she now sat motionless on the big chair, wrapped in shawls and shivering.

Hannah's gray-streaked red hair whipped around her face in the fierce gusts that drove Maude and Jane into each other's arms for warmth as they waited for the herb-woman to tire so they could take their turn. Hannah finally stepped out of the shallow trench, breathing hard and sweating from the exertion, even in the chill. Maude picked up the shovel, but it became clear that she wasn't strong enough to do much good. Jane took her place. Despite the autumn rains the ground was so hard that she quickly wore a blister even on her work-roughened hands.

"I'll get some rags," Hannah said. "Perhaps if we pad the handle you'll be able to work a little longer." Jane nodded her thanks as Hannah left. She leaned on the shovel handle and then resumed chipping away at the hard earth. *Halseys have high standards.* Mamma's words, so frequently repeated, echoed in her mind. *Ladies may take care of the household and tend to the sick, and they may do fine sewing, even make butter and cheese, but heavy work is for others.*

Taking care of the household no longer meant supervising a staff, as it had when Mamma was a young woman, and when Mamma talked about tending to the sick, she didn't mean boiling sheets that a dying man had been lying in. To Mamma, sewing meant embroidering tiny patterns on a dainty nightgown, not patching worn-out linens. Making butter and cheese so that young gentlemen might admire your arms while your sleeves were rolled back was different from working in the dairy every day so that you and your sister don't starve. And now Jane was digging a grave. *Do ladies dig graves, Mamma?* she wanted to ask. She set her lips grimly, determined not to cry in front of Maude, and she tossed the small bit of dirt in her shovel as far away as she could manage.

It landed with a dry thud on the toe of a boot. A man's heavy leather boot.

A squeal of terror rose in her throat. Someone had found out that they were here, alone, defenseless, with no man to guard them, and was coming to rob them of what little they had, and then kill them. She stood frozen, unable even to lift her head. Where was Hannah? Why hadn't she come back?

"Janie?" Maude sounded peevish. "What are you—" Then she fell silent as she, too, saw the dark form at the edge of the clearing.

Maude's voice woke something in Jane. Here, next to the graves of the brother and sister who'd lain in this spot for years, she would not lose her last sister. She held the shovel like a weapon and forced herself to look up. The outline of a man's shape was silhouetted against the pale sky.

"Who are you?" She tried to sound as cold as Isabella. "Who are you and what do you want?"

The man took a step forward. He was tall and broad-shouldered, and his dark curly hair was long and unkempt. Jane recognized him; he was the man she had spoken to when she had passed out tea to the roofers. "You're the one who's been leaving us whey and milk, aren't you?" His voice was rough but kind.

Surprised, Jane let her shovel droop, and nodded.

"We're grateful that you remember us," he went on. "Your milk has saved many of us in these times of want, including my own sister's child." Jane's knees weakened as relief flooded her. He seemed to mean them no harm, even though he was a man of the woods. The man nodded at the bundle of linens. One of Harry's hands had fallen out of the sheet and was curled, yellow and rigid, in the dirty snow. "You've had a death here, I see. I'm sorry for your loss, Miss, but you can't dig that grave. Go on back to the house." Jane looked at Maude, who nodded eagerly, evidently thinking of the warm fire that awaited them in the parlor.

"I'll do it, Miss. I'm more used to handling a wood ax than that shovel there, but I can do better than a girl. The ground isn't hard if you're used to working it. Once I break through to the soft under-soil I'll make short work of it. It will be a way of thanking you for saving me from having to dig one of these for my nephew. When I'm through, I'll send my son up to the house with the shovel."

From the forest shadows behind the man, a boy stepped out. Jane recognized him, as well; it was Will, the boy whose dark curls had nearly covered his face the day the roofers had argued with Harry. His hair was shorn now and his face was gaunt, making his large, dark eyes look huge. He ducked his head and then nodded shyly. Jane nodded back wordlessly. She suddenly felt timid and told herself, *Don't be silly. It's just that boy who worked on the roof.*

"I'm sorry for your loss," Will said. He reached out his hand, and Jane, confused, put her own in it. His hand was warm and rough, and he held hers briefly before dropping it.

"Oh, it's not— He wasn't—" Jane was angry at herself for being tongue-tied, and besides, she didn't know how to tell him that Harry wasn't her real father without sounding heartless. In her confusion she led Maude away. *Stupid, stupid!* she told herself. *Why not stay and talk with him?*

"They're helping us because they respect our family," Maude said confidently as soon as they were out of earshot.

Jane shook her head. "I don't think that matters anymore. They're helping us because they're our neighbors, and we can't do it ourselves." She wished she could go back and respond more graciously to Will's sympathy, but it was too late.

"It's because of our ancient name," Maude persisted stubbornly. Jane just shook her head without answering. Maude could protest all she wanted to and the ancestors could whisper at her all day and all night, but they wouldn't convince her that the name Halsey meant anything special.

They met Hannah at the door. "Did you have to give up?" she asked. "I can take another turn." She strode down the hill. Jane called after her, but Hannah was already speaking to the man, who was by now up to his knees in the hole. The two adults looked up at the house and then at the sheet-wrapped bundle on the ground as they conferred some more. Then Hannah turned and came back up the slope. "Let's wait in the barn until he's done," Hannah said. "It's a little warmer in there." She didn't need to say why they couldn't go back in the house. Hannah knew as well as they did what their mother would say if she knew they had been talking with one of the people of the woods.

The barn wasn't as warm as the parlor would have been, but at least they were out of the wind, and there was Baby's flank to snuggle up to. Jane felt herself sliding into sleep when a gentle hand shook her shoulder. "Come," Hannah said. "It's time to get your mother and the girl."

They all stood at the graveside while Mamma murmured some words of prayer. They would have to wait until the priest returned in the spring to hold a proper service. She couldn't tell from Isabella's blank face and unblinking eyes if she knew what was happening. After it was over, they turned and trooped silently back toward the house, Isabella in the lead. Mamma put a gentle hand on her shoulder, but the girl shook it off without looking up. Mamma didn't try again.

When they reached the door, Jane knew she couldn't go inside, back into the stench of illness and death and the sight of that empty bed where Harry's corpse had lain. "I—I need to go to the dairy," she said. "I just remembered..." Before anyone could ask what she had just remembered, she fled to the little stone building perched above the stream.

The familiar, comforting smell of cheese and butter rather than the sight of the dead man, rather than digging his grave, rather than the sight of Isabella's ashen face and dry, glittering eyes, tore a sob out of Jane's throat. She closed the door so that only weak sun rays came through the tiny window high in the stone wall, and cried until she was light-headed, and then she cried some more. Every time she thought she was finished, a fresh sob jerked her chest.

Finally, just as suddenly as it had started, Jane's weeping ended. *Mamma will be wondering where I am,* she thought wearily. She didn't want anyone to follow her here—she didn't think she could bear being questioned—and she picked up one of the cheesecloths to dampen in the stream outside in order to wash the traces of the tears from her face and bring down the puffiness of her eyelids.

She opened the door and nearly jumped back at the sight of a figure standing there. Harry's ghost? But instantly she knew her mistake and recognized Will, the last person she wanted to see in her misery.

"Are you all right, Miss?" he asked.

"What do you want?" Her words were tight from her recent weeping and from being startled, and she was glad that she was still in darkness so that he couldn't see her face, streaked and swollen with tears, as she knew it must be.

He held out the shovel. "Didn't want to take it into the barn," he said, his voice suddenly hard. "Didn't want anyone to think I was there to steal one of your fine cows or goats."

"No one would think—" Jane stopped herself. She took the

handle. "I'll put it away." She tried to hide her weariness and her storm of crying, and was relieved that she sounded cool, almost detached.

"Suit yourself," he said indifferently, and turned away. Jane knew she should feel irritated and Mamma would expect her to say something to make this forest boy mind his manners, but she couldn't muster up the energy to care that he had addressed her so insolently. She watched him walk back down to where he and his father had dug Harry's grave, his broad shoulders hunched against the wind, which had picked up and now was blowing icy little drops of rain into her face as she stood in the open doorway.

When she finally sighed, closed the dairy door tight, and made her way up the hill, the sun was barely above the trees. As she trudged up to the house, she glanced behind her. Nothing. Nobody. Then why did her back feel the prickle of gazing eyes as she went?

9

The next day, Hannah filled a bucket with water and slopped it over the floor of the parlor. She and Jane rolled up their sleeves to their elbows and their skirts to their thighs. They scrubbed the wooden planks with a heavy brush that Hannah had unearthed in the kitchen. Hannah dug sand from near the river and scoured the pots with it until they gleamed.

The work took Jane's mind off the bundle that they had deposited in the cold ground, and off the boy who at one moment seemed to want to befriend her and at another treated her with indifference, even coldness. She threw open the windows of the South Parlor when Mamma was in the dairy, despite Isabella's protestations against the cold, and aired the room thoroughly, turning over the cushions and thumping them. Under Hannah's direction, Jane and Maude dragged the mattress on which Harry had died far away from the house and set it on fire. Thick black smoke poured out along the ground, barely rising into the air and stinging their nostrils as the damp straw struggled to burn.

Hannah took Maude out to hunt for medicinal herbs and edible roots, and Maude came back showing more animation than she had exhibited for months, talking about how you had to be careful what you picked and how you picked it or the fairy-people would do something that caused the medicine not to work, or even to be harmful.

"Why do the fairy-folk want to hurt us?" Jane asked Hannah.

"It isn't that they want to hurt us, Jane. They're playful, is all, and they can be spiteful, like little children. If we do something that they don't like, they'll do something to pay us back, or if they're bored, they'll play a trick just to be irritating. Any harm isn't done on purpose."

"So you have to be careful," Maude said, with an air of superiority, now that she knew something that Jane didn't. "Don't bother them and they won't bother you."

"But they sometimes take our babies and leave their own behind, don't they?" Jane looked at Hannah.

"I've heard of that," the woman said, "although I've never known it to happen."

I wish the fairies had taken Rose instead of her dying, Jane thought. Even a changeling sister would be preferable to the loss. She sometimes felt incomplete, as though a piece of her had died along with her twin, even though she couldn't remember her. How much easier it would be if she had someone like Rose she could really talk to, not Mamma, who refused to face the reality of their lives, or Maude, who was too young to understand it.

After Hannah had been there a week, they sat in the South Parlor drinking an herb tea that Maude had concocted. Mamma had finished hers and was nodding by the fire as

Hannah showed Maude how to clean and bandage a blister that had burst on Jane's palm.

Hannah took Jane's hand in hers and inspected the work. "Your grandmamma would have been proud of how hard you're working," she said, glancing at Mamma, who showed no sign of hearing.

Jane was startled. "Grandmamma Halsey?" She had only hazy memories of an old lady in lace and velvet who had died shortly before Papa had left for good.

Hannah nodded. "She had so much energy, and couldn't stand to see things not done properly." After a pause, she continued, "You look more and more like her every day." She nodded at Maude. "Both of you."

"Like Grandmamma? But everyone says what a handsome woman she was!" Maude exclaimed, and both Jane and Hannah said, "Hush!" But Mamma didn't stir.

Hannah leaned in closer and spoke quietly. "And so are you. Maybe you're not pretty like what's fashionable, or even like Isabella." The three of them glanced out the window at the drive, where the girl wandered aimlessly, kicking at pebbles. "But you're tall and strong, and you have lovely hair, at least when you take the trouble to comb it." She put a finger under Maude's chin and tilted her face up. "And clear, smooth skin and beautiful smiles." Maude grinned, and Jane tried to see her sister with a stranger's eyes.

"You always say that," Jane said. "But I don't think it's true."

Hannah smiled. "No girl your age thinks she's pretty. You just wait a few years."

The conversation turned to a clinical discussion between the herb-woman and Maude concerning the difference between the treatment of blisters and of burns, and Jane lost interest. She went to milk Baby. She hoisted the bucket—it was getting lighter at each milking, which worried her—and took it to the dairy, intending to check on the cheese, which usually progressed slowly in the cold weather. Maude had come to the dairy while Jane was in the barn and was now skimming that morning's milking. Good thing that Jane had come in at that moment; there was no telling how much of the sweet cream would have disappeared down Maude's throat if nobody was looking.

"Do you think Hannah's right, that we're pretty?" Maude bent farther over her task.

"Don't let your hair get in it," Jane said. She pulled the curls off Maude's cheeks and held them behind her neck. "I don't know," she said. "Hannah loves us, so she thinks we're nice to look at. But Isabella doesn't like us, and she said so, too, that day her comb got broken. So maybe...maybe it's true."

Jane hardly ever thought about what she looked like, since hardly anyone but her mother and sister and Hannah, who was like a second mother, ever saw her. Her face was just her face, and her body was her body—a body that was capable of shoveling out a stable and taking care of delicate newborn puppies and chicks and milking a stubborn cow. She looked down at herself. She had always walked past the glazed mirrors in the upstairs hall without a glance, but from what she could see now, her legs were long and straight and the outline of her body dipped in and out in a way that made her think of the portrait of Mamma in Papa's empty room. Was that beauty?

She didn't think that Mamma, at any rate, would say it was. Mamma always admired the more delicate kind of girl that they saw in church—a girl named Lavinia, for one, the daughter of one of Mamma's former friends, who now pretended not to know her. Lavinia and her younger sister had skin that must rarely be exposed to the sun, and their hands were smooth, not rough with the calluses and blisters that farm work raised on Jane's palms.

Jane sighed. If Hannah wasn't just being kind, she was blinded by her affection for them. Maude's arms were muscular from all her churning over the years, and now her face was red with exertion. She seemed to feel Jane looking at her and paused in her work. "What?" She sounded indignant.

"Nothing." Jane left Maude and went about her own chores.

After Hannah sent word home that Harry's infection had spread no further, Hugh and his father came to the house. They repaired the broken pump in the kitchen, replaced rotten wood in the pantry with sound planks, and laid hay, mown from the little left in the yard, in the barn. When Jane brought them some of Maude's herb tea, they put down their tools and drank it gratefully.

Hannah's husband gave his empty mug back to Jane and surprised her with a warm squeeze of her hand. "You call on us if you have need of anything," he said. "We don't have much but our labor, but you can have all that we can spare."

Jane nodded her thanks, unable to speak for the sudden stinging in her eyes and the hard place in her throat. She glanced at Hugh, who was silent, as always, but who was looking at her with something like compassion in his hazel eyes. Why would Mamma say that Hannah's family was not fit for them to associate with? When did any of the fine people she used to know help them? And what of that man, Will's father, who had dug Harry's grave? Even though he was one of the people of the woods, he had proven himself more of a friend than the people Mamma used to go to parties with.

When Hannah and her family left late that evening, it seemed like all the life in the house went with them.

10

It was the hardest winter Jane could remember. Mamma said that there had been a worse one when she was a girl. But in those days there had been servants to ride deep into the forest and fetch dry wood to stack in huge piles for cheerful fires, and there were woolen blankets and hot things to drink whenever anyone wanted them. Now it took all day to find a few logs that weren't half-rotten, that could dry out in a day or two and provide some weak and smoky heat in the fireplace. They still had blankets, but they were damp and riddled with moth holes, and their mustiness made Maude sneeze incessantly.

Despite the chill and damp outdoors, Jane preferred the forest to the house. At least among the trees nobody complained, nobody whined, nobody looked at her as though she should somehow know what to do. She took to wandering in the woods—never very deep—even when she knew that she would find nothing to eat.

One morning she saw a late honeybee, coaxed out of its hive by an unusually sunny sky, and followed it for a while in the small hope that it would lead her to its tree. Hannah would probably know how to remove the honey without getting stung. But she soon lost it and was about to turn back when she thought she heard something moving in the brush. She paused on the path, decided she must have been mistaken, and was starting to move on when something grabbed her wrist and yanked her, sprawling, behind a tree. She drew in her breath to scream, but a hand clamped itself over her mouth and whoever was holding her hissed, "Hush! King's men!"

A burst of sound, and two horsemen thundered past her. She caught a glimpse of faces set in grim purpose, of drawn swords, of cloaks billowing behind the riders as their mounts sped past, their legs flashing, the large animals tearing down the path just where she had been standing. They disappeared, leaving her with her heart thumping even faster, she felt, than those gleaming hooves had pounded.

The hand on her mouth loosened, and she whipped around. She found herself looking into brown eyes and said furiously, "What do you think you're—" when a short, hoarse cry sounded deep in the woods, farther down the path. Furious words followed, protestations, then the crack of a blow, and then an oath. The words died on her lips. What could it mean?

She didn't have to wonder long. A horse's snort, the creak of leather, and then the thud of hooves—much slower than before—reached her ears. Laughter, men's mirthless laughter, as though in mockery or triumph, followed, and then, returning in the direction where they had disappeared just a few moments earlier, came the two horsemen on their sleek mounts. The second was followed by a man on foot, who stumbled on the uneven path. He was thin and ragged, and his hands were bound in front of him; the rider held the other end of the rope and tugged the man—no, a boy, tall and lean, but a boy nonetheless. The first horseman now carried a longbow, and a quiver of arrows hung over his shoulder. Jane knew in an instant what had happened: the boy had been caught poaching, shooting game that belonged to the king.

The boy caught sight of her even as she pressed herself back against whoever had dragged her behind the tree. His eyes looked wild, and he opened his mouth, but no sound came out of it.

Jane waited until she was sure they were out of sight and hearing, and then she wrenched herself out of the hands restraining her. She staggered to her feet and turned to face her captor. "Who are you and what..." She stopped. It was Will.

"You're welcome," the boy said coldly as he, too, rose to his feet. "Would you rather I had left you to be trampled? Or to be taken by the king's men?"

She was almost too astonished to speak. "Why would the k-king's men want to take *me?*" she finally sputtered.

"Why not?" he asked. "You were here near a poacher, so you were probably helping him."

"A poacher? I'm not a poacher!"

"The king's men don't know that, and it's easier to pick you up and punish you than to ask questions. That's what they do, now that the old king has turned over the forest to his son."

Jane was speechless with indignation.

The boy kicked at a bush and scowled. "It's not fair. They make it too easy for poachers, so that anyone in want is so tempted that he can't resist."

"What do you mean?"

"They slice the back of a deer's hind leg so that it can do

no more than hobble, and leave it near a path. They stay near and watch for someone who is so in want that he'll risk capture for the chance of food. Sooner or later someone comes by, like Edmund, the boy whom they caught, and he shoots the deer. Then they take him for poaching."

It did sound unfair, but still, the law was the law. "He shouldn't kill the king's deer," Jane said. She realized that she sounded more prim than she intended and tried to amend what she had said. "What I mean is—"

The boy didn't wait to hear what she meant, but spat, "His father's dead and his brother can't hunt anymore—can't even work, since he broke his leg falling off *your* roof."

"His brother was that man?"

"Jeremy. Edmund has to find food for all of them. Something you would know nothing about." And before she could answer, he had disappeared into the woods.

Something I know nothing about, she seethed inwardly as she made her way back to the house. *What does he think we live on? Who does he think finds food for us?*

That afternoon, Jane, still raging at the rudeness of the boy in the woods, found an old black dress in Mamma's wardrobe upstairs and cut it down into a mourning frock for Isabella. She fashioned a black hair ribbon out of a piece of lace that had gone around the dress's hem.

"Why can't I wear my mother's gowns?" Isabella tugged at the black sleeves that came down nearly to her fingertips. "I'm almost big enough for them. This one is so *ugly.* And black doesn't suit me." It was true; her pale beauty faded next to the harsh fabric.

"You're in mourning," Mamma said. "Out of respect for

your father, you must wear black for a year. It's not supposed to suit you. I am wearing black as well, and it doesn't suit me either." She didn't ask where the black silk had come from, and Jane didn't offer the information.

After Maude found two chickens frozen in the coop, she and Jane brought the rest into the house and set them to roost in the empty pantry. Despite the mess and the smell, this arrangement made for less work, since no one had to go out to feed them and hunt for their eggs. They feasted on the dead chickens. Jane tried to put out of her mind the fact that with two fewer to lay and with the short days and scarce feed, they would be lucky to find one egg a day until spring. One egg, and four people to share it.

They still had the cow and goats to tend to. They had moved the butter-churn and cheese-making materials indoors so the milk wouldn't freeze. Without it, they would starve. Mamma sold Harry's big coach horses, saying that they had no need of them, and Jane had to fight hard to hold back tears as they trotted down the drive one last time, blond manes flowing, heads tossing as though with joy at leaving. They were so beautiful, and there was so little beauty left to them. Mamma managed to pay off Harry's debt in the village with the gold that they brought, and even came home with some flour and tea. But when that was gone and Mamma talked about selling Isabella's little carriage and pony, the child grew so hysterical that she changed her mind.

"We'll keep them for now," Mamma told Maude and Jane after Isabella had sobbed herself into a restless sleep. "They were his last gift to her, after all." *Yes, his last gift,* Jane thought, *along with the candied fruits*—the mere thought made her mouth ache with longing—*and the sparkling glass shoes and the silk hair ribbons.*

Mamma wrote letter after letter to banks, to Harry's relatives, and to his old business acquaintances. No reply came. Whenever Jane left the house to do the milking or to clean the barn or to turn the animals into the field or let them in again, she saw Mamma's face at the window, or Mamma standing in the doorway, looking down the road, and Jane knew she was waiting for a messenger. Once, when the sound of hoofbeats reached them as they sat down to a meager midday meal, Mamma flew to the door, her hand to her throat. But it was only a peddler, and Mamma was nearly rude to him when she turned him away. The disappointment on her face was so wrenching that Jane had to look away, and she distracted Maude with questions about the hens so she wouldn't notice that Mamma sat down heavily in the big chair and stared at nothing.

Isabella, huddled so close to the small fire that she was practically in it, spoke for almost the first time since her father's death. It was an unusually cold day, bright with piercing sunshine and new frost. Isabella had wrapped herself in a blanket as she crouched on the hearth. She reached for a stick, but Maude said, "Don't. There won't be enough for tomorrow."

Isabella didn't look up. In a low but penetrating voice, she said, "You must not let me freeze to death. My father would never allow it. My father would buy me—"

"Hush." Jane spoke so sharply that Isabella obeyed.

Finally, on an evening that was so bitterly cold that Isabella and Maude consented to sit together under the last warm blanket, Jane was returning from the barn, hoping that Maude was making something for supper, when she heard a single horse on the road. King's men again? She stood still, expecting the hoof beats to continue on down to the village, and when the sound grew louder, she stepped into the drive.

The rider drew up when he saw her. "This Halsey Hall?" He jerked his head up toward the house. Jane nodded mutely. The man leaned down and held out a small piece of paper, folded and sealed with a blob of green wax. "Take this to your mistress."

Jane didn't bother to correct him as she took the paper from him. "Do you want to wait for an answer?"

He turned his horse around and kicked at its sides. As he moved away, he called over his shoulder, "I was told there wouldn't be one, and no money to pay to carry it back. Is that true, or does your mistress have enough to pay a messenger to ride across the border?"

Across the border! The message must come from someone Harry had known, his banker or a friend, or someone else who would finally loosen his money from the bank. Jane hurried back home, hardly noticing the pail banging painfully into her shins. She left it on the steps, mindful even in her haste not to let any of the precious milk slop out, and ran into the South Parlor. "Mamma!"

Mamma stood and snatched the letter from her. She ran her thumb under the seal, breaking the wax. Her lips moved slightly as her eyes darted back and forth across the page. A frown creased her forehead, and she turned the page over, saw there was nothing there, and reread the message.

"Mamma?" Maude squeaked. Any words of comfort Jane might have spoken stuck behind a lump of fear in her throat. Mamma raised her head, and what Jane saw frightened her even more. Mamma looked so strange. Her eyes glittered as though with fever, and a bright red spot stood out on each cheek. She turned her eyes in Jane's direction but didn't seem to see her. Her hand fell to her side and the paper fluttered out of it as Mamma walked slowly, slowly from the room and into her own chamber. The door closed behind her without a sound.

As soon as she was gone, Jane leaped on the paper. It took her no more than a minute to read the cruel words.

Madam,
I have been instructed by Lady Mathilde, to whom you have written twice, to tell you that she is not, as was claimed by Master Harry Delaville, the godmother of the child you describe as being the daughter of Lady Mathilde's "friend" Serafina. This Serafina was indeed known to Lady Mathilde; however, the lady was not her friend, but her paid companion. When the lady married Master Delaville against Lady Mathilde's wishes, Lady Mathilde broke all ties with her.

Lady Mathilde wishes no ill to the child and has made inquiries on her behalf with the bank that handled Master Delaville's affairs. Far from leaving a fortune to the girl, he died in debt. Lady Mathilde has made good those debts, but finds herself unwilling further to extend herself on behalf of the daughter of an ungrateful servant. She instructs me to tell you that she will receive no more letters from you and that any emissaries you send to her will be turned away.

And then there was a scrawled signature that Jane didn't even try to make out.

The other two girls stared at her as she folded up the paper and tucked it into the pouch at her waist.

"What is it?" Maude asked finally, her voice just above a whisper.

"We'll get no help from Isabella's godmother," Jane said. "Come on. It's time to make supper." Together they went to the pantry and surveyed the nearly empty shelves. Maude picked up the last of the biscuit, and as they made their way back through the freezing kitchen, a little scratching sound came from the South Parlor. The rats and mice must have been as hungry as they were, to be bold enough to come out of their holes and nests during the day.

But the sound was neither rats nor mice. It was Isabella sitting in the fireplace, her fingertips restlessly stirring the cool ashes. "What are you—" Maude stopped at the sight of the pale, drawn face that Isabella raised.

The green eyes looked blankly in Jane's direction but did not seem to focus on her or on anything else. "I'm cold," the girl whimpered. "So cold."

They left her alone while Jane went outside and retrieved the pail. They made a meager meal out of stale biscuit and thin milk, saving for breakfast the eggs that Maude had found. Isabella wouldn't leave the fireplace, so Maude brought her portion to her. Isabella ate it as daintily as if it had been pheasant. When night fell and the sisters went to bed, she was still there. And when they woke in the morning, it was to find Isabella sound asleep on the hearth, her cheek resting on a bed of cold cinders.

11

Jane broke the surface ice from the washing basin with the back of her hairbrush and washed her face quickly in the stinging water. She rubbed herself dry with a rough cloth that brought some blood back to her cheeks and then passed it to Maude. Her sister took the towel, and without looking at Jane, she asked, "May I go to Hannah's house and ask her husband for some fuel?"

"No." Jane knew her voice was hard.

"But, Jane—"

"There is nothing dry in this whole area. They have no more wood than we do and no more food. We can't have Hannah's family freeze and go hungry so that we may warm and feed ourselves." Jane's tone must have told Maude that no arguing was possible. Her sister's quiet resignation chilled Jane more than arguing would, more than the icy water in the basin had.

In the barn that afternoon, Jane dropped a handful of hay into the pony's manger. Poor little Mouse. It was fortunate that she didn't need to eat much, or she surely would have starved by now. As it was, the ribs showed through her shaggy winter coat. The goats had stopped producing milk. Jane rested her head against Sal's skinny neck, and he nibbled her hair gently. Isabella hadn't stirred from the fireplace all day, and she looked away when Maude tried to coax her out. Jane felt a twinge of pity for the girl. She must be so miserable, so frightened. What could—

She started as the big horse lifted his head and swung it to the side. He snorted, nostrils flaring, his ears upright. "What is it, Sal?" Jane rubbed his neck. "There's nothing out there." She spoke to calm herself as much as the horse. What would she do if thieves were to come? They had nothing worth stealing, but hungry men might be capable of anything—taking their little bit of furniture for firewood, she thought, or even murder, if they were angry at finding no plunder.

She held her breath. She thought she heard singing far, far off, but Sal had never seemed to notice fairy singers. What could be bothering him?

Sal's ears swiveled back and then forward, and his bony neck even arched a little. One huge hoof pawed the ground, and he tossed his head and snorted again. Then Jane heard it, too: faint and far away, the sound of a hunting horn. She held still and listened. It came again, a bit louder, tinny yet somehow rich, plaintive but also exciting. Sal whickered and moved restlessly from one side of his stall to the other.

The horn sounded again, closer, and now Jane could make out distant shouts, as well. She hurried back to the house with her pail of milk, leaving a small amount in the bucket next to the path. It steamed gently in the chilly air before she covered it, and she had to fight against the urge to drink the few drops herself. In the parlor, as she poured what remained of the thin liquid into four cups, she asked Maude, "Where's Mamma?"

"She's still in her room," Maude said. "I peeked at her, and I think she's asleep. Why?"

"I heard hunters in the forest. And Sal acted like he wanted to go right out with them." Maude handed a cup to Isabella and kept one for herself before sitting down at the table with Jane.

"There aren't any hunters in the forest," Isabella said dismissively from the cold fireplace. It was the first time she had spoken. Maude rolled her eyes. "There aren't," Isabella insisted. "These are the king's woods, and the king is too old to hunt. Nobody else would dare. If poachers are caught, their right hands are cut off."

The baying of hounds and thudding of hooves reached their ears. "What's that, then?" Jane couldn't resist saying as all three ran out into the dusk. Jane caught up a shawl and wrapped herself and Maude in it as they stood in the snow of the drive, straining to see what was coming. Jane gestured at Isabella, and reluctantly Maude held open a corner of the shawl to her, but Isabella wrinkled her tiny nose at the frayed piece of cloth. "Fine," Jane muttered. "Freeze to death."

And then a glorious sight burst upon them. One instant the drive was empty save for their three hunched figures, and the next it was filled with long-eared dogs milling around and nipping at each other; horses, brown and white and gray and black; and gentlemen and ladies in heavy winter hunting clothes in jewel tones of scarlet and blue and green and gold, with shiny long boots and woolen cloaks whose mere sight made Jane feel warm. A merry-looking boy blew short blasts on a silvery horn.

The hunters took no notice of the girls, standing silent in the shadow of the porch, but talked and laughed as a young man on a white horse pushed his way through the crowd. His dark green hood had fallen back, showing a head of bright gold hair, pale blue eyes and a pouting mouth.

"So, they've lost the scent, have they?" He lazily swung his riding crop down at a hound. The dog dodged the blow, wincing, and tucked its long tail between its legs. A lady laughed.

"Let's dismount here and have the people give us refreshment," one of the young men suggested, but another, looking up at the house, exclaimed, "You'll get no refreshment here! This is old Halsey Hall, isn't it?" He pointed at Mamma's family crest carved in the stone above the door: a greyhound under an oak tree, its branches intertwined into an *H*.

One of the ladies said, "Is it really? My mother used to talk about the splendid balls they had here when she was a girl. I always thought Halsey Hall was such a funny name. Why won't they give us refreshment, Frederick?"

"Didn't you know?" a man answered, reining in his horse so that it walked backwards to where the ladies were talking. "Lady Margaret Halsey married Daniel Montjoy. Surely you've heard of him?"

The lady rolled her eyes. "Who hasn't? The handsomest man in the kingdom, my mother used to say! Their wedding was the most beautiful anyone had ever seen."

The gentleman spoke again. "Montjoy went through all her money before he drank himself to death. Just look at the place." They stared up. Jane followed their gaze to the empty window frames, the broken chimneys, the grass growing between the stones of the high walls. She tried to speak, but her throat was too tight to allow words out.

"Didn't Lady Margaret marry again?" one of the ladies asked. "Some man who made a fortune in foreign lands—"

Before the speaker could finish, Isabella's clear voice rose above the din. "That was not *some man*. That was Harry Delaville. It's true that he made a fortune. A huge one. I am his daughter." Heads turned in their direction. Silence fell, except for the stamp of a horse's hoof.

"His daughter?" someone finally asked. "Where is your father?"

Isabella lowered her eyes. She made a small gesture and then said, with a choke in the middle of her words, "The fever—"

The riders drew back. "He's ill?" one asked, as another nervously edged his horse toward the path to the woods.

"He died some weeks ago," Isabella said, and the company relaxed. If he had been dead for weeks, the danger of infection would be over. A few drew closer, looking curious. "I made him soup, and fed him, and bathed him, and tended to his every need—" Jane clamped her hand over Maude's sputtering mouth "—but he died." Isabella's voice shook.

"You poor child," said one of the ladies. "You took care of him?"

"Oh, yes," Isabella said simply. "In between my other chores. I had to milk the cow and feed the chickens, and sweep, and do the laundry." And she started to cry. One of the ladies dismounted and knelt by Isabella, who wept into her shoulder.

"And who are these girls?" The lady wiped Isabella's face with her sleeve and glared up at Maude and Jane.

"Oh, those are my stepsisters," Isabella said dismissively.

The others looked at them as though surprised that someone was there. They must be a sight, Jane thought—two ragged girls huddled together in front of the ruin of their house. Jane tried to curtsey, but she became entangled in the shawl. She stumbled, and nearly fell. She stood upright again, conscious of every eye on her. "I—" she began.

"Why do you not share your shawl with your stepsister?" asked the lady sharply.

"I—I offered it," stammered Maude. "She didn't want it."

"I'm cold." Isabella looked up appealingly at the lady.

"Of course you are, darling." The lady glared at Maude. She took off her own bright blue cloak and wrapped it around Isabella.

The young man on the white horse spoke. "Isn't there a hunting lodge near here?" Jane nodded. "I believe my father and I stayed there when I was a boy on my first hunt," he said. Then, to Isabella, "You have no living relatives?"

Isabella somehow managed to drop a beautiful curtsey, even wrapped up in the heavy cloak. "No, sir."

"And you are your father's only child?"

"Yes, sir."

"And your mother?"

"Dead." Once again Isabella's voice caught.

"If you have a fortune," broke in one of the gentlemen, "why is the house in such disrepair?"

"My father hired workmen to fix it. After he died, my stepmother dismissed them without paying them."

The young man on the white horse persisted, "You are your father's heir, then?" Isabella nodded. "What is your name?"

"Isabella Delaville." Isabella raised her eyes to his. Her golden hair looked even brighter with flakes of snow falling into it, and her pale face glowed in the fading light. The young man stared down at her. The people around him shifted in their saddles, exchanging glances, and the horses stamped in the snow.

The man swung down from his mount. He dropped lightly to the ground, crunching the snowy gravel under his booted feet. A groom seized the white horse's reins; his rider seemed to have forgotten about him.

The young man approached Isabella, who dropped her eyes modestly and folded her hands in front of her. He gently unclasped them and held them in his own gloved hands. He didn't seem to realize how cold she must be, standing there in her light dress and no overcoat, while he was robed and cloaked in velvet and furs. "I'm—Bertrand," he said. "Do you like music, Isabella?"

"Oh, yes," she said. "But it's been so long since I heard any."

Jane and Maude looked at each other. Music? What on earth?

But someone else had understood. One of the men hastily unstrapped a lute from his back and tuned it rapidly, blowing on his fingers to warm them. He struck up a slow tune, but Bertrand snapped, "Not a funeral dirge, man! Play something lively!" And instantly the lutenist swung into a happy melody.

Bertrand bowed to Isabella, who curtsied so low that Jane wondered if she would be able to rise again. Bertrand took her fingertips and gently helped her up and then, slowly, carefully, led her in a dance.

It was the most beautiful sight Jane had ever seen. The snow was turning rosy in the light of the setting sun, which also brought a touch of color to Isabella's wan cheeks. She moved as lightly as the snowflakes that had begun drifting down, and the notes of the lute were so sweet and so sad and happy at the same time that Jane felt her throat close with tears. Maude wept openly at her side.

The melody ended, and the young man stood still and stared at Isabella, who curtsied once more. "Sir—" one of the ladies began, but she stopped when Bertrand raised his hand to hush her. Slowly he lifted Isabella's fingers to his face. He pressed his lips to them, and then turned her hand over and kissed the palm. Isabella's face glowed like a candle. Jane's heart ached as she watched them, and she found herself thinking of Will, and of how warm his hand had been in hers, next to Harry's grave.

Still they stood, until finally an older man said, "Sir, your father must be getting anxious. It will be full dark soon, and—"

With obvious reluctance, Bertrand dropped Isabella's fingers and mounted his horse. Isabella stared up at him. "Come!" he finally barked to the company. He pulled on his reins so that his horse wheeled in a tight circle before plunging back into the darkening woods. With a great deal of commotion, the other riders, too, urged their horses forward. The dogs were the last to go, and they ran baying through the woods, dodging around trees and nipping at one another before disappearing into the shadows.

12

Jane worked and worked at Baby's udder, but no stream of milk spurted into the pail. Not even a drop came out. The milk had been growing scanter each day, and Jane had stopped dividing it between a portion for them and one for the people of the woods. There was so little that almost as much stuck to the sides of the bucket as what she poured out. She stopped, forced to admit to herself that it wasn't that Baby was refusing to let her milk down, but that there was nothing left.

She burst into tears, her head resting against the cow's bony side. What would they do now? The milk, little though it was, was all that was keeping them this side of starvation. She knew what a real farmer would do, but slaughtering Baby was unthinkable. *No,* she thought as she sat up and rubbed the tears off her cheeks. No, they would all starve together.

Jane opened the doors between the stalls to allow the animals to crowd together for warmth. She shoveled out the old straw and gave the goats and poor little Mouse just a handful of hay each, with a bit more for Sal. In a very few minutes it was all gone, and Baby, as usual, butted her with her hard head.

"Nothing for you there today." Jane laughed shakily, pushing away the animal's big face. The hunger and sorrow in the dark brown eyes went to her heart almost as much as the sight of Maude shivering in the big empty hall. She scratched Baby briefly between the ears, but a head scratch was not what the cow wanted, and she lowed a deep, mournful moo. Jane stood rubbing the angular neck, once so firm and glossy, while the cow thrust her muzzle with resignation into the empty manger and then grunted and lowered herself to lie down.

Back at the house, the other two girls looked at her in silence as she came into the parlor with no milk bucket. Maude dropped her gaze to her lap, and Isabella turned back to the patterns she was tracing in the cold ashes. Mamma, wrapped in her shawl, stared out the grimy window, her mouth a thin line in her thin face.

The situation was no better in the pantry. Jane poked into every corner, lifted the lid off every box and bin. There was nothing, not even a shriveled apple or a crumb of biscuit. They had finished their small store of cheese days ago.

In the South Parlor, Isabella was still huddled by the hearth, no doubt imagining that she was sitting near a warm fire. The girls glanced up at Jane and then down again, obviously reading the despair in her face.

At the sight of their dull eyes, Jane made up her mind. "Come, Maude." Maude rose, wrapped herself well, and followed Jane out the door. Mamma and Isabella did not even look up as they left.

They trudged through the muck that had once been the familiar path to the home of Hannah Herb-Woman and her family. But even before they reached the small house, they knew something was wrong. Maude took her sister's hand and Jane squeezed it.

They emerged into the clearing and stood hand in hand, staring at the boarded-up hut. No smell of smoke, no clucking of chickens, no barking of Hugh's friendly dog had reached them on the path. Still, she was unprepared for this utter emptiness.

Maude finally broke the silence. "Where did they go?" Her voice was barely above a whisper.

"How should I know?" Jane's fear made her snap, and then she softened as she saw the fear in her sister's eyes. "They probably went someplace where Hugh's father could find work. If—" She hesitated, and then went on carefully, "If something bad had happened, they wouldn't have taken the time to close up the house." She opened the door to Hannah's drying shed. "And see? She took all her herbs and the chickens, too. That shows they had time to prepare. They'll be back." Maude looked unconvinced.

They turned into the forest and went in deeper than they ever had before, deeper than Jane had gone the day she had dropped her basket. Maybe they would come across a frostbitten apple, or maybe a squirrel had hidden a cache of nuts last fall and had forgotten to collect them when the hard weather hit. Perhaps, like the children in one of Mamma's tales, they would wander until they died and were covered by leaves.

The trees shot straight up, the tangle of branches making it impossible to see the sky. The canopy was so dense that even on a sunny day, little light must reach the ground, and the forest floor was bare of grass and underbrush. The thaw that had set in a few days before had stripped the ground of the small amount of snow that might have penetrated this far.

Jane was sure she saw signs that someone had recently been there: broken twigs near the path, a dent in the soil that might be a footprint but might not. She was about to move on when something glinted from a clump of weeds. Making sure that Maude was busily foraging and not looking at her, she parted the stems and picked it up. It was a buckle—just a simple buckle of the kind that would fasten someone's boot or shoe. She tucked it into the pouch at her waist.

A few times a twig cracked, and once a rustle in the branches seemed to indicate that someone was near. Each time, the girls jumped, and Maude clutched at her sister. Jane remembered that dark figure behind the tree. But they saw no one except an occasional squirrel or soggy-looking bird.

After a long, wet search, they had gathered only a handful of rain-soaked nuts. Then Maude stumbled on a clump of mushrooms, raising their hopes, but after that they found nothing else. In a small clearing, Maude sat down on a fallen tree, unmindful of the damp that seeped through its rough bark into her skirt. It started to rain, a cold gray drizzle that was barely more than a mist, but that seemed to reach into their bones with its icy fingers.

Jane sighed heavily and reached down to her sister. "Let's go back."

"In a minute," Maude answered flatly. Jane stood and waited, but Maude made no move, so Jane began to move off, knowing that Maude would never stay in the woods by herself.

"That's the wrong way," Maude called after her.

Jane stopped and looked around. "No, it's how we came."

But suddenly she wasn't certain. She took an irresolute step forward and then stopped again. Surely she would have noticed that large, dog-shaped rock if she had passed it on the way into the clearing—wouldn't she? But it didn't look familiar. She turned and hesitated. This must be right. She glanced over her shoulder through the brush that grew on the edge of the clearing, back into the forest of tall, straight trunks straining upwards to the sky.

"We have to go over there." Maude pointed behind her own shoulder.

"No," Jane said. "We didn't come that way." Maude pushed herself up off the fallen tree and started in the direction that she had indicated. Jane ran after her and seized her arm. "We must stay together. No matter which way we go, we *must* go together." Maude shook off Jane's hand and stopped, looking in one direction and then in another. The rain was falling more heavily now. It tapped on the bare branches in the denser part of the forest. Large, cold drops fell with increasing regularity on their uncovered heads. The smell of damp earth grew heavy as the ground became wetter.

Maude turned her rain-streaked face to her sister. "Oh, Jane," she whispered. "We're lost." She flinched as a large drop hit her square on her nose. Jane looked about her. It was true; she had no idea which direction to take. She tried to remember a landmark, but the trees, monotonous in their sameness, stretched around them in all directions. Oh, why hadn't they brought Betsy with them?

"It's all right," she told Maude, although her heart shivered within her. Were they going to wander through the woods until they lay down exhausted and died? Or would someone—or something—find them first? Jane forced herself not to think of the tales Mamma told them about gnomes and witches, about men dressed in green who lived in the woods, wild men who would carry the two of them off to a different world—a lovely world, to be sure, but one where they would be lonely, for no humans inhabited it.

And just as she imagined that world, she heard, far off, a few notes sung in a human voice. *Was* it human, though? Could fairies sound like people when they wanted to? It was so faint that she thought she must have imagined it. But then the same notes were repeated, just a hair closer and a shade louder.

"What was that?" Maude whispered. "Fairy singers?"

"Only the wind," Jane wanted to say, but the lie stuck in her throat.

A sudden crackling in the branches made them leap into each other's arms and then stand rooted to the spot, quaking and clutching each other. "What was *that?*" Maude asked again, this time in a startled gasp. Jane forced herself to loosen her grip on her sister. She slowed her breathing with an effort and pried Maude's fingers off her arms.

"A squirrel," she said without conviction, but Maude shook her head.

"It was too loud to be a squirrel," she insisted.

"A deer, then." Jane didn't succeed in convincing even herself. A deer would have been as startled at the sight of them as they were at the sound of it and would have run off, but whatever this was, it had not moved again.

Jane tried to move in the other direction, pulling Maude's hand, but her sister refused to budge. "I'm not going. Not until I know what that was."

"It was nothing," Jane said.

"It was something," Maude retorted. "*Nothing* doesn't make

the branches shake." Jane looked at the thicket, and sure enough, several of the twigs were trembling. Even denuded of their leaves, the branches were so thick and intertwined that she could not make out what was causing the motion.

"We'll go a different way," Jane said.

Maude shook her head. "That's the way we came. I know it is."

There was nothing else to do. Surely if whatever was in the thicket intended them harm, it would have come out and attacked them by now. Wouldn't it? Perhaps it was a badger that had found itself too far from its hole to make an escape and was waiting for them to leave. Or an injured deer that couldn't get away. Or—she didn't like to think what else it could be. "I'll just take a look," Jane said. She forced herself to walk straight there without hesitating, pretending to feel no fear. She peered into the brush.

"There's nothing here," she called to her sister. "I told you there was—"

She stopped. Because there *was* something there. And whatever it was, was looking back out at her.

13

Brown eyes stared up at Jane, and fingers held back the branches of the shrub. Before Jane had a chance to say anything, to jump backward, to call out to Maude, the figure leaped up and tore into the forest. It was a girl, Jane realized, a tall and slender girl, running over the sodden leaves.

"What is it?" Maude had crept up to Jane unheard and touched her on the arm.

Jane jumped and turned on her sister, fear making her vibrate. "Why did you do that?" she cried, shaking Maude by the shoulders. "Don't ever do that!" Maude started to cry again. "Oh, Maude," Jane said impatiently, and then stopped. For the strange girl had halted by a tree, almost out of sight.

Maude followed her sister's gaze, snuffling. "What is it?"

"Don't you see her?" But now the girl had disappeared. "She was right there." Jane pointed at the tree where the girl had paused.

Maude peered suspiciously into the woods. She swiped the

wet hair off her face and rubbed her nose with the back of her hand. "Who? I don't see anybody."

"Well, she's gone now," Jane said crossly. "But there was a girl in the bushes and she ran into the forest. She stopped by that crooked tree." She hesitated, knowing that Maude would be frightened by what she said next. "She looked at me like she wanted us to follow her."

"No!" Sure enough, Maude seized her sister's hand and tried to pull her away. "No, Jane! We can't go with her! What if she's a fairy? What if she takes us to her kingdom to live for a hundred years and when we come back Mamma will be dead and Hugh and..."

Jane didn't know anything about fairies except what she heard in the stories that Mamma and Hannah told, but in her brief glimpse of the girl, she had seen grimy fingernails and a clumsily mended tear in the sleeve. She didn't think that fairies got dirty or wore garments with big rips held together by coarse thread. One of the girl's shoes had flopped as she ran—perhaps it was missing a buckle, the one that Jane had found? No, the girl was a mortal. "We have to follow her," she told Maude, and without waiting for an answer, she started walking.

Maude caught up with her. "But what if—"

"Anything's better than staying in the woods. Better than dying in the woods," she amended grimly. This time Maude didn't argue but fell into step behind her.

Jane reached the tree where the girl had stood, and looked around. A flash caught her eye, and she turned just in time to see the slender form vanishing over a knoll. "This way." She set out again.

"I still don't see anything," Maude said, but Jane didn't have the strength to answer.

They trudged for what seemed like hours. Jane felt a blister rise on her heel and then pop, but she was too tired and cold to care. She caught glimpses of the girl every time they reached the spot where she had last seen her. They almost forgot why they were following her, or to be curious about where she was leading them. The rain stopped, then started again. Maude slipped and rose covered with mud, but lacked the will to wipe it off.

"Jane," Maude said when the sun finally showed itself. Jane grunted in reply. "Jane!" Maude said more loudly. "Isn't that our hunting lodge?"

Jane paused. It had been a long time since she'd been to the lodge—there was no reason to go there, really; it had been stripped of furnishings and draperies even before Papa had left. What she saw now was a small stone house. Brush and ivy had grown over much of it, and there were gaps in the red-and-white tiles that made up the gaily patterned roof. Still, as she looked more closely, she knew that Maude was right. This was the lodge that Papa and his friends had used as a base when they went out in search of deer and boar and other game, in the days when the old king ruled wisely and allowed his subjects free use of the woods.

"Do you remember the way home from here?" Maude asked uncertainly.

Jane nodded. She'd better remember; the girl had truly disappeared this time. Why had she brought them to the old lodge? Was it because she knew that they could find their own way home now?

A short time later, the girls pushed open the heavy front

door of Halsey Hall and for once didn't make the effort to close it behind them. What did it matter? There was no warmth to keep in and there was nothing to steal. Besides, closing it would take more energy than they could muster.

Mamma was nowhere to be seen, but Isabella still crouched in the fireplace, sifting the ashes through her fingers. She looked up as they entered. "You're all muddy, Maude. Mud-Maude." She laughed.

"And you're covered with cinders." Maude listlessly emptied the nuts from her pouch on to the table in front of Jane. "Cinder-Ella."

"Don't call me that, Mud-Maude," Isabella said.

Maude stuck out her tongue at her and filled the saucepan with water. Jane picked up the last sticks of wood and stood by the hearth as Isabella scrambled out. Despite the younger girl's constant complaints of the cold, she had never learned how to make a fire. Jane piled up twigs and struck at the tinderbox until a spark lit the wax-soaked string. Soon the fire was burning weakly, and Ella stretched out her chapped fingers to it.

Maude came back from Mamma's room. "Asleep already." Mamma had been going to bed earlier and earlier. Jane suspected that this was so she could leave more food for them without showing that she knew they were in want. Jane smashed the nuts with a frying pan, loosening the shells. Maude balanced the saucepan above the fire and sat down next to Isabella, who was now staring dully at the pale flames.

"Maude, move over," Isabella said crossly. "You're taking all the fire." Maude didn't answer. "*Move,* I said," Isabella repeated, and she gave Maude a shove. Maude put out a hand to catch herself and knocked over the saucepan, spilling the water and extinguishing the flames. Isabella gave a shriek. "My *fire!*" she wailed, and scrabbled at the soggy ashes until her fingers were black.

"Oh, Isabella," Jane said heavily. It was obvious that the fire was out and would stay out, too, until the wood dried. In this weather that would take at least a day. None of them had the energy to look for more sticks, which would be wet, in any case. Jane pushed the nuts into three small piles. "Come here, both of you, and eat something." They ignored her, and Isabella continued to scold Maude. Jane knew she should stop them, but she just didn't care enough to make the effort, and she nibbled on a nut. Maude gathered a reserve of energy from somewhere and pulled Isabella's hair.

"Get your hands off me, Mud-Maude!" Isabella cried, and she slapped Maude's face.

"Cinder-Ella!" Maude slapped her back.

Jane didn't say anything. *Let them fight,* she thought. *At least it will warm them.* The two girls stood facing each other and glared, and then they turned to the table. Each ate her portion of the nuts, Maude sniffling loudly, Isabella maintaining a dignified silence.

Jane thought that she would fall asleep easily after their ordeal. Instead, she lay wakeful between the two younger girls. Since they had stopped keeping a fire in the evenings, the nights were so cold that Isabella had been sharing their bed. She never said a word to them, and every morning when Jane awoke, Isabella had already risen and was seated at the hearth, pretending that she had been there all night.

Jane stared at the ceiling, listening to the others' even breathing. Who was the girl who had led them home? And had she really been leading them, or did she just happen to pass by the hunting lodge?

The questions turned over and over in her head until she fell asleep.

14

Jane woke alone in the big bed. Finally, weak sunshine came in the window. At least she wouldn't be doing her chores in the rain today. She pulled on her boots—she had slept in her clothes—and ventured into the South Parlor, where Isabella and Maude sat close together under a shawl, their hatred of each other less potent than their desire for warmth. They looked at Jane wordlessly as she passed through the room. Mamma must have still been asleep, for she was nowhere to be seen.

Jane didn't need to check on the hens roosting in the pantry; she knew that Maude wouldn't let her beloved chickens starve as long as even a handful of grain remained to them. She headed to the barn, hoping that her memory was faulty, that she really hadn't fed the animals the last of the fodder the day before.

She pushed open the barn door and saw what she knew she would find—animals that looked at her with a spark of hope in their dull eyes, quickly quenched, and no fodder left. She made her way into Baby's stall. The cow didn't even bother to poke her nose into Jane's clothes to see if she had brought a treat. Somehow this hurt Jane more than if she'd had to disappoint her, and weak tears ran down her face as she knelt next to the animal, her arms around the bony neck.

The little pony stood with her legs wide apart and her head down, and didn't raise it when Jane scratched her between the ears. As Jane left, Mouse lowered herself to the ground and lay there, her limbs tucked under her, her neck bony under her shaggy winter coat. Jane wondered if the day when sweet little Mouse would lie down and be unable to rise again was far off.

Jane picked up a half-rotted acorn and bit into it. The bitter taste made her gag, and she dropped it into the wet leaves. Her foot slipped on a damp rock, and she fell, tearing her stocking, which had been mended so many times that she doubted that anything of the original garment remained. She lay in the mud. *I should just stay here,* she thought as the wind shook freezing drops of water on to her face. *I could go to sleep and never wake up, and not have to worry about Mamma or Maude or Isabella.* But tempting as that thought was, she knew she couldn't abandon them, and with an effort, she rose and went back, dragging her feet, into the house.

Voices came from the South Parlor—angry voices. Had someone come in while she was away? Fear gave her the energy to break into a trot, coming to a halt when she saw that it was Mamma who was talking, or rather scolding, while Maude sobbed, hunched over in the big chair.

"In the *house!*" Mamma said. "Animals in our house—the house that our ancestors built, that you were born in, the house where Grandmamma died and where Papa and I held our wedding feast! What are you thinking? Turn them out immediately!"

"But Mamma," Maude wailed. "It's too cold outside—they'll die!"

"We are not farm women," Mamma said through gritted teeth. She clutched Maude's ear and pulled her to her feet. "We are not peasants who keep livestock in our home."

Maude wriggled and tried to pull away, but Mamma had an iron grip on her. She shook Maude, who cried, "Ow! Ow!"

Jane couldn't stand it. Mamma seemed unaware of how much pain she was causing, unaware of everything except her outrage that chickens were roosting in her parlor. She took Mamma's arm. "Let go of her," she said as calmly as she could. Mamma kept shaking Maude but glared over her shoulder at Jane, who drew back at the sight of her face—white, with gaunt cheeks and staring eyes.

Then Maude whimpered, and Jane pried Mamma's fingers off her sister. Mamma looked at her and then at her own hand as though not understanding what had happened, and then she picked up her skirts and fled from the house.

Jane wrapped her arms around her sister and sank into the big chair, drawing Maude with her. They were so thin now that they both could fit, sitting side by side. "All right, Maudie?" she asked quietly. Maude nodded, and her sobs quieted. "How did Mamma find out about the chickens?" Mamma had to have been aware that chickens had been roosting in the pantry for some time now. Something must have happened to force her to acknowledge that fact.

Maude started to cry again. "I was worried about Delilah." Delilah was the fiercest of the chickens; she wouldn't let anyone except Maude reach under her to search for an egg. She was also Maude's favorite. "She acted like she was cold, so I brought her in here and held her on my lap." Her lip trembled. "And then Mamma came in, and..."

Jane stood. She was bone-weary, and she ached where she had bruised herself in her fall. She was cold, and she was hungrier than she had ever been in her life. Most of all, she was tired of taking care of everyone. But she knew she had to. She didn't cry; she didn't have that luxury. She had only one hope left and had to take advantage of Mamma's absence, which wouldn't last long.

She hadn't climbed the stairs in a long time. Her arms trembled with weakness as she hauled herself over the dangerous spots, and when her hands slipped on the banister or her foot didn't land squarely, she paused until her heartbeat slowed to its normal pace. She didn't dare look down as she inched her way past the long gap in the middle where she had to place her feet carefully, slowly, on the supports that had once held steps.

The disapproval in her ancestors' expressions hardly registered as she made her way through the dim corridor past their tight-lipped faces. *You go out hunting mushrooms and nuts in the rain, and then we'll see how dirty you get,* she thought as she passed a damsel decked in a lavender frock that always made Jane think of springtime and flowers.

Jane paused at Mamma's door. She knew that a few silk gowns still hung there; but the fabric was so thin that Jane doubted they would make any difference against the cold, even if the cloth was still sound enough to be sewn, so she sighed and continued down the hall. She stopped again. Papa's door.

Since her last visit, more dust had gathered, coating all the surfaces. The disturbance of the door's opening made some of it rise in little swirls near her feet, and she sneezed. Rain had come in through a crack in the window, and the smell of mold was stronger than she remembered. The riding crop still lay on the floor—what would disturb it, after all? She looked up, and there was Mamma smiling down at her from the portrait on the wall, stepping forward eagerly, her plumed hat as fresh and jaunty as her expression. Jane walked up to the portrait, dust eddying around her feet, and studied her mother's likeness. Where was that Mamma? Where had she gone?

"I'm doing my best," she whispered, and flinched at even that little sound in the tomblike silence.

The large wardrobe in the corner was closed and locked, but its key was in the door. She had to open both doors wide so that the feeble light from the window would penetrate enough for her to see inside.

Not much was left, but what was there was free of dust and mouse nests, since the doors were so stout and tight. She did find what she was looking for: Papa's riding boots. On one of their visits, Maude had for some reason tried to put them on. Her feet were too broad for the elegant boots and although she had jammed her toes in, willing them to fit, she'd had to give up. Jane had wrestled them off her and landed with a thud on her bottom when the foot finally freed itself, causing the first laughter heard in that room for years.

Jane took out the boots and then closed the doors of the wardrobe. She ran her hand over the smooth surface of the wood, admiring its rich color. Many generations of wax were rubbed into it, giving it the illusion of depth and life. A thought came to her. Still clutching the boots, she ran down the corridor. "Maude!" she called down the stairwell. Her voice boomed and echoed. No answer. "Maude! Come here!"

Isabella's pale face, streaked with gray, appeared around the doorway to the South Parlor. She looked up mutely, and Jane shivered. If only she could find someplace where the girl would be taken care of, maybe she would talk again and find something to do other than playing with ashes and cinders.

"Where's Maude?" Jane demanded. Isabella looked over her shoulder toward the large front door. Why wouldn't the girl speak? "Out?" Jane guessed impatiently. No answer. "Isabella, is Maude outside?" Isabella nodded. "I need you to find her." Isabella's face remained blank. Jane had to suppress the impulse to leap down and slap that stony face, slap it until it showed some expression. *Why* wouldn't Isabella behave normally?

"Firewood!" Jane called down with a sudden inspiration. She was startled by the fierce look that passed over Isabella's features. "Get Maude and tell her to come up. I found firewood."

While she waited for her sister, Jane emptied the wardrobe. She tried not to look at what she was removing, but she couldn't help recognizing the jaunty hat, the metal flask, the rusty hunting knife. To the small pile she added the woolen shawl that Papa used to wear around his shoulders as he stretched his long legs out to the fire after a long day of hunting. It had been bundled into the bottom of the wardrobe and smelled musty, but it would still be warm.

"What firewood?" Maude's voice came from the door. She sniffled.

Jane added the last item, a box of bird shot, to the heap on the floor and straightened her back. She pointed. "This."

"Oh, Jane," Maude protested. "Papa's beautiful wardrobe!"

"Papa is dead," Jane said flatly. "And this wood is dry and soaked with wax. It will burn beautifully."

"But we can never carry it downstairs," Maude said.

"I know," Jane replied. "Help me."

Together they shoved the massive piece of furniture through the door and down the hall. It creaked and groaned, and the screech as they pushed it over the flagstones made Jane's teeth ache. Their arms and shoulders shook by the time they paused at the top of the stairs. Jane peered through the gap to where Isabella stood, staring eagerly up at them.

"Get back in the parlor," Jane commanded. "And then do *not* move a step until we come get you."

"What are we going to do now?" Maude asked. For answer, Jane set her shoulder to the square frame of the wardrobe and heaved. It slid forward a few inches and then stopped.

"Help," Jane managed to choke out, and Maude bent over and added her weight to her sister's. When the heavy piece of furniture stood poised on the very edge of the landing, they straightened and looked at each other.

"Papa's beautiful wardrobe," Maude whispered again. Her objection was only a token one, Jane knew, and she ignored her.

It took but a little effort to push the wardrobe over. At first it tipped slowly, suspended; and then with a speed that made them gasp and leap backward, clutching each other, it hurtled forward with a wrenching sound, skidded on the few steps remaining at the top of the flight, and then plunged through the gap. The crash boomed and echoed through the empty hall. Mice skittered out of and then back into their holes along the edges of the wall, and from the ballroom came the chirping of birds. Jane stepped back, feeling oddly exhilarated.

"Can we do it again?" Maude's eyes glittered.

But Jane was worried what their mother would say at the sight of a huge heap of highly polished and carved firewood, so she shook her head. Best to burn the evidence. "This will have to be enough for now." She dropped Papa's riding boots and the shawl down the gap. The boots bounced off the wood and landed with dull thuds on the stone floor. Then the girls made their slow, careful way down, being even more cautious than usual in case the shock of the heavy wardrobe smashing into the supports had loosened them.

Jane left Maude carefully laying a fire. She put the boots in the spot where she used to leave the milk and whey. When she returned that evening, the boots were gone.

The next day she left Papa's shawl, and that evening she found a dead rabbit, frozen nearly stiff, in its place. She brought it in and thawed it while Maude fetched a shriveled onion and wood-hard turnip which she had miraculously found where they had fallen into a bin that had long been unused. They made a stew, feeding the rabbit's small purple entrails to Betsy, who snapped them up and licked their fingers. The scent of the cooking meat nearly drove them wild while they waited for the tough vegetable to cook enough to chew. They ate the stew with their fingers, sucking the meat off the little bones. Isabella managed to look dainty even while gnawing on the end of a bone, rabbit gravy on her chin, and Mamma took enough notice to remind her to wipe her face. That night they slept well for the first time in weeks.

Papa's wardrobe burned bright and hot, but too quickly, due to its dryness and to the years of beeswax that servants had rubbed into it. They went back upstairs several times to find more fuel. Maude tried to wrestle the heavy shutters off their hinges, but the hardware was rusted almost solid and she gave up. So instead they pushed down Grandmamma's rocking chair and a small table that stood in the corridor. The ancestor in the portrait hanging above the table glared down at Jane when she slid it away from the wall, and she muttered, "Oh, leave me alone," as she carried the dainty thing to the stairwell.

For now their firewood needs were met. But the people of the woods left them food only occasionally, and often they had nothing to eat except an egg. Once a chicken was clearly on the point of dying, so Jane wrung its neck as she remembered seeing servants do long ago, and they had stew, and then soup made of the bones. Christmas came and went with no pig haunch to roast. The disappointment drove Jane nearly wild, and for several nights she dreamed that she was about to sink her teeth into a chunk of pork, dripping with juice and covered with crackling skin, only to wake up with her stomach feeling as though a knife had transfixed it. Isabella was so thin that she was almost translucent, and Maude seemed to be all knobby bone. Mamma spent most of each day sleeping.

Jane considered. That girl in the forest had been slender, but not as thin as they were. She'd shown a great deal of energy as she fled through the woods—didn't that mean that she was eating, at least a little? Maybe Jane could find her. She didn't know what she would say when she did, but she couldn't just sit here and wait as they all grew weaker and weaker until they died one after the other.

The thought of getting lost among the trees was almost more than she could bear, though. She could make a trail of white pebbles, like the children in a tale that their long-gone nanny had once told them. So she wrapped herself up warmly and set about hunting pebbles to show her the way home. After an hour, she threw aside the small handful in disgust. She would never be able to gather enough. White stones were very hard to find, which, after all, was what made them useful as trail markers.

Maude had watched her with interest, even finding an occasional pale rock after Jane explained what she was doing. When Jane tossed away the few she had found, Maude went back in the house, to warm up, Jane supposed. But she reappeared a few minutes later, dragging one of the red velvet drapes that hung around the doorway to the ballroom. The fabric was so rotten that the girls had given up trying to use the cloth for warmth, even as a wrap.

"What are you doing?" Jane asked, too tired and dispirited really to care.

"Look!" Maude seized one of the golden tassels that formed a fringe along the edge of the drape. She gave it a swift yank, and it came off easily. She showed it to Jane triumphantly. "We can tie them to branches to mark a trail."

A little while later, Jane set off toward the hunting lodge, clutching a makeshift pouch of red velvet that held dozens of brightly colored tassels. In her pocket were two precious needles—her last—and a ball of brown thread. Maude had wanted to accompany her, but Jane convinced her that there was no point in both of them exhausting themselves. "If I find food, I'll come back and get you," she promised. Maude agreed with a scowl, and Jane left alone. *At least if I get lost only one of us will die out here,* she thought as she passed the hunting lodge.

She tied the first tassel to a branch at her eye level, just barely in sight of the hunting lodge. She stepped back to look at it and felt a surge of fear. What if mischievous fairy people untied the tassels so that she couldn't find them? Or worse, what if they took them down and then retied them to the wrong branches, leading her farther and farther into the dark woods until she was lost so deep among the trees that nobody would ever find her, not even her bones?

She had no choice but to keep going. Here, alone in the forest, she allowed herself to think the thoughts that she kept hidden even from herself when she was with the others. What if Mamma wearied of their hard life and drudgery and went on a walk and never returned? *Mamma would never do that,* Jane thought. But Papa had done it. What made her so certain that Mamma would not? She stopped and realized that, lost in thought, she had not tied a tassel in a long time. She carefully retraced her steps and found the last one. *I mustn't do that again,* she thought.

And then she heard it again—the singing, sweet yet sad, that had so often floated into her window late at night. Only this time it was closer, and she could make out individual voices. Not the words—she was still too far away for that—but a sense of the melody and the meaning. These were fairies; she knew they were.

Then she heard a distinctly human sound: a baby wailed, and a woman's voice broke off from her singing to murmur something soothing. Someone else—a man this time—sang a few more notes. Where was it coming from? She stood on tiptoe, although she knew that wouldn't help, and strained her ears. The voices were distant, but she thought she could tell where they originated. She started off in that direction, remembering to tie her tassels every time she was almost out of sight of the last one. The voices suddenly hushed. She started toward them but stopped. She would never find them.

"Help me!" she finally called, and her voice broke into a harsh sob. She swallowed hard and then went on, "I'm Jane Halsey from up at the hall. We're starving." Nothing. She lingered another minute. Her exhaustion told her to lie down and go to sleep, and never return to the dank, crumbling house. She resisted with an effort, turned around, and was starting back on the path home when she heard something moving swiftly toward her. She stood frozen to the spot until a figure became visible, coming quickly up the hill.

It was that girl, that same girl with the large dark eyes, and she was running up the slope toward Jane. The girl stopped short, but without any apparent fear, when she saw Jane looking at her. Her face was more serious than it had been before, and this time, instead of disappearing, she beckoned. Jane took a step in the girl's direction, and at her encouraging nod, she took another step and then another. They walked for only a few minutes, the girl slowing whenever Jane fell behind.

She never would have seen the hut if the girl hadn't stopped in front of it. Fashioned out of logs and what looked like dried mud, it blended in perfectly with the woods. Vines grew up its walls. It was tiny but looked stout and well built. The girl ducked and went inside, and as Jane neared the hut, she heard the murmur of voices and the fretful whimpers of a baby fighting sleep.

Jane tried to follow her, but the earth tipped under her feet and a cloudy blackness spangled with silver whirled before her eyes, and she felt the cold ground strike her cheek, and then she knew no more.

15

Jane found herself half sitting, half lying, propped up in a pair of strong arms while someone spooned hot herbal tea into her mouth. Her vision cleared, and she saw that the cup was held by a woman with stern but gentle eyes. By the light of two windows and the embers in the nearby fireplace, Jane could see that they were in a hut very much like the one that Hugh shared with his parents. It was small but neat and tidy, and Jane's empty stomach gave a wrench as a savory smell reached her from the iron pot nestled in the coals.

She tried to sit upright, but the woman pushed her back gently into the arms that were holding her.

"You're the girl from up at the Hall?" the woman asked abruptly. Jane nodded. "Why don't you leave milk and cheese anymore?"

"The cow and goats went dry." Jane cleared her throat as her voice squeaked. "They're starving. We're all starving."

The woman looked her up and down, and then spoke to the person behind Jane. "Find a basket and put some food in it, Annie." The arms holding her loosened their grip, and Jane, glancing down, recognized the clumsily mended tear in the sleeve.

Jane caught the girl's—Annie's—wrist and said, "First, let me fix that." She sat up, reached into the pocket tied around her waist, and pulled out the thread and needles. *No charity,* she told herself. This time it wasn't the ancestors talking; it was her own pride. She wouldn't take food from these people who clearly needed what they had unless she gave them something, no matter how small, in return.

Annie glanced at her mother, who nodded, and then she held out her arm while Jane sewed a seam. The girl watched with interest, and when Jane was through, she could hardly see that there had once been a rip there. Annie extended her sleeve to her mother, who inspected the work. The woman looked at Jane with real warmth this time, and said, "While my daughter finds you some—" she hesitated, and then went on "—some refreshment, perhaps you would like to occupy your time?" Jane nodded, and suppressed a smile. The woman might not have the fine manners that Mamma had tried to teach her and Maude, but she had the delicacy not to remind Jane that it wasn't refreshment that Annie was bringing; it was life-saving provisions.

She wouldn't be occupying her time doing fancy needlework, she saw, as the woman placed a pair of heavy woolen work trousers in her lap. The large tear that split the knee ran all the way across from side to side. She stitched a smooth seam and shook out the trousers, then held them up and surveyed her work with satisfaction. She took another sip of the now-cool tea and looked around her. A baby, wrapped in what Jane recognized as her own father's shawl, the one that she had left on the path, lay asleep on a pallet near the fire. A wooden screen stood between the child and the hearth. There was also a large table with four stools set around it and two small beds. A ladder led to what must be a loft, where the adults slept, she guessed.

The woman, who had been stirring whatever was in the pot on the hearth, handed Jane a shirt and said, "Is it possible to make this bigger? My son is growing so fast," and at those words the door burst open and two men—no, a man and a boy—came in.

The boy was saying, "Mother, is something wrong? I called you—why didn't you answer? And where's Annie?" Jane half rose, holding the shirt in one hand and the threaded needle in the other.

"Hush, Will," the woman said. "We have company."

They turned, and Jane felt ill as she recognized the boy. Why did she keep seeing him? The boy was taller now. Even broader in the shoulder, too. She could tell by the way he looked back at her that he recognized her, too. She dropped her gaze at the hostility in his.

"Why, it's the girl from up at the Hall," the man said in a tone of friendly inquiry.

Should she curtsey? No, perhaps not. "I'm Jane Montjoy."

"Jeffrey Forester," the man said. "Will, make your bow."

The boy didn't bend or even look at Jane. "Why's she here? Haven't the nobles done enough—"

"Hush," the woman said, more sharply this time. "This girl never did you any harm." The boy turned abruptly and stomped outside, slamming the door. His father made an exasperated sound and followed him.

"I'm not a noble," Jane said awkwardly. "And I didn't mean to harm anyone—"

"I know." The woman laid a work-roughened hand on hers. "He has some mistaken ideas about those who live with plenty and those who don't have enough."

"I don't live with plenty. Truly, we don't have any food or firewood or—"

"I can see that," the woman said. "We didn't know you were in such need, or we would have helped earlier. And now, please share our meal before you go home." She took the iron pot, which turned out to contain stewed root vegetables—turnips, parsnips, and carrots—off the fire and placed it on a thick pad on the table.

Will and his father came back in, and Will set out five bowls and plates. His mother ladled thick porridge onto the plates and passed them around. The father served himself out of the pot and passed the ladle to Annie, who helped herself and passed it on to Jane.

Jane thought she would faint at the sight of the food but shyly spooned out only a small portion for herself. Will was about to take the ladle from her when his mother said sharply, "Here, child, take more than that," and scooped out a large dollop and plopped it onto her porridge.

Will made a grunt that sounded impatient as he looked at the dish and then up at his mother. "I had mine before you came home," she said. "You take what's left." She watched as he emptied the vegetables from the bowl onto his porridge.

The baby made a fussy waking-up sound, and the mother went to tend to it. While her back was turned, Will scraped the remaining vegetables from his plate onto his mother's. He glanced up before Jane could look away from him, and he glared at her with such ferocity that she felt herself grow red and lowered her head to her food so that no one would notice. *I didn't ask her to feed me,* she thought. *It's not my fault there's not enough.*

Will and his father stood. "Time to get back to work," the man said, and told Jane she was welcome to visit whenever she liked. Jane appreciated his delicacy in not saying what his son was so obviously thinking, that if she visited at mealtime, there would be less food for the rest of them. Will didn't say goodbye, despite his mother's command. Instead, he slammed the door without a word as he followed his father outside.

Meager though their meal had been, it was still more than Jane had eaten in the past several days put together, and she felt stronger and more clearheaded than she had in quite a while. She stood when the others did and started to help clean up, but the mother stopped her. "I can do this quicker by myself," she said, laying the baby in a cradle near the fire. "If you wouldn't mind showing Annie how you sewed that seam..."

For the rest of the afternoon, Jane tutored Annie in the art of mending, showing her how to take tiny, almost invisible stitches, how to catch the last sound threads together, how to follow the curve of an edge so that the join of two pieces would lie smooth rather than pucker. She even embroidered a decorative flower over a hole in a shirt.

Annie laughed, a deep chuckle, as she shook out the shirt. "I doubt Will would like a flower right on his shoulder!" She had a pleasantly husky voice.

"I didn't know that was his." Jane tried to take the shirt back to cut out the flower and put something less delicate in its place, but Annie held it out of her reach.

"No, now that I think of it, he'll be pleased with it. He likes everything that grows." Annie laughed as Jane tried again to grab it, and to her own surprise, Jane laughed, too.

Soon Annie managed to sew a seam with reasonably straight stitches, and she beamed when Jane praised it. She bent her head to her work with renewed enthusiasm, and Jane glowed inwardly that someone cared for her opinion. "You mustn't let Will bother you," Annie said after they had worked a while in companionable silence. She was squinting cross-eyed at a needle as she tried to poke a thread through its tiny eye.

To cover her confusion, Jane took the thread from her, clipped off its ragged edge to make a sharp point, and handed it back. When she had regained her composure, she asked cautiously, "What do you mean?"

"Got it!" Annie's tongue poked out of her mouth as she carefully drew the thread through the needle.

"What do you mean, I shouldn't let him bother me?" Jane asked.

"He doesn't mean anything by being rude," Annie explained, knotting the end of her thread. She let her hands rest on her lap, as though glad of a chance to stop the finicky work. "We know everyone so well. Everyone we usually see, I mean. He's not used to being around grand people like you."

"Grand? *Me?*" Jane could hardly speak for astonishment.

Annie didn't seem to hear her. "That's why he acts so stiff with you. He's shy. When it's just us or people he knows, he's different."

Jane didn't believe it, and she didn't know why Annie felt the need to explain her brother to her, so she didn't reply. Instead, she picked up the gown she had been shortening and said, "Look, when you sew a hem, you don't want the stitches to show through on the other side. So pick up a few of the threads with the point of the needle—"

Annie hemmed most of the skirt under Jane's direction, and when the baby woke again, Jane picked the child up. "Boy or girl?" she asked as the baby's big eyes stared at this unfamiliar face.

"Girl. Frances." Annie surveyed her work and then held it up so that Jane could see a pucker.

"Take out those last three stitches," Jane instructed. "You pulled too tight. Leave the thread looser." Annie sighed and did so, grumbling about how long it was going to take to work her way all around the skirt.

"Was that you, that day in the forest?" Jane asked.

"What day?" Annie didn't take her eyes off her sewing.

"When I was walking in the forest—were you looking at me from behind a tree? And did you leave a basket of mushrooms and apples in our field, and then find some cheese on it?"

Annie shook her head. "No, that was Will. He told us about it after he came home."

Will? It didn't seem like something he would do, given how he felt about "nobles." Jane looked down at the tiny face again as the baby put two fingers into her mouth and sucked them hard, her eyelids drooping. She brushed her lips against the soft hair and inhaled warm baby scent. *Just like Robert,* she thought.

Annie's mother came to take the baby from Jane. "She's a love, this one," she said as she gazed at the little face. "But I fear her teeth are going to cause her trouble. Hannah Herb-Woman left me some of her remedy, but I doubt there's enough."

"My sister has been helping Hannah," Jane said timidly, not

knowing how much actual use Maude could be. "She might know which herbs to use and how to prepare them."

"I'll remember that when the time comes, and thank you." The woman laid the baby down just as the door banged open, and the man and the boy came in again.

"She's still here?" the boy asked, not looking at Jane.

Huh! she thought. *Annie calls it being stiff and shy. It's just plain old rudeness. He's not uncomfortable—he's proud. Proud and conceited.*

"Hush, Will," his mother said sharply. "You'll wake the baby. Jane has been teaching your sister how to sew a straight seam."

Annie muttered something unintelligible that nevertheless managed to express her feelings about sewing a straight seam, and her brother grinned. It was astonishing how different it made him look, but as soon as he caught Jane's eye on him, the smile vanished and his scowl reappeared.

"He's right, though," the man said. "It's getting late, and it's no short walk back to the big house. William will go with you. Will, take the young lady as far as the hunting lodge."

"Me?" Will exclaimed at exactly the moment that Jane said, *"Him?"* She lowered her head and hoped they hadn't heard her. Just because the boy was rude didn't mean that she had to stoop to his level.

"Yes, you," his mother said sharply. "Annie's finishing up her seam, and I doubt that you and your father found much dry wood to cut, so you should be fresh and ready for a walk. No argument now," she added, as Will opened his mouth.

So, after thanking her hosts and packing up a small bundle of clothing to repair, Jane left, accompanied by a silent Will, who was carrying the basket of "refreshments" that his mother had given them. Jane had seen the woman put in dried beans, a cabbage, and smoked fish, along with a little pot of what Jane hoped was lard or goose fat for cooking with, a sack containing grain or flour, and even a few lumps of precious charcoal, wrapped in leaves to prevent their dust from soiling the food, nestled in the bottom of the basket.

They walked in a silence that grew more and more awkward the longer it lasted. Jane cast about for some neutral topic of conversation, even while knowing that her mother would find it only fitting that she and this woodcutter's son would have nothing to say to each other.

But it was Will who broke the silence when the hunting lodge came into sight. "My father asked me to tell you that he regrets that he didn't leave you meat from the Christmas pig this year." He sounded awkward, as though reluctant to pass on his father's apology. "We didn't have any ourselves. Late in the fall the king's men found our livestock and took all the beasts."

"Took them?" Jane asked, shocked. "They took them? Why?"

Will didn't meet her eye. "We live in the king's forest. Whatever is in it belongs to him. If the soldiers had found us as well as the pigs and the goats…" He left the sentence unfinished and extended the basket, still without looking at her. She took it in both hands. Before she could thank the boy, he had vanished.

16

Just like a fairy, Jane thought as she trudged to the door, and her mouth crinkled into a smile at the thought. Will was even less fairylike than his sister. The last few yards to the house were difficult with the heavy basket.

The big front door was ajar. Why did the hall look different? It suddenly seemed so enormous, so cold and so filthy. But she knew that the hall had not changed; it was her own eyes that were different after her time spent in the cozy little hut in the woods. She saw now why Hugh had always stopped and gaped on the rare occasions when he came in here, usually after being ordered by Maude to be a third in some game they were playing. She knew that it wasn't only the hugeness of the hall that had astonished him; it was the ruin and the mess of it.

She entered the South Parlor. The others were sitting by the hearth, staring dully at the small flames. Maude glanced up as Jane came in, then back at the fire, and then, realizing that her sister was carrying something, up again, with a bit of light in her eyes for the first time in days. "What's in there?" she asked.

Isabella rose to her feet and stumbled a little. Without thinking, Jane caught her elbow. "All right?" she asked.

To her surprise, Isabella didn't pull away and even smiled with trembling lips. "Just a little—a little light-headed," she said. "Thank you."

"You're welcome." Jane tried to hide her surprise at Isabella's civility. It had been a day full of surprises.

Mamma sat in the big chair with her feet drawn up and a shawl around her. She, too, appeared different. Jane noticed new lines in her face, new gray streaks in her frowsy hair, a new trembling of her pale lips. "Maude, make Mamma some tea," she said as she turned away. She couldn't stand to see it.

That evening they feasted. It would have seemed a scanty meal just a few months ago, but tonight a shared half cabbage boiled with smoked fish, and some hard biscuits made of brown flour and lard, felt like luxury. Mamma didn't even seem to notice that they had not laid a cloth on the table and that they ate without bothering to take the tiny nibbles she usually insisted on. While Jane and Maude cleaned up, Isabella put all the coal in the fireplace before Jane could stop her, and they sat by the flames for a long time, warming their hands, feeling their cheeks flush in the blessed heat. Maude told a rambling story about a boy and a giant, clearly making it up as she went, and when she had drawn to an unsatisfactory close Isabella said shyly, "I know some tales, too."

"You *do?*" Maude sounded shocked. "Why didn't you ever tell them before?"

Without explaining, Isabella began, "Once there were twin princesses. Both were beautiful, but one had a warm heart and the other only a cold stone where her heart should be...." When the story came to its satisfying end, with the warm-hearted princess wed to the king of a neighboring country after many trials and the coldhearted one left to tend sheep in a lonely field, Maude begged for another.

"She's too tired." Jane saw Isabella's eyes drooping. "Let's go to bed."

The next day, and then almost every day after that, Jane found food—under an upturned bucket, weighted with stones to protect it from wild beasts—on the path, and almost every day she also found clothing to mend. One day she carefully cut open the seams of Maude's long-outgrown church dress and sewed the few whole pieces together into a gown for the baby, guessing at the size as best she could.

Maude tried to help, but her stitching was clumsy, and Jane knew that the work had to be done well. Keeping warm and dry in this damp early spring was just as lifesaving as having enough to eat. She was not taking charity or stealing food from the mouths of the people of the woods if she left a pair of woolen stockings, holes smoothly darned, on the path and found a precious piece of salted pork waiting for her the next day. Each was helping the other and making a fair trade. So she sewed tight seams and made sure that the patches were as firmly placed and smooth as if they were part of the original garment.

The hollows in Maude's cheeks began to fill in, and Isabella's skin no longer looked as though a strong light would shine through it. Jane found that she had more energy and did not need to sleep half the afternoon. Even Baby lost her skeletal look after a bale of hay appeared in the barn one day, although Jane knew that the cow's milk would not return until after she'd had another calf. She faithfully fed and watered the animals, turning them out in the pasture to crop at the few tender shoots of grass that were finally coming up. The chickens went back outside and pecked eagerly at bugs. Maude brought in a few brown eggs almost every day.

And almost every day Jane had some sewing to do. She found she enjoyed the challenge of mending a complicated tear, of lengthening a dress whose wearer had grown tall despite the severity of the winter. She knew that many of the clothes she had been given did not come from the family she had met—the little girl's dress, for example, and the trousers made for a man stouter and shorter than the woodcutter. She saved scraps cut from one garment to patch another, and her stitches became even neater, stronger, and less visible. Isabella joined her, showing a talent for embroidery that hid a stain and could change a man's work shirt into a girl's smock.

One day Jane left a pair of heavy work trousers on the bucket and picked up the loaf of bread wrapped in a clean rag that she found under it.

"Miss!" A tall figure emerged into the open. It was Annie. "My mother asks if there is any way to make this wider." She handed a bundle of brown cloth to Jane. Jane unfolded it, revealing a woman's dress. It was of finer fabric than most of the garments that the people of the woods had been giving her for these weeks, and it even had a bit of fancy stitching around the neck and at the ends of the long sleeves.

"It's her best gown," the other girl explained. "Now that spring is almost here, Father Albert will be coming back. Mother hasn't been churched since before Frances was born, and she wants to wear this when services start again. She hasn't had it on for years, and now it's too small."

Jane held up the dress and looked at the seams. There wasn't much fabric to let out, but she thought she could see ways to make at least a little difference. "I'll try," she said.

The next day she inspected the dress. She carefully snipped apart the bodice and the full, gathered skirt. If she took out some of the gathers, she might be able to make two strips from the skirt that she could then seam into the sides of the bodice, adding a few inches. The skirt wouldn't be as full as before, but it looked like there would still be enough for some pleats that would ease the fit around the woman's hips. Then she could… Her fingers moved almost as quickly as her thoughts.

She turned the skirt inside out, so that the most faded spots would be hidden, and sewed up the hem at the back, where the wearer must have trodden on it and created a ragged spot. Maude stitched the pleats, measuring them with a piece of string to make sure that they came out even. She had always been clever with that kind of thing.

And now it was done. The work had been long even with Maude's help, and it was past the hour that Jane usually left repaired clothing on the path. She suddenly decided to take it to the woodcutter's hut rather than waiting a day. She was eager for Annie to see her success with her mother's gown, she told herself. The days were starting to lengthen, and she would have more than enough time to walk to the cottage, leave the dress, and return home before dark.

The rain had finally stopped, and faint sunshine poked through the branches, which showed a little green on their tips, as if they had been dusted with green powder. Jane's golden tassels still hung limply from some of the lower limbs. Odd how she had lived so close to the people of the woods her whole life and had even occasionally seen them in church, but she had never before known how close to her home some of them lived. Once, she remembered now, on one of her rare visits to the village, she had seen a family that might even have been the woodcutter's, but she had paid them no attention. She had not even really noticed them until now.

She was struck again by how nearly invisible the little cottage was. She went to the door and knocked, softly at first, in case the baby was asleep, and then louder when there was no answer. Silence.

A step behind her made her whirl around. It was only Will, surveying her with what looked like suspicion. He carried a wood ax over his shoulder. They stood in silence, each eyeing the other, until Jane extended her hand, showing him what she was carrying. "Your mother's dress. Your sister asked me to—"

He nodded, then reached past her and unlocked the door. He pushed it open and stepped back to let her inside. "She'll be here soon."

Jane took this to mean that she was to wait for the mother's return. Who was this boy to tell her what to do? "I'll just leave it here." She stepped into the dark cottage and laid the gown on the table.

"She'll be here soon," the boy repeated, turning back to the woods. Then he did a very surprising thing. He sang. It wasn't a full song, just a few notes, and they were strangely familiar.

"Fairy singers!" Jane blurted. She blushed as Will looked at her quizzically. "I mean, you're the people who sing in the night."

"In the daytime, too, but it's quieter in the woods at night. You can hear us better." A few notes, in what sounded like a woman's voice, came back from the hill behind the cottage.

"It's how we talk when we're separated," he explained. "Like the huntsman's horn that tells the others that the hounds have found the game. My mother says she's on her way home. Did you really think we were fairies?"

"That's what our grandmother and our mother always said it was." Jane hoped the boy couldn't tell how embarrassed she was.

"I've lived in these woods all my life," the boy said, sounding amused, "and my father before me, and his father before him. And none of us have ever seen a fairy. Not that I don't think they're in the forest," he added hastily, looking around as though worried that someone might have heard him, someone who would be angry that he doubted their existence. "It's just that they're too shy to show themselves when they don't have to. I don't think they'd draw attention to themselves by singing."

Jane was spared having to go on with the awkward conversation by the appearance of the woman, carrying the baby in a sling. Jane stepped forward. "Here's your gown." She unfolded it and shook out the creases. "I had to alter it a little to find enough material to make it fit you." The woman picked it up and held it against her front. It did look large enough now, and the change from gathers to pleats would suit her ample figure.

"You'll stay for a meal," the woman said. Jane knew that Mamma would expect her to say no, she wouldn't, but the thought of food made her light-headed.

The father and Annie came in, Annie smiling when she saw Jane, the father giving her a nod before sitting down at the table. The woman filled the wooden plates with porridge into which she had stirred dried peas and herbs this time. They had all cooked together into a savory, pale green mass.

Jane ate as slowly as she could, but the taste of the porridge made her suddenly ravenous. The woman, without asking if she wanted more, ladled out another spoonful.

When Jane rose, her bowl finally empty, she saw to her dismay that the sun was casting long shadows. "I have to go," she said, her mind suddenly filled with the stories that Mamma had told about witches who trapped wandering strangers and trolls that came out of their caves only after dark, when respectable people were in their beds.

"William will go with you," the man said as before. Without a word, the boy stood and shouldered his wood ax. Did he even take it to bed with him? Jane wondered. And what if she didn't *want* him to go with her?

But of course she needed someone, and Annie was busy with Frances. Jane had rarely been out in the woods alone, and never after dark. She wasn't sure whether she would be able to find her way when the few familiar landmarks would be obscured by the night. This fierce-looking boy was better than no escort at all. So she thanked them for her supper, took the basket that the woman handed her, and set out for home.

When they reached the hunting lodge, she paused. Should she thank the boy? At least say goodbye? But he had turned away and was headed back down the path.

"Stop!" Jane called, without really knowing why. He paused and then turned—slowly, as if to tell her that she couldn't tell him what to do.

"Why do you hate me?" she asked. Her voice squeaked, making her sound like a pitiful child and not the dignified young woman that Mamma kept telling her she had to be. She cleared her throat and tried again. "I've never done anything to you."

"Oh, you have." His confident tone infuriated her.

"Never!"

"You and your family," he said. "Here you live in this—this—" words seemed to fail him, and he waved his hand in the direction of her house "—with everything you could ever want, and you take food from us. *You* don't know want. *You* don't suffer hardship." He glared at her. "You didn't pay us when we repaired your roof, even though Jeremy's family has had to do without his work ever since he fell off it. And we've heard about your house. Floors of polished stone. A separate room just for dancing in. A bedroom for each person." He laughed without humor. Words poured out of him as though he had been thinking them for a long time. "And of course you don't want to let someone like me into your house, after you've been in mine and eaten food that we couldn't spare—"

"I never asked for food," Jane said. "Not after that first day. We were starving and freezing. And I've worked..." She paused. Halseys didn't work, did they? But what else could she call it? "I've worked for every scrap of food I've had since then."

"Starving? Freezing?" The scorn in Will's voice curled her toes. "How can you say that, when you live in a place like that?"

She didn't know want? She didn't suffer hardship? She thought of plump little Frances and saw again the dead body of little Robert, so small that the priest's man had carried him to his grave tucked under his arm like a loaf of bread. How could she ever convince this boy of the truth about how she lived? Would Mamma ever forgive her if she did, if she let a boy of the woods know how miserable their lives were? A derisive snort from Will made up her mind. "Come with me. Come see the plenty and comfort that we live in."

"I don't need to."

"Oh, you do. You think you know something, but you're wrong. And you think you're better than we are—"

"No, it's you who think that!"

She shook her head violently. "You think that just because my parents and grandparents had money and owned a lot of land, that we're somehow not as good as you because you live in the woods." This time he didn't answer, and she felt a small glow of satisfaction.

Jane suddenly regretted that Will had goaded her into asking him in. She didn't want him to see the staircase fallen into ruin, to smell the decay, to hear the scuttle of mice and rats, to hear Maude whining about not having any food, to see her sister and stepsister huddled on the hearth. But she *had* asked him, and now she continued up the path.

They stopped on the drive. "Well?" Jane asked.

"What?" Will looked at the house, still visible in the last rays of the sun.

"Don't you *see?*" She pointed at the ivy growing up the walls, its little roots, she knew, pressing into tiny cracks in the stone and pushing them apart, making them wider until they weakened the very bones of the house. Bird droppings streaked the few panes of glass that were still in the big windows. She glanced at Will.

"So?" he asked. "I've seen it before. I worked on the roof without getting paid, remember? It needs some repairs and some cleaning. I don't—"

"Come inside," she said, too galled now to care if it upset Mamma. They climbed the broken steps and passed through the big door, now always left standing ajar, and then into the front hall, where the fragments of the staircase swept up one wall and across to the big landing. The remaining tasseled red velvet curtain still hung on one side of the large door that led off to the ballroom. The blank space where the other one used to hang made the doorway look like a child's mouth with a gap where a front tooth should be.

The stink of rats and mice was even stronger than Jane remembered. Perhaps with the warmer weather all smells became heavier, or perhaps more of the filthy beasts were living under the stairs and in the angles of the doorways. Or was it that she was smelling her home with an outsider's nose? She found Will's expression difficult to read. Surprise, certainly, and perhaps disappointment that this grand house was not what he had heard about all his life.

"Where do you live?" he asked, and she led the way into the South Parlor.

She pushed open the door to the familiar scene. Maude, stretched out on the big chair that had been Harry's favorite, glanced at Jane and then stared at the boy without speaking. Jane saw to her relief that Mamma was absent, sleeping, probably. She also saw that her sister's hair was so tangled that the knots would probably have to be cut out rather than combed, and that her clothes were much too small and were so ripped and stained that nobody, not even the people of the woods, would want to wear garments made of the scraps they were rapidly falling into. Maude's hands were red with sores from being cold and damp for so long. *Do I look like that?* Jane asked herself in a sudden panic.

But it was Isabella who drew the boy's attention. She squatted, thin and bedraggled, in the hearth, tracing shapes in the cold ashes with her small and filthy fingers. Their meager store of fuel stood next to the fireplace. They could not afford to kindle any of the sticks until the room grew colder after the sun set.

Isabella looked up, and Jane could tell that she had seen the boy. Her red eyes glared out from her soot-streaked face, and her long hair was gray with ashes. A shawl wrapped about her disguised her thinness to some degree, but her pointy little face hinted at how much flesh she had lost over the long winter, despite the extra food they had been receiving for the past few weeks.

"What's the matter with her?" Will whispered.

"There's nothing the matter with me." Isabella addressed Jane. "What is he doing here?"

Jane felt herself blush. "He's a—he's a…" She sought for the right word. Will looked at her in silence, a small smile curving his lips, as though he wondered how she was going to finish. "He's a neighbor," she finally managed. Isabella's silvery laugh showed what she thought of this description.

The sound seemed to wake Will from a trance. He took a step into the room. "What's the matter with her?" he repeated, louder this time. "What's her name?"

Maude spoke. "Ella. Cinder-Ella. Or you can call her Ash-Ella." She, too, laughed, but without mirth.

Jane took Will's arm and drew him out of the parlor. "You see?" she asked, not caring that it sounded like *I told you so.*

"I do see. But I don't understand—you've always acted as though you thought you were better than the rest of us."

"What did I do?"

"The way you never said hello when we came to work on your roof. The way you looked at my father when you were digging the grave for that man. And when my father and I dug the grave for you, you were too proud to say anything to me."

"Too *proud?*" That day she had been so frightened of Master Forester that she could hardly speak to him. And then she had been crying in the dairy when Will had come to return the shovel. She remembered how tight her voice had been to hide her tears. Had that made her sound proud? She flung words at him. "I'm not the proud one—*you* are."

"Me?" His voice squeaked. He cleared his throat. "What are you talking about?"

"It's not my fault I live in a big house and my ancestors used to have servants. It's nothing to do with me. You act like I'm not good enough for you to know, just because my family doesn't work with their hands." She spread her fingers. "I *do* work with my hands. But even if I didn't, I'm just as good as you, and when you walk me home you don't talk to me—"

"I didn't think you wanted me to."

"I wanted you to."

There was an uncomfortable silence, broken when Will suddenly looked her straight in the eyes and grinned. "So, we've both been wrong."

She nodded warily, concerned about where this was going.

"I thought you were proud, and *you* thought *I* was proud."

She nodded again.

Will stuck out his hand. "Friends?"

She wasn't sure what he wanted her to do, but she put her fingers in his. His palm was rough and dry and pleasantly warm, as it had been by Harry's grave that day. "Friends."

He held her hand longer this time, and for some reason it felt natural. She didn't want to remove it. She looked up at him and saw that he was smiling. Then he brought her hand to his lips, just as the hunting boy had done with Isabella that snowy day, and kissed it gently. It was over so quickly that she thought she must have imagined it.

"I have to go home," he said. "It's getting dark." Before she could stop him, he disappeared through the big door, and she heard his boots thump on the stairs as he ran down them.

She lingered in the hall, looking at the back of her hand, which his lips had touched. It didn't look any different, although it tingled; and when she pressed her own lips to the spot, she tried to imagine what it would have been like if instead of that swift kiss, he had pulled her to him and bent his head to her face and—

"Jane? What are you doing?" Maude stood in the doorway.

"Nothing," she managed to say, and she pushed past her sister and put the basket on the table in the parlor. "Let's see what Mistress Forester sent this time, shall we?"

17

Maude took obvious delight in instructing Jane about which of the plants sprouting everywhere were useful as medicine and had to be picked now, which had to be left until flowers or berries grew on them, which had no use, and which were poisonous and should not be harvested. "There's not much that grows around here that will kill you," Maude informed her sister, "but some will give you a bellyache. Just ask me before you pick anything I haven't told you about." Jane suppressed a smile at Maude's self-important tone and followed her instructions.

"What's this one for?" she asked, humoring her sister.

Maude glanced where Jane was pointing and dismissed it with a shrug. "Nothing. But that dandelion over there—juice from the stem helps wounds heal, and a tea made from the leaves can calm your stomach. But if you drink too much—well, you'll spend all night in the privy."

"What's good for babies getting their teeth?"

"Teething?" Maude pondered. "Chamomile. Why?"

"Do you have any?"

"I have some dried. I think it's still good. Why?"

"I just need some. Can you make it up for me?"

"Why, Jane?"

"For a baby who's teething! Why else?" She softened. "Please, Maude. She cries all night." This wasn't strictly true; little Frances Forester had been perfectly content the last time Jane had seen her. But she felt a sudden desire to visit the Foresters' cozy hut. *I miss Annie,* she told herself. *Maude is being irritating.*

Maude gave Jane a small pouch of powdered chamomile and instructions on how to mix it into a paste with water and rub it on the baby's gums. As she took it, Jane said, "If Mamma asks where I am, tell her—"

"She won't ask," Maude said glumly. It was true; Mamma hardly seemed to notice their existence anymore and rarely even spoke.

Jane gave her sister a quick hug. "Don't worry. Now that spring is coming, things will get better. You'll see."

"I hope so," Maude muttered as she turned back to her plants.

At first, Betsy accompanied Jane, but when the dog became distracted by a scent or a sound and dashed off through the trees, Jane didn't bother calling her back. She was no longer afraid to come this way, at least not in the daylight. The people of the woods were too shy to approach her, and the fairies must be equally timid, for she had never seen one. Annie had told her that there were no bears or wolves in this forest, and the outlaws lived far away, on the other side of the castle.

As she approached the hut, she was surprised to hear talk and laughter, and the creak of wagon wheels. She emerged from the trees to see the woodcutter's horse, a brown giant named Bartholomew, harnessed to the cart that normally Master Forester filled with wood to sell in the village. But today it was loaded with people: not only Mistress Forester and the baby, but an elderly couple who lived nearby, and several small children. Annie was helping the last of them in, a chubby boy who had to be perched on the lap of the old woman. Annie climbed up to sit next to her father, who slapped the reins on the horse's back, and Jane was pleased to see how well Annie looked wearing a brown dress that Jane had patiently helped her to sew.

"What are you doing here?" She hadn't seen Will ride up on a shaggy spotted pony. She felt a mixture of embarrassment and anger at his curtness. Did he still resent her? What did she have to do to prove that she didn't hold herself above them?

"I was bringing something for Frances. It's for teething. Mix it with warm water and rub it on her gums." She flung the pouch at him. It fell short, but she didn't stop to pick it up. Let *him* get it. It was for his sister, after all. She tried to stride away with dignity like Mamma, but tears of rage stung her eyes, and she stumbled on the rough ground. She kept her footing with difficulty but hadn't gone very far when she heard the pony trotting up behind her.

"Wait," Will called. "Jane, wait."

Well, at least he knew her name. She stopped but didn't turn around, afraid that he would see her tears and think he had hurt her feelings, when in fact he had infuriated her. "What do you want?" she snapped.

He came around in front of her and pulled the reins to stop the pony, who dropped his head and cropped at the grass. Jane refused to look at him.

"I'm sorry," Will said. "I didn't mean that the way it sounded. I was surprised to see you, that's all."

"Why?" His apology had dried her tears. "I've been here before. And it's not like I can send word ahead that I'm coming!"

"It's just that I thought you'd be in the village by now."

"The village? Why would I be there?" She looked down the road, where the wagon was disappearing. "Is that where everyone's going? Why?"

"Don't you know what today is?"

"No, I don't. Should I?"

"Why, it's the twentieth of March—St. Cuthbert's Day. I thought everyone knew about the fair!" When Jane didn't answer, he exclaimed, "Don't tell me you've never been!"

"Yes, I've been," she said. "But not since I was small."

Papa had taken her. Mamma had stayed home; she must have been expecting Robert, Jane realized now, and Maude was too little for the bustle of a fair. Jane had sat on Papa's shoulders to watch the puppet show, and he had bought her so many sweets that she couldn't eat them all, and they had laughed at a monkey and had seen a two-headed lamb. Then some men had called to Papa from a tent, and he told her to sit and wait for him, and after it grew dark she gathered up the courage to go in and look for him among the noisy men and the short-tempered women carrying tankards. He was asleep on a bench, and when she tried to wake him he had grumbled and pushed her away, so she sat on the ground, which was wet and sour with spilled ale, until the morning, when he awoke. At first he groaned and didn't even seem to recognize her, but then he found their carriage where the coach horses had remained harnessed all night and were so tired they could barely drag the carriage home, and Mamma had sobbed and clutched Jane to her and screamed at Papa over her head.

She became aware that Will was talking to her. "What?"

"You should come," he repeated.

"Oh, it's much too far to walk." She was puzzled at the offer. "But thank you."

"I'll take you on the pony. I'm not going to stay long. I'll get you back long before nightfall."

Suddenly there was nothing that Jane wanted more than to go to the fair with Will. Maude was right—Mamma wouldn't even notice she was gone. And with Mistress Forester there, Jane wouldn't be unsupervised. Still, was it proper for a girl from Halsey Hall to go to a country fair, accompanied by a boy of the woods?

"There will be jugglers," Will said. "And musicians and—"

Jane made up her mind, feeling a thrill at her own boldness. "All right. Thanks." Will reached down and hoisted her up behind him. "Can he carry both of us?" Jane asked as Will clucked and turned the pony's head.

"Easily," he said. "Hold on, now—we have to trot to catch up."

Hold on to what? she thought, but the answer was obvious, so she tentatively put her arms around his waist; and when Will lightly kicked the pony's sides he broke into a bouncy trot, and she clung more tightly, breathing the warm scent of leaves and trees and sap that rose from Will's skin.

When they slowed to a walk behind the wagon, Annie turned and called a greeting to her, a broad grin flashing on her sun-bronzed face, and Mistress Forester said, "How nice that you're coming, Jane." Jane smiled and waved, glowing inwardly at the welcome.

They fell behind as Will allowed the pony to stop and graze a few times, and once he dismounted to ease the pony's burden as they climbed a small hill. He didn't talk much, but when he did, his tone was cordial, and Jane found herself wishing the way to the village was longer.

But they arrived in less than an hour. Will reined in and was looking around to find a place to leave the pony when they heard his name being called. Jane turned, holding on to Will more tightly—for balance, she told herself—and saw that coming toward them were Ralph and Alys, a brother and sister who lived near the Foresters. She had talked with Alys once when she and her brother had come by the hut. She was lively and talkative, and appeared to enjoy making people laugh at her witty stories and her imitations of local people. Jane hadn't exchanged more than a few words with Ralph, who seemed to be a particular friend of Will's, and felt shy as he approached. The brother and sister looked very much alike, with shining auburn hair and teeth so white they flashed when they spoke or laughed, which was often.

"Your father asked me to tell you to tie your pony to that tree." Ralph pointed to where Bartholomew stood in the shade, unhitched from the wagon. "He paid the boy a penny to watch over them while the family's gone."

"Thanks," Will said. "Jane, why don't you wait here while I take care of that? You must be tired of riding."

She wasn't, as long as she could sit pressed against Will, but Ralph reached up to her with a friendly smile, and she allowed him to help her down. She was stiff and knew she'd be sore the next day. She was about to follow Will when Ralph said, "Looks like a good fair this year. There's a dancing bear and a puppet show."

"Oh?" Jane felt foolish. She stopped and tried to think how to answer. She was so unused to speaking to anyone new that she had no idea how to carry on a conversation. What did one talk about with young men? What would Mamma say to him? "I…I've never seen a bear."

"He's like a huge dog," he said. "With long claws and big yellow teeth. But don't worry—he's wearing a muzzle and the trainer knows how to handle him."

They seemed to have run out of things to say. "I have to go find Will," she said, but he laid a hand on her wrist to detain her.

"I think he's busy." He sounded amused, and she followed his gaze to see Will laughing with Alys. The girl laid her hand on Will's wrist as though to emphasize something she was saying, and then the two of them laughed again, Alys's curls bouncing.

"Oh." Jane felt a sudden ache in her chest. When she could trust her voice, she said, "Thank you for your assistance." She knew she sounded haughty, but she couldn't help it. "I need to go find Annie now." She turned and plunged into the crowd, hoping to lose herself so quickly that Ralph wouldn't be able to follow.

Stupid, stupid, stupid, she scolded herself. What made her think that Will was being anything other than polite when he offered to let her ride with him to the fair? Of course he would leave her to find Annie and would spend time with his friends, especially the lively Alys, rather than with someone who threw medicine pouches at him.

Jane rubbed the back of her hand across her eyes. She stepped on what felt like a foot, but the throng was so thick that she couldn't tell whose it was. A man cursed and looked around to find someone to blame. She turned away from him and found herself looking into Will's face.

"Where are you going?" he asked. "I thought you were going to wait for me while I arranged about the pony!"

"It's all right." She hoped her voice wasn't trembling. "I can find Annie on my own."

His brows drew together. "Find Annie?"

"Yes." She inhaled a shaky breath. "She must be somewhere down—"

"So you wanted to be with Annie today?" Before she could answer, he tightened his lips and turned away.

For an instant she imagined how horrified Mamma would be if she called out for a boy, especially in public, or even worse, if she told that boy that she wanted to be with him. But she didn't care. She was sick of not saying what she was thinking, of hiding the truth from Mamma, from Maude, and now, from Will.

"Will!" She ran after him. He stopped and turned. She swallowed and forced herself to speak. "I didn't want to be with Annie. I thought you wanted to be with Alys."

"With *Alys?*" His incredulity would have made her smile if she hadn't been so desperate for him to believe her.

"I saw you talking and laughing with her, and Ralph said—"

"Oh, Ralph said something, did he?" Will smiled and shook his head. "He was just teasing. No, I like Alys well enough—I've known her since she was a little orange-haired baby, and she makes me laugh. But even if I liked her in a different way—which I don't," he added hastily, "there would be no point. Alys is destined for the convent."

Jane didn't realize her mouth had dropped open until Will

put a gentle finger under her chin and closed it. "The convent?" was all she managed to say.

"I know—hard to believe, isn't it? She's so merry, it's hard to imagine her keeping a vow of silence. But she says she has a calling, and even though her parents are against it, she's determined to leave for the house of the Sisters of St. Benedict as soon as spring planting is over. Ralph told me last week that they insisted she come to the fair today. I think they're hoping she'll change her mind when she sees the fun she'll be missing."

Jane still couldn't speak.

"Let's see where that music is coming from," Will said, and he turned toward the sound of the pipes.

Jane followed, but the throng was so thick that they became separated almost instantly. Will reached back for her hand and pulled her close to him, and together they wove their way through the crowd. She twined her fingers in his.

The music turned out to be a group of pipers and fiddlers and drummers who were playing a tune so lively that when Will led her into the circle of dancers, she didn't hesitate to join them. Her feet remembered the steps that Mamma had taught them two winters before, when the firewood had run low and they had danced to keep warm.

Every few minutes someone would break free of the circle and dance in the middle to cries of "Hup! Hup!" from those still twirling around. Jane was surprised when Will sprang into the center, and astonished when he performed leaps and acrobatic moves that brought admiring shouts from the other dancers, especially the girls. When someone took his place in the center of the circle he waited until the dance brought her close to him and took her hand again instead of rejoining the circle at the nearest point. She felt herself flush with pleasure.

The tune finished with a crash of drums. Will and Jane collapsed, laughing, into each other's arms. Jane suddenly became conscious of his embrace and pulled away. "Where do you suppose we could get some water?" she asked, pretending to be busy gathering her hair off her face.

"The well's down there." Will gestured with his head and started to make his way through the crowd ahead of her. On an impulse she reached for him again. As her fingers slipped into his, Will turned his head, smiled at her and clasped her hand tightly, tugging her along.

After they had drunk their fill, Will spent a copper penny to take a chance on winning a prize by shooting a target with an arrow. He missed badly, but his strong woodcutter's muscles helped him at the next stall, where he did well enough at slamming a weight with a huge mallet that he won a length of red ribbon. "That will look well on Annie," Jane said.

"It will look even better on you." His fingertips brushed hers as he handed her the bright ribbon. She awkwardly tied her hair back off her face, feeling her cheeks flame and hoping that he would think her color came from the dancing. "Perfect," he said.

"Thank you." She wished she could think of something more to say.

Will led her to the stalls where foods of all kinds were being sold. "What do you like?" he asked.

"It all looks so good," she said. "You choose. I don't know the vendors."

Will returned shortly with two small cakes dripping with honey and topped with crushed nuts. They settled under a tree, and he handed her one. She closed her eyes as she savored the rich flavor. She didn't remember ever eating anything so sweet.

Will chuckled, and she opened her eyes. His face was closer than she'd realized. "What?"

"You look like Frances when she's about to fall asleep with a belly full of milk."

She grinned at him, and suddenly, but so naturally that she felt no surprise, his lips were on hers, and he was clasping her waist and gently pulling her closer to him. The sweetness she tasted was part Will and part honey, and she put a tentative hand on his cheek. He turned his head and kissed her palm, and then her forehead, and then each eyelid, and then her mouth again. She was as breathless as she had been after the dance, and her heart hammered against her ribs.

He pulled back a bit and smiled at her. His brown eyes held little sparkles of green, like the forest floor in spring, and his teeth were white and straight, except for one that was slightly crooked. For some reason this small imperfection made him even more handsome. She reached out to his cheek. "Will—"

A giggle nearby made her drop her hand and look up. Two girls stood a few yards away. Jane recognized them in a flash of panic: they were daughters of one of the families that had once been cordial to her mother but now snubbed her. The girls wore new spring dresses, and each had a warm shawl and shiny boots. Jane sprang to her feet and smoothed out her clothes hurriedly.

The older, a sharp-nosed girl with cold eyes, clucked her tongue in reproof. "Oh, these woods people," she said to her sister. "They're just like animals."

The younger girl rolled her eyes. "Why don't you go back to the cave you live in?"

Will had risen to his feet as well and started to say something when the older girl said, "Why, that's not a girl of the woods! Lavinia, isn't she one of the Montjoy girls, from Halsey Hall?"

The younger one gasped in mock horror. Her hand fluttered over her heart as though she felt faint. "I think it is! Mamma was right—she says her mother lets them behave like savages. Look at her with her fair finery in her hair and wearing her best gown!" The older girl snickered.

Jane's heart thumped again, only this time not from the pleasure of Will's caresses. She tried to speak, but no words came from her mouth.

"Wait till I tell Mamma," the older girl said. "She'll want Lady Margaret to know what her daughter is doing."

Jane finally found her tongue. "Oh, don't tell your mother!" she begged. "Please!"

"What's the harm?" Will asked, his voice suddenly hard. "Let them do what they want. Come, Jane, let's go."

But Jane couldn't move. Hearing that her daughter had been kissing a boy of the woods, especially in public, might kill Mamma. She heard words tumbling out of her mouth and was unable to stop them. "You're mistaken—we weren't kissing, we were just talking. Don't tell anyone! I wouldn't kiss him."

The older of the girls looked at Jane thoughtfully, as though considering what she was saying. Jane squirmed under her penetrating gaze. "All right," the girl said finally. She wagged a finger at Jane. "But you should be more careful. Your family is one of the oldest in the county. You cast all of us in a bad light with that kind of company." The two girls left, their heads together as they whispered and giggled.

Jane went weak-kneed with relief. She sat down and said, "Oh, thank heaven. If Mamma found out—"

Will wasn't listening. "We were just talking?"

"I had to say that! My mother—"

"Your mother would be ashamed that you were kissing someone like me, is that it?"

"No!"

"You're from one of the—one of the oldest families in the county, and I'm just a boy of the woods." He was nearly shouting. "You were ashamed of me in front of your fine friends. And here I thought that we were… I should have known better. You people, you Montjoys and Halseys, you think we're nothing. We're just here to do your work and not be paid." She grabbed his wrist and he flung her hand off. "I'll take one of the children home with me on the pony. That will leave enough room in the wagon for you to ride home." His tone was so bitter that she winced.

He stormed off so quickly that in an instant he was lost in the crowd, and even though she ran after him and called and called until her voice was hoarse with shouting and with tears, she didn't find him, and when she went back to where Bartholomew was standing near the wagon, the pony and Will were gone.

18

One evening, Jane went upstairs to see if there was anything left to burn. The few books left were so damp and moldy that they would throw off more smoke than heat. All the wooden furniture that they could wrestle down the stairs had long ago turned to ashes. Maybe there was something in the cupboard in Papa's chamber.

She rooted around among the few things he had left. The smell of his shaving soap lingered, making her remember the feel of his scratchy face against hers. She replaced it hastily. There were some pipes and a broken knife next to a whetstone. She was putting the stone back when it occurred to her that Master Forester might need one for his wood ax. No, he certainly had one—every woodcutter owned a whetstone. But did Will?

The thought of Will made weary tears start to her eyes. She slid the heavy stone into the pouch she wore around her waist. It would be a good excuse to visit the hut. If she could only talk to him—but somehow he had always "just left," according to Annie, whenever she went to the little house in the forest. Her heart felt as cold and hard in her chest as the whetstone did in her pouch.

Jane heard a distant pounding of hooves and looked out the window listlessly. It didn't matter who was going by on the road. It wouldn't be Will—neither Bartholomew nor the pony could run as fast as that. Down the road, near the river, a horseman was riding. He must be on his way to the village. She stood on tiptoe and peered at the cloud of dust that the horse was raising. To her surprise, the horseman turned his mount up their drive. She abandoned her search for tinder and clambered down the stairs, the whetstone thudding against her thigh.

Mamma was staring at nothingness, and Ella was asleep in the big chair in front of the fire, but Maude and Jane ran to the hall and wrestled the heavy door open. They stood gaping on the porch as a horse thundered to the house. A man, magnificent in purple velvet, dismounted and stood holding the reins, looking up at the house.

Mamma appeared in the doorway, pushing a stray lock of hair back into place. Together they watched the man reach into the bag at his waist and pull a large scroll out of it.

Maude nudged Jane and pointed at Mamma. Jane stared in astonishment. Despite her shabby clothes and cracked shoes, Mamma held herself like a queen as she looked down her long nose at the messenger. The strange glitter in her eyes had been replaced by a haughty stare, and she stood as composed as a statue.

The messenger removed his hat and made a deep bow. "Lady Margaret Delaville, formerly Montjoy, formerly

Halsey?" Mamma inclined her head in assent but still said nothing.

The man held the scroll out to her. She continued to stare at him. He appeared confused and then took a few steps forward, knelt on one knee, and extended the paper to her with his head bowed. Mamma read it rapidly, holding the parchment at an angle to catch the last rays of the sun. Jane saw her suppress a smile. Mamma said nothing but nodded as though in satisfaction, then rolled up the scroll and handed it back to the messenger.

"What is it?" Maude whispered to Jane. Jane shrugged impatiently. All she had seen were large letters and a purple signature.

But the man had heard her. "A royal ball, Miss. All the young ladies of quality in the vicinity must attend, by the king's command." He turned to Mamma. "You have two daughters?"

"Yes."

"There's also—" Maude started.

"There's also our other sister and our brother," Jane broke in, shooting Maude a fierce glance. Didn't Maude know anything? Mamma would never let Isabella go to a ball while she was still in mourning. The man might not understand this, and he might enforce the king's command to the letter, and Mamma would be furious. Such a breach of propriety was against everything suitable for young ladies. Better to pretend that Isabella didn't exist.

"Where are your brother and sister?" the herald asked.

Jane pointed down the hill. "There. In the graveyard."

"I meant living," the man said patiently, as though to someone slow of wit. "Just living daughters of the house."

"We're both here," Jane said. "There are no more living daughters of this house."

No sound came from inside. *Thank goodness Isabella's asleep,* Jane thought. *She would never miss the chance to speak to someone so important-looking.*

The herald wrote on the scroll. "Montjoy—two. Names?"

"Jane Evangeline," Mamma said, "and Maude Arianna."

The man made a few more marks and then handed a smaller scroll to Mamma. "Don't lose that. It's your official invitation. On the night in question, all the ladies on this list—" he tapped the stiff parchment of the larger scroll with his fingernail "—must come to the palace or they will be answerable to His Majesty." The man mounted his horse and cantered down the path as though he couldn't wait to leave the crumbling mansion.

"Why didn't you tell him about Isabella?" Maude asked.

Mamma didn't seem to hear her. Her eyes danced, and she clasped her hands like a girl. Jane eyed her warily. She couldn't remember the last time Mamma had been so animated—almost hysterical, in fact. "A ball! At the palace! I can finally present you correctly. A royal ball, Janie—just think of it! Think of the young men you'll meet, perhaps someone who is there to find a wife to be mistress of his grand hall." Jane didn't answer, and Mamma gave her shoulder a playful shake. "What, so excited you can't talk?" Jane groaned, but quietly, so that Mamma would not hear.

"Why didn't you tell him about Isabella?" Maude repeated.

"Don't be silly! Isabella is in mourning. It would be a disgrace if she were to attend a ball. It's not really proper for me as a widow, either. You girls must attend, though, and you need a chaperone, so I must go, propriety or no. Who knows when you'll get another chance to meet someone suitable? Besides, the king himself has ordered it."

Jane still couldn't speak. What was Mamma thinking? How could she and Maude be presented at a court ball? Didn't Mamma realize that Jane had never attended a party, hadn't even seen people dancing in a ballroom since she was four years old? All she knew about balls and hunting parties and soirees came from Mamma's descriptions of long ago. Hunting parties—if those people who had come by on just such an outing that winter had treated them with so much contempt at their own house, how much worse would they be when Jane and Maude appeared at the palace in rags and without knowing how to behave?

And as for meeting a suitable young man—what young man would ever look at her or her sister? If by some miracle a young man asked her to dance, what would they talk about? Terror rose in her throat as she thought of the contemptuous stares that would be leveled at her until she felt she was going to choke. She envied Isabella, who would have to stay home whether she wanted to or not.

Somehow she thought Isabella would *not* want to stay home. If only they could change places!

"I think I know what the ball is for." Mamma's voice shook with excitement. "It's so the prince can meet some girl. I heard about it in the village a few weeks ago. People were saying that the prince fell instantly in love with a girl he saw last winter."

Isabella! Jane thought with a jolt. *He wants to meet Isabella!*

"The problem," Mamma went on, "is that they haven't been properly introduced. I imagine he arranged this ball so he could meet her." She paced back and forth. "We have two weeks to get ready. You have to practice some simple dance steps, and you need to work on your curtsey, and we have to go over your deportment." She laughed and seized her daughters' hands, twirling them around. "You'll be the loveliest girls at the ball—just wait and see!"

19

Maude and Jane carefully cut apart the ball gowns they had chosen from among the few whole ones in Mamma's wardrobe. Jane had waited until Isabella was asleep before examining the contents of the box marked "Serafina's gowns," but she needn't have bothered; Isabella's mother must have been as small as her daughter; the gowns had impossibly tiny waists and narrow sleeves.

Mamma stayed away while the girls measured each other, Maude figuring out the best way to use the scraps by making two sleeves out of the back of a wide skirt and turning the pieces of a bodice to make a new one. They would have to add darts and tucks that would make the fabric lie smoothly, since their bodies had changed so much since the last time they had made clothes for themselves.

The actual sewing was easy in comparison. They were making no flounces, no fancy pleats, no cunning gathers. Mamma could attribute this simplicity to ladylike modesty if she wanted; Jane knew that it came from her own desire to be invisible.

Jane sewed tight, even seams and they tried the gowns on. They had to take one long piece apart, reset it and sew it again, but even that went quickly. They worked in a feverish near-silence, occasionally murmuring only "Give me the scissors," or "Can you thread this needle?" Finally all that was left were the hems, and Maude was capable of doing them by herself, as they were straight lines that required no special skill.

Jane flexed her tired right hand open and shut to ease the cramping. She slid her fingers into the pouch at her waist. The whetstone was still there; every time she thought about taking it to the hut, her courage failed her. She laid her hand on the table to stretch the wrist, and her fingers brushed against a length of white satin that had been the underskirt of one of Mamma's gowns. She turned the glossy fabric over. It had been kept from stains and damage by the length of cloth that had lain over it all those years. It was also pretty and soft, and Jane hated the thought of not using it. The piece was so small, though. She started to fold it up regretfully and then remembered what Annie had said when she had asked Jane to alter her mother's dress. Mistress Forester hadn't been churched since Frances was born. That meant that the baby hadn't been christened either.

The new priest was bound to come back soon. Was there enough of the white fabric to reach to Frances's fat little toes? Jane held it up. Yes, and she might even be able to piece it in such a way to leave enough for a cap, too. It wouldn't take long. And if she took it to the woodcutter's house, she could just happen to mention that she had found a whetstone, if they were in need of one.

The fabric was slippery, so she cut it with care, estimating the baby's size, remembering to add a bit, since surely she had grown since Jane had last visited. She laid the pieces together and was satisfied with the result.

"But I don't *want* to go to the ball," Maude said as though she and Jane had been in the middle of a conversation, startling her sister out of her thoughts. "What if the prince wants to marry me?"

"You?" Jane was astonished. "Why would he want to marry *you?*"

"I don't know—but if he did, what would I do?" Maude persisted. "Would I have to marry him?"

"I suppose so." Jane hoped that the way she mumbled around the pins held in her lips masked her exasperation. She slid the pins into the fabric and threaded her needle. She made the stitches tiny so that Frances wouldn't catch her toes or fingers in them.

Mamma hadn't found any happiness with either of her two husbands. So why was she so eager for her daughters to marry? Even if Jane did happen to meet a suitable young man, she knew that no young gentleman would have any possible interest in her, a fortuneless girl living in a ruin. And Mamma would never let her marry someone who wasn't a gentleman, of the class that she and Papa had grown up with. In Mamma's day, young people met one another at balls and parties, out hunting and at festivals in the palace—places where Jane and Maude would never go.

"But what would I do if he *did?*" Maude sniffled, and Jane put down her work and passed her a handkerchief.

"You'd have to marry him if he asked you. He's the prince."

"But I can't!" Maude wailed, burying her face in the handkerchief. "I'm going to marry Hugh!"

"You are?" Jane resumed her work.

"His parents wouldn't care that I don't have a dowry. Hannah's already taught me about herbs, so I can be an herbwoman like her. Nobody would have to know I was a Halsey, and they would buy my herbs and Hugh can be a herdsman like his father."

"Hugh said all that? I didn't think he said that many words in his whole life!"

"I said most of them," Maude admitted. "But he thought it was a good idea. I could tell."

"Mamma would lock you up forever rather than let you marry Hugh," she said.

"She wouldn't let you marry that woodcutter boy, either!" Maude retorted.

"What? Marry the woodcutter? What are you talking about, Maude?" Her face turned hot, and she quickly looked down at her work to hide the redness that she felt spreading across her cheeks. "I'm not going to marry any woodcutter!"

"You like that boy, though."

"What boy?" Jane pretended ignorance. "Oh, you mean Will Forester?"

Maude nodded and stuck her needle back in the fabric. "You like him." It wasn't a question.

"I do not." Jane glared at her sister. "He's proud and short-tempered, and he thinks he's better than everyone else."

Maude shrugged. "He's nice. Remember how he helped with Harry?"

"He didn't do it because he's nice—his father told him to!"

"But he did it. And he works hard. And he's handsome."

Jane didn't answer but stabbed her needle into and out of the fabric, hardly noticing where it went.

"Don't you think he's handsome?" Maude persisted.

"I suppose." Jane paused in her work. Will was rough and brown from the sun, and his shoulders were broad, not like the slender men in the portraits that hung upstairs and in the ballroom. He had a wide smile, not the elegant simper of those gentlemen, and a firm way about him that somehow Jane couldn't imagine her painted ancestors sharing. She couldn't shake the memory of the sweetness of Will's lips on hers, the green sparkles in his eyes and that small imperfection of the crooked tooth.

"You're talking nonsense." Jane looked her sister up and down critically and changed the subject, away from the uncomfortable topic of whether Will was handsome. "I don't think you have anything to worry about with the prince." She softened her harsh words by adding, "Nor do I."

They worked in silence punctuated by an occasional sniffle from Maude. Jane sewed the tiny puffed sleeves into place. She cut in half the ribbon that had once secured this underskirt around the wearer's waist, and stitched the two pieces onto the opening at the back of the neck so that Mistress Forester could tie it closed. It wasn't fancy, just a simple white robe with small sleeves and a scalloped hem. Still, she thought it would suit Frances quite well. "I have to go out," she told Maude, who nodded without interest.

In the hallway, Jane pulled her wrap from the hook. Maude must assume that she was just going to the privy and would wonder where she was when she didn't return. *Just don't tell Mamma I'm gone,* she thought as she slipped out the door.

She knew she shouldn't leave Maude at work when there

was still so much to do, and when Mamma was liable to come in any minute to try once again to show them how to curtsey without looking like bobbing butter churns. She stopped in the middle of the path and half turned back, then faced front again, then back. "This is silly," she said out loud. "Either go or don't go."

She didn't realize she had made up her mind until she found herself entering the forest on the by-now familiar path. She passed a few of the remaining gold tassels hanging from tree branches. She strode confidently through the clean-smelling woods, hearing and understanding the various rustlings around her without fear. It was hard to remember the Jane of just a short time ago, the Jane who was so ignorant about her neighbors and so fearful of the little she knew.

There was the dog-shaped rock that had sent her into such confusion when she and Maude had gotten lost; it was embarrassing to think how close to home they had been all the time. There was the bush that Annie had hidden behind, no doubt chuckling to herself as Jane stood timidly in front of it, clearly terrified at what she might find when she parted the branches.

The small hut emerged into view. No smoke came from the chimney, so the family must be out. She told herself that this was no matter; she would leave the dress on the kitchen table. They would know where it had come from. She tried to deny the feeling of disappointment that almost brought tears to her eyes. *How stupid!* she thought as she tried to lift the latch to let herself in.

It was locked. Well, she would just leave the whetstone and the christening robe out here, on that stump—no, it was too dirty for a white dress. On the stool by the front door—and just then a bird flew overhead, and Jane thought of droppings. She had been so careful to keep the little gown clean, washing her hands before working on it, using her least-rusted needle to sew it with. She supposed there was nothing to do but return home and try again another time.

"What do you want?"

Jane whirled around. It was Will, and she suddenly felt ridiculous. "I—I didn't want to leave this christening dress for Frances outside. The door was locked," she explained. She held out the little dress, feeling flustered as she remembered the conversation she had just had with Maude.

He took the christening robe and glanced at it, then at her. "Mother will be grateful." His eyes were hard.

She pulled the whetstone out of her pouch and extended it to him. "And I found this. I thought you might need one."

His fingertips brushed hers as he took it, and she jumped a little. He turned the stone over in his hands without looking at her. "I do need one. Thank you."

She wanted to explain about what had happened at the fair, about how she was just trying to get rid of those girls and stop them from saying anything to her mother, that she truly wasn't ashamed of kissing him, but she could find no words.

"I'll just go home, then," she managed to choke out, and hardly seeing her way through her tears, she fled. He didn't try to stop her.

20

Jane sat on her bed, Maude in the one chair that remained in their bedroom, and they sewed until it became too dark to see what they were doing. Their store of firewood was running low again, and the only fire laid was in the South Parlor. Until now they had worked on their gowns in secret after Isabella had fallen asleep so that she wouldn't ask questions, but there was no time for secrecy anymore. "Come, Maude," Jane said as she gathered up the long skirt so it wouldn't trail on the floor.

In the South Parlor, Isabella sat and stared at the fire. Her hands were idle, as usual. She gazed suspiciously at the brightly colored cloth that the two girls shook out as they got ready to finish their alterations.

As Jane's needle flew into and out of the rich fabric, she remembered her second walk home with Will, the time when it had seemed as if they might be friends someday. They had spoken little, and only about everyday things, but Will had made her laugh and had listened thoughtfully to everything she said. She remembered the ride to the fair, and then the way he had kissed her. She wiped her eyes with the back of her hand when Maude wasn't looking.

"What are you doing?" Isabella asked.

"Sewing," Maude said shortly, keeping her eyes on her work. Jane could hear the smirk in her voice.

Isabella fingered the gleaming fabric. "Why are you sewing silk? Where did you get it?"

Maude jerked away, stabbing herself in the thumb with her needle. "Ow! Look what you made me do! Go away, Cindergirl." She sucked on her thumb, glaring at Isabella.

"Why are you sewing silk?" Isabella persisted.

"We're making ball gowns," Jane answered.

"*Ball* gowns?" Isabella squeaked. She burst out laughing. "Are *you* having a ball? In there?" She stood up and gestured toward the ruin of the ballroom. "Who are you inviting? Mice?" She laughed again. "Mice!" She shook her head.

Jane bit back a sharp retort and concentrated on her work. She wondered which ancestor had worn the dress she had just finished hemming. The harsh blue-green might have looked well on a white-skinned black-haired beauty, her paleness set off by the bright color, but Jane knew that her tan skin would look yellow and awful against it. Still, it was the only one of Mamma's old gowns with pieces large enough to be cut into a dress for her, and anyway, it was too late to change. Maude wouldn't look any better in her salmon-pink, she thought, glancing at her sister, but she had insisted on it. At least the blue and white of Mamma's dress suited *her*, it having been made especially for her years earlier, before Papa had gone away. Mamma had shown no surprise when she found it spread out on her bed.

"Mice!" Isabella said a third time.

Her scorn made Maude color deep red. "Not mice." She bowed her head over her work and glanced up furtively at Isabella as she said, "Counts. Dukes. The *prince.*"

"Oh, yes," said Isabella. "The prince." She laughed.

"It's true," Maude said, ignoring Jane's warning looks. "He's giving a ball tonight and bids all the unmarried ladies of quality in the neighborhood to attend."

Isabella stood stock-still. "You're lying," she said uncertainly.

"It's true," Jane answered.

"No, it isn't," Isabella insisted.

"It is," came Mamma's voice from the door. Maude started guiltily, then bent over her sewing, a flush rising up her neck to color her cheeks. "I told the girls not to tell you, Isabella, because I knew it would disappoint you not to go."

"I'm not to go?" Isabella asked. "But if the prince says *all* unmarried ladies—"

"You're in mourning," Mamma said. "You can't go to a party for a year."

"My father," Isabella said, and paused, her thin chest heaving. She made a visible effort to control herself. "My father would want me to have this opportunity. He would want me to meet people of my own kind, not roofers and wild people who live in the woods."

Mamma said nothing but looked stunned. To break the unbearable silence, Jane put down her needle and said, "Shoes! What shoes are we going to wear?"

"Grandmamma's dancing slippers are still in the chest in her room!" Maude said suddenly. Jane tried to shush her, but Maude went on eagerly. "And they're big enough. Remember, Janie? The last time you tried them on—" She subsided as she realized what she was saying.

Jane felt a mixture of fear and excitement. Now Mamma would have to admit that she knew where the silk had come from, that it was not yard goods chosen to suit them, purchased in the city and carried home by servants, wrapped in delicate tissue. She would have to tell them that they were to wear Grandmamma's dancing slippers, if they had not dried out and stiffened in the years since they had been worn.

"I wish I had thought of shoes earlier," Mamma finally said in a tight voice. "Every cobbler in the city must be working day and night to ready dancing shoes for the ball. All the young ladies will want new ones." *That doesn't make any difference to us,* Jane thought. *We don't have money to buy new dancing shoes that we'll wear only once, even if the cobbler was sitting idle, waiting for customers.* "It's a good thing you made the dresses long enough to sweep the floor. Janie, you can wear my shoes." Jane looked at Mamma's feet. Her thick clogs were cracked and scuffed.

"What about Maude?"

"She'll just have to wear her boots," Mamma said. "She's too young to dance, anyway. She and I will sit and watch you, Jane, as the counts and dukes lead you onto the dance floor." Isabella rolled her eyes, and Jane felt like doing the same.

Maude's boots, like Jane's, were old and worn, and even if they had been new, they would still have been farm boots. Jane shuddered at the thought of her sister walking into a ballroom filled with elegant ladies and gentlemen, wearing an ill-fitting gown in a color that did not suit her, and farm boots on her feet. She glanced at Maude and saw her own thoughts mirrored on her sister's face.

Jane stood. Mamma might continue to pretend that all was as it had been when she was a girl, but Jane had had enough. "Come, Maude." She strode from the room, her sister at her heels. Mamma didn't even ask where they were going.

Another step had rotted through since their last foray to the bedrooms, so it took longer than usual to climb the stairs. They had no time to pause for ritual but immediately began inspecting the shoes. Maude pulled a dancing slipper out of the chest. She turned it upside down and shook out a mouse nest. "Too smelly." She tossed it aside.

"I'm tired of this." Jane held up a pair of shoes that must once have been crimson, but that now were faded to a dull red-brown, and put them with the "maybes." "I'm tired of pretending, and tired of being a Halsey. Most of all," she added bitterly, "I'm tired of not talking—of not saying anything important, not telling Mamma how hard we're working, just so she can keep on pretending." Tears burned her eyes and nose. She wiped at her cheeks furiously.

"Everything was fine until *she* came along." Maude put high-heeled gold slippers in the "yes" pile that Jane had started. Jane moved them to the "no" pile.

"It wasn't fine," Jane said angrily. "We pretended it was until Isabella and the man came here." Simple dove-gray shoes with low heels would do, she thought, and she tried one on. Grandmamma must have had long feet, as the fit wasn't bad, so she added them to the "yes" pile.

"I want her to leave." Maude's lower lip was stuck out in a pout. "She doesn't like living with us. But even her own relatives don't want her."

"Maybe her mother's friend will change her mind about

taking her in," Jane suggested. "Maybe she'll come and take her away, or arrange her marriage to some young man."

"That kind of thing doesn't happen," Maude said. She stood. "Janie, we have enough shoes. Can't we go to Mamma's room? I want to see her jewels."

Jane started to answer, "They're not real," but suddenly a thought was born in her mind. She sat still. If she moved, she would dislodge it, so she held her breath and let it grow. *Yes,* she thought. *Yes, it might work.* Excitement swelled in her chest. "Maybe…"

"Maybe what?"

"Maybe I can do something to *make* it happen," Jane said slowly. She sat in silence a few more minutes and thought. Her plan wasn't formed, but at least it was beginning. Ella would go to the ball if she could, wouldn't she? There might be a way to make that possible….

She went into the corridor, leaving Maude sitting on the floor trying on shoes. She stopped and looked at Great-Great Grandmamma Esther and then at Great-Grandpapa Edwin, and then at the others, Halseys and Montjoys and everybody else, who stared down at her in disdain or off into the distance with superior detachment. Jewels twinkled in their clothes, on their fingers, in their hair. Jewels that looked like the worthless ones in the box in Mamma's room.

She smiled. *Yes,* she thought. *Yes, I think I can do it.*

"And there's nothing," she said out loud to all of them, "*nothing* any of you can do to stop me."

She went back into Grandmamma's bedchamber. "Come on, Maudie. Let's go downstairs. We still have to do our hair."

"Do you think I could use Isabella's comb?"

Jane shook her head. "Don't even ask. It's not worth the trouble. Don't forget the shoes!"

21

They were surely the only people going to the ball in a rickety farm wagon, Jane thought as they joggled over the road. Mamma had decided that Saladin was up to the long drive to the palace. At each jolt, Maude bounced against Jane.

For the first hour, Mamma had told them over and over again how to behave. "Don't be too eager to accept an invitation to dance," she warned them. "A lady must be reserved. Don't stuff yourselves with food. Hold your heads high and don't look at your feet while you dance."

"Yes, Mamma," they said, and "No, Mamma."

When she had repeated the same instructions several times, she fell silent, but not for long. "Susanna Spencer will surely be there." They knew she was not really talking to them now. "She has a daughter about your age, Jane. I went to the baby's christening, but we've lost touch since she moved to the city. Susanna was a lovely girl. And Papa's friend Marcus Baxter—I think the lady he married had some daughters. It would be good to see Marcus again."

Jane didn't care who would be there. She wouldn't have wanted to see anyone except Annie, but Annie wasn't what the prince would call a "lady of quality," and of course she wouldn't have been invited. She watched the traffic on the road. Carriages pulled by elegant horses, their backs gleaming even in the weak evening sun, sped past them. The air chilled rapidly as darkness fell, and as they neared the end of their journey, the first stars shone above them while a full moon rose over the trees. Jane stared at a brilliant star until her eyes burned, whispering, "Please, grant my wish. Please. Please. I'll never ask for anything again. Grant me this one wish. Please."

She stuck out her leg from under the blanket and inspected her foot. The ancient gray silk shoe was so cracked that she doubted it would last the night. *I don't suppose I'll have to worry about wearing it out by dancing,* she thought. *The prince is looking for only one girl, and that's not me. I'll spend the evening sitting with Mamma and Maude, watching the prince dance with lovely ladies in new gowns that suit them. If I dance with a gentleman even one time, everyone will see my ugly dress and my broken shoes, and they'll be able to see I don't know how to dance like them, and nobody will ask me again. I'll go home and live with Mamma until we die.*

She wondered what Isabella was doing back at home. They had left her with a good fire and broth for supper, but the girl hadn't spoken to them or even moved as they finished their preparations. Was she still sitting in the big chair, staring at the flames?

Surely Isabella had to get up at some time, if only to go to the privy. When she did, she would see the sparkling gems that led out the back door. Tempting her with their glitter.

They were just the glass and paste jewels that Mamma used to wear to costume parties and fancy-dress balls, but Isabella would think they were diamonds, as Maude used to believe when the girls looked at them in the jewel box upstairs. The light from the lantern that Mamma always hung by the back door at dusk, as though to light Papa's way home, would make them sparkle like real gems.

Jane closed her eyes and pictured Isabella following the stones to the stable, where little Mouse stood harnessed to the yellow carriage, her coat brushed, her hooves gleaming. Jane had pulled out a dainty white gown from the box marked Serafina's Gowns. She'd hidden the dress in the barn until they were ready to leave for the ball, and then, when she went to tend to the animals for the last time that day, she'd hung it where Isabella would have to see it as soon as she stepped through the door. The girl would think that some fairy had put it there. Jane was confident that she would have no trouble driving gentle little Mouse. Isabella knew the way to the village, and once there, all she had to do was follow the train of coaches as they sped from there to the palace. It was not the most direct route, but it was the only one Isabella knew, and it would do.

People lined the streets to watch the partygoers on their way. It had been so long since there had been any type of celebration that they cheered when anyone came by, even a farm wagon drawn by a broken-down old hunting horse. "Lady Margaret!" a woman shouted as they entered the village. "It's Lady Margaret and the two young ladies!"

The girls sat up hastily. People that Jane recognized from church and from her infrequent trips to the market wore broad grins as they waved with enthusiasm. Mamma waved back regally and distantly, as though people cheered them every day. “You look lovely!” called out a girl about their age. *Do we really?* Jane wondered. Maude appeared to have no such doubts, as she grinned and waved back. Jane tried to look at her sister critically. Her dark hair was smooth and glossy, her eyes sparkled with the excitement that also lent a pink glow to her cheeks, and her teeth were straight and white. Maybe Hannah was right—it wasn't the type of beauty they saw in the paintings, but maybe they needn't be ashamed of how they looked.

They passed through the village and entered the open country again. Jane lay back down against the hay and thought of Isabella.

Oh, please let her find it, Jane thought. *Let her come to the ball, and let the prince fall in love with her and marry her and take her away. Then it will be just me and Maude and Mamma again, the way it ought to be.* She knew she should be ashamed that she was tricking Isabella and that Mamma would be very angry if she knew, but she couldn't stop a swell of anticipation and excitement from rising in her chest like a bubbling stream. And it was what Isabella would want, she told herself—to meet the prince and be taken away from the crumbling mansion, and from her and Maude. She closed her eyes and wished again.

When Jane opened her eyes, Mamma was maneuvering the wagon into a crowded drive. She was so wrapped up in her shapeless cloak that her form was hidden, and her hood was drawn over her hair, but still, anyone could tell that she was not a common coachman, and some heads turned. Mamma urged Saladin forward but was forced to stop by the crush after only a few paces.

The courtyard was bright with hundreds of torches, some

stuck into the ground, many more attached to the walls of the enormous building that loomed above them. They illuminated everything so that even though the night was full dark by now, people cast flickering shadows.

And there were so many people! Ladies were helped down from coaches as delicately as if they were made of blown glass, and gentlemen barked orders at the coachmen and the stable hands who scurried from stable to carriage and back again.

A uniformed man bustled up. "Deliveries at the rear. You tradesmen should know that by—" He stopped short as Mamma stepped down from the wagon, and her hood fell back, revealing her swept-up hair and her imperious face with its strong jaw.

"Get out, girls," Mamma commanded. Mutely, they climbed down. Jane's legs were stiff, and Maude groaned as she moved.

"See that my horse is fed with your best oats." She handed the reins to the man and swept past him, leaving him staring at the old hunter. Jane did her best to imitate her mother's imposing posture, but almost immediately she stumbled and nearly fell, so she abandoned the attempt, fearful of splitting her shoes.

They climbed the smooth stone steps. The house—of course, she reminded herself, it was the palace—gleamed a chilly white, and candles glittered in each large window, taking the place of the stars overhead, whose glow was obscured by the torches.

They were in the midst of a crowd. Everyone else wore a warm wrap and long gloves, but even in her silk dress and threadbare shawl, Jane was in such an agony of nerves that she hardly felt the cold. Would she have to dance with someone who would sneer at her as soon as he realized that she didn't know the steps to their formal dances, and that her clothes were old and her shoes cracked and scuffed? What would the music sound like? Would there be strange foods that she would have to eat and pretend to enjoy? She envied Isabella, at home in the warm South Parlor, with broth for supper. She pushed the thought aside. *I have to do this,* she reminded herself. *I am a Halsey.* But the thought of her dead ancestors held no magic.

The man standing inside the door was richly dressed, and Jane started to drop an awkward curtsey, sure that he must be the king or some important noble. Mamma pulled her up briskly, and she tried not to blush at her mistake. Mamma handed the man their wraps and told him who they were.

"Lady Margaret Delaville and the Misses Montjoy," the man repeated in a loud voice. Nobody paid any attention, and they made their way down the wide hallway. Deep rugs in rich colors lay under their feet, and the walls were crowded with portraits of people with such severe expressions that they made the painted Halsey ancestors look benign by comparison. Most of them wore crowns, but they held their heads so erect that they obviously didn't feel their weight.

Like most everyone else, Jane, Maude, and their mother hurried past the closed doors lining the corridor. They were silent while the others laughed, exchanged greetings, asked one another questions. Mothers tugged their daughters' sleeves straight and smoothed hair, brown and blond and black and red, straight and curly. Girls broke from their parents and clustered in little groups, whispering and talking and shrieking with laughter. Young men surveyed the crowd and commented on people's appearances. Nobody called out a greeting to them; nobody exclaimed over their finery or complimented them on their hair. Either they weren't as pretty as Jane had been starting to believe, or nobody cared about pretty girls if they weren't wearing fashionable clothing and wore their hair plain instead of twisted and braided into more elaborate patterns than Mamma could manage.

Jane surveyed the dresses of the women around them. They were of shiny fabric in many colors, and at first she thought that Mamma's blue-and-white gown fit in well. Then she noticed that the style of the other ladies' gowns was quite different, with less lace and more embroidery than Mamma's; that the skirts were broader and the sleeves puffier. She glanced at Mamma's dress, which had seemed so fine at home, and saw that next to the others it looked flouncy and narrow. She dropped her gaze before Mamma could see the shame in her eyes.

Jane heard a stifled giggle and a whisper. Despite her best efforts not to look, her eyes were irresistibly drawn to a corner where several young ladies were standing. Among them were the two sisters who had surprised her and Will at the fair, and the younger one was pointing at Jane and whispering excitedly to another girl, who held her hand over her mouth, her eyes wide with shock and amusement. They fell silent, their expressions a mixture of smirks and disapproval; and when Jane turned her gaze away, trying desperately to pretend she had merely been looking aimlessly around the room, she heard them explode with laughter that brought a reprimand from someone's mother.

Jane held tight to Maude's hand as they pushed through the crowd, and tried to keep the tears from spilling out of her eyes. *I hate them,* she thought. *All of them.* She squeezed between two men and found herself in a wider spot. She paused to catch her breath and panicked when she didn't see Mamma.

"Maude!" She raised her voice to be heard above the hubbub. "Where's—" But then she saw Mamma. She was smiling, talking to a woman with gleaming blond hair tied into complicated knots, who was holding the hand of a pretty girl in a pale pink dress. The lady was not smiling back at Mamma, and she even seemed to be pulling the girl away. When the other woman turned her back on Mamma, Mamma stood rooted to the spot, her hands dangling at her sides, her face bleak, as the crowd milled and pushed around her.

Jane raised her free hand and waved to Mamma. "Here we are!" she called.

Mamma looked toward her voice, and then with a frown she joined them. "A lady does *not* raise her voice in public." She pulled both girls almost roughly down the hall. Maude stumbled and stepped on the white slippers of a lady who said something harsh that Jane didn't catch, and Jane nearly bowled over an old gentleman in her path. The hall ended in a doorway as wide as their barn door at home. People had formed a rough line and were taking turns going through it.

Jane squirmed her hand out of Mamma's tight grasp. "Who was that lady?" She rubbed her sore fingers.

Mamma looked away, but Jane had already seen that her lip was trembling, and most unexpectedly, a tear threatened to spill out of one eye. Mamma pulled a rag, carefully folded to hide its worst stains, out of her sleeve, and dabbed at her face. "It was someone I used to know," she said at last. "Susanna Spencer. She was my bridesmaid. But now..." Her voice trailed off, but Jane didn't need to hear the rest. Now Susanna Spencer didn't want to have anything to do with Mamma.

Mamma, with her cracked nails, her old clothes, her anxious expression, was not fine enough for the elegant lady and her beautiful daughter.

Jane slipped her hand back into Mamma's. Mamma held it, but more gently this time, as the crowd moved and shifted, and the three of them managed to step through into the light. Jane caught her breath at the sight of the broad landing of gleaming white marble with a gold railing that had purple velvet wrapped around its supports. Mamma dropped a deep curtsey before starting down the steps. Jane and Maude did their best to follow suit, bobbing awkwardly. Their hours of practice seemed to have made very little difference. *I'm glad no one's looking at us,* Jane thought, moving cautiously onto the top step. Panic made her freeze. What if she slipped and fell down all those stairs in front of all those people?

She wished that Will could see the ballroom. He would never think of her family as privileged again. The lofty ceiling was painted with a bright scene of angels blowing on trumpets, and torchlight made the gold in their wings sparkle until it looked as if they were moving. The polished floor reflected the bright colors of the ceiling, the walls and especially the gowns of the beautiful ladies moving across it.

Music, sweet and lively, floated up the stairs to where Jane stood frozen. She swallowed and dared to look down. The room was so bright, and the colors were so vivid that it took a moment to sort it all out. In the raised gallery at the other end of the room, men wearing black suits sawed at violins, tweetled on flutes, tapped on drums. They looked oddly somber while making such a merry sound. The dancing men had none of their gravity. Instead, they laughed and talked, as did the ladies, who seemed merely to skim the floor, moved backward and forward gracefully, bowing and holding hands, then letting go and gliding away. How did they do that so lightly, so effortlessly? It had been so simple with Will, just around and around in a large circle, moving with a few simple jumps and turns that she had picked up quickly, nothing like these complicated moves. The dance steps that she and Maude had practiced with Mamma in the parlor must have been as out of date as their gowns.

Maude poked Jane. She came to herself and started down the stairs. Mamma had told them sternly that they were not to cling to the banister like little children, but to walk down straight and proud, as befitted the daughters of Halsey Hall. Jane prayed that she would not slip. Maude clutched her arm so tightly that Jane resigned herself to bruises tomorrow. She said nothing. If *she'd* had something to grip, she would have held on to it as hard as Maude did.

Just as they reached the bottom, the music stopped and the dancing halted. A babble of laughter and talk arose.

"Look at the *food!*" Maude raised her voice to be heard above the din. "I'm so hungry, I could eat it *all!*" At that moment the music died, and in the sudden silence her last words rang out.

"Oh, no," Jane groaned. A few people near them snickered, and Mamma glared at Maude so fiercely that Jane, standing at her side, winced.

At some invisible signal, the ladies, including Mamma, sank to the floor, their skirts spreading around them until the pavement looked like a field of flowers. The men bowed so low that Jane thought they would knock their foreheads on their knees. Confused, Jane did her best to curtsey as deeply as the ladies around her. Maude was standing upright, looking anything but flowerlike in her harsh pink dress, and staring in bewilderment at the multitudes, who must have appeared to her to have been overcome by a sudden attack of dizziness. Jane yanked Maude's arm, tugging her down.

"Why are we curtseying?" Maude whispered in her ear. "Mamma didn't say anything about—" A trumpet blast from above interrupted her. Without lifting her head, Jane strained her eyes to the top of the stairs and saw the man who had read their names earlier. He stood as straight as a pine tree at the very center of the top step.

"His Imperial Majesty, King Manfred!" Wild cheers and applause erupted when a tired-looking old man, leaning heavily on a cane, stepped forward. He raised his free hand and waved at the crowd. Even from that distance, Jane saw the tremor that shook him.

Under cover of the noise, Mamma leaned over and said to Jane, "He looks even worse than I'd heard. Poor man. He used to be so hearty." She shook her head, even as she continued to applaud.

When the noise died down, the man spoke again. "His Majesty, Prince Bertrand."

Jane raised her hands to clap again, but lowered them as she saw that everyone else was standing still, arms at their sides. No cries of "Huzzah!" greeted *this* name. Jane glanced at Mamma, whose face held a grim expression. Then she took a deep breath and looked back up the stairs.

There stood a beautiful young man with blond hair.

"Janie!" Maude tugged at her sleeve. "That's the boy—"

"I know," Jane said. "Hush."

She had dared to hope for this ever since Mamma had told them about the prince falling in love with a girl he had met only once that winter. She had wished on every first star, on every chance happening that seemed to offer luck.

This young man with the sulky, handsome face was the one who had come riding to their house when they were starving and freezing. The boy who had stared so long at Isabella and had questioned her about her family's fortune, and had danced with her as snowflakes fell around them. Jane breathed out a sigh that seemed to arise from her toes. Wishes *do* come true. At least some of them.

But still more had to happen. Isabella still had to find Jane's trail of jewels and make her way to the ball, or Jane's careful plan would come to nothing. Unnoticed, Jane moved to the window. The stars were still invisible in the torchlight. She turned her gaze to the spot in the heavens where she had seen that first star twinkling.

"Please," she whispered. "Please."

22

The music started again and people moved across the floor. Maude tugged at Mamma's sleeve. "I'm really hungry." Her voice rose in a whine. "Can't I get something to eat?"

"You don't look like you go hungry very often," said a slender girl standing next to them. She was wearing a dress of such pale rose that it reminded Jane of a cloud at sunrise—almost white, but if you looked hard you could see the color. Maude's cheeks flamed in a blush. It was true; it hadn't taken her long to gain back the weight she had lost over the long winter, and in her too-tight salmon-pink dress she looked like an overstuffed sausage. Jane tried to imagine the girl with her impossibly thin waist cutting wood or digging honey out of a tree buzzing with bees and burned to say something to her, but she had turned away and was talking with a gentleman.

"*May* we eat something, Mamma?" Jane asked.

Mamma was clearly about to say no, but then her face softened. "Just taste, girls. A lady doesn't make a glutton of herself, especially in public. Most especially a Halsey lady."

Before Mamma had even finished, Maude took off almost at a run, pushing her way through the crowd. Jane followed more slowly, wishing her sister would show a bit of dignity. She caught up with Maude in front of a table crowded with heaping platters of food. Tiny silver fish lay in rows on rounds of toast, savory-smelling cheeses alternated with pickled vegetables in colorful spirals on a golden dish, fruits—where had they found them this time of year?—were arranged in geometric shapes. A black-clad man sliced honeyed boar and piled the dripping pieces onto a board where the juice ran off on to the white tablecloth.

Jane stared at the table, wishing she could eat now that there was finally a bounty in front of her, but her stomach was so tight with apprehension that the thought made her sick. A servant scurried past, carrying plates of uneaten food back to the kitchen. Last winter, she and Maude and Isabella could have eaten all day on what was left on them. Jane stepped aside to let the servant past, and the hurrying woman glanced at her without pausing, looking surprised at the courtesy. Jane recognized her; she was a friend of the Foresters', who, Jane knew, had lost three of her four children in the famine. What must the woman think, seeing all this food wasted? What would Mistress Forester think? What would Will think?

Maude, of course, had gone straight for the sweets and was staring open-mouthed at a giant tower of pastries. They were in fanciful shapes: rabbits, swans, frogs, all colored bright pink and blue and yellow, nothing like the plain honey cake topped with crushed nuts that Will— *Stop thinking about him*, she told herself fiercely. She reached a tentative hand toward one as Maude stuffed a yellow frog, speckled with green, into her mouth. Before Jane could take a nibble of her blue swan, Maude's face registered distress.

"What is it, Maudie?" Jane asked. Maude shook her head. Her cheeks bulged, and she could communicate only with her eyes—and Jane could not understand their message. Maude made no attempt to swallow but looked around in increasing agitation.

Jane finally guessed the trouble. "Do you need to spit it out?" Maude nodded mutely. Jane sighed. First, there had been that embarrassment because of Maude's greed, and now, she wouldn't even eat the sweet she had been begging for. Jane looked around without success for a bowl, a cloth, anything. Housekeeping items were likely kept hidden away, so the guests wouldn't be bothered by the thought that human hands, not fairies, had created this spectacle.

"Come with me behind that curtain." Jane pulled Maude with her. She parted the purple velvet hanging behind the banquet table, and hoping that nobody—especially Mamma—was observing them, she ducked behind it.

Worse and worse. The curtain, instead of discreetly blocking off a serving area, as she had assumed, appeared instead to be a temporary partition between the ballroom and an annex. Most dreadful of all, the area was filled with men, some sitting at a table, others leaning over the seated men's shoulders, talking, laughing, pointing.

The men took no notice of the two girls shrinking back into the curtain. Their voices were raised, and Jane saw cards flashing. Unexpectedly, a memory flew to her—of her father and other men, crowded around a game like this one, with cards and coins and bottles covering the table. Then, as now, the men seemed excited as the cards flew.

"Janie!" It was Maude, in a stage whisper. "I spit it out in the corner. Let's go before they see us."

But Jane was mesmerized. Almost, almost she could see Papa as he had been then, handsomer than any of the men now seated at the table, more elegant, more lightning-quick in his movements. She blinked back tears.

"Jane!" Maude's voice had become more urgent, and Jane shook off the memory. She pawed at the velvet, looking for the opening. They were entangled in the heavy cloth when Jane realized that the noise in the small room had been replaced by silence. She gave her sister's hand a warning squeeze, remembering how furious Papa had become when she had interrupted his card games. These men seemed hot-tempered, from the snippets of conversation she had heard, and most of them wore sharp-looking swords at their sides.

A voice rose from the table. Jane thought she recognized the speaker. It sounded like Prince Bertrand. "What are you saying? What do you mean, there's nothing left? Of course there is something left! My father—"

"It is by your father's orders that I speak," came the thin and raspy tone of an old man. "His Imperial Majesty has retired to his chambers. Before he left, he made it clear to me that you are to be advanced no more credit at the gaming table. He said—"

"Nonsense. The treasury is full. My father is an old, sick man and will die soon." The prince didn't pause as the others gasped and murmured protests. "And then it will all be mine. So you're risking nothing by allowing me to borrow against my inheritance."

The other voice hardened. "Your father, Your Majesty, is indeed an old man. His health, as you say, is poor. But the treasury is far from full. So many died in the fever and famine of the winter that more than half the taxes remain unpaid."

"So we will collect them now that the fever has passed."

"We cannot," the old man answered. "Many people who owed money did not survive the winter. You cannot collect taxes from a corpse."

"There must be something you can do, Lord Chamberlain. I share my father's faith in you. Sooner or later, the treasury will be full again. In the meantime, surely one of these men will extend me credit."

Silence.

"Come, which of you wishes to become the favorite of your future king?"

More silence.

Finally, "You already owe a great deal of money to each of them," the old man's voice said. "Your father—"

"My father!" The prince's voice rose. "Stop talking about my father! *I* am your prince!" The girls heard chairs overturning, and shouts rang out. Jane pawed frantically at the curtain and finally found an opening, but they had twisted so much that they found themselves looking once again into the little room. She froze at the sight of the prince holding his sword high in the air. Three men held him back as he lunged for an old man who knelt before him with his head bowed.

"Now!" Jane whispered, and the girls fumbled at the curtain and slipped back into the ballroom. They scuttled to a row of chairs against the side wall. Between the matrons fanning themselves in the ever-increasing heat and the girls too plain to be asked to dance, they managed to find two chairs next to each other. They slid gratefully into them, Maude panting with exertion, Jane relieved that they had made their escape.

Maude stared at Jane, wide-eyed. "Is the prince going to kill that old man?"

Jane shook her head, although she was far from sure. "I don't think so. Lots of people were holding him back." The thought of that peevish face and shrill voice sickened her. She remembered how quiet Will was, and how, when he did speak, his voice was calm and thoughtful. She thought of the confident way he handled his wood ax. Not like that spoiled boy with his vicious-looking sword.

Suddenly she was relieved that Isabella wasn't there. If she had somehow found the trap that Jane had set for her, if she had managed to drive the little orange carriage here, perhaps the prince would have believed her lies about her father's fortune. What a nightmare it would be if Isabella did marry the prince; anyone who married him was in for heartbreak, and Isabella had suffered enough.

Maude's voice broke into her thoughts. "That pastry was *awful.*" She pulled such a disgusted face that Jane poked her before anyone else could see it. "The cream was curdled, and there was mold on it. I thought it was decoration, but then I could taste that it was mold."

Jane squirmed as her hastily stitched collar scratched her neck, but subsided as her chair's legs squeaked in protest. Was this what everything was like here in the palace, then? A spoiled, murderous prince, rotten food, furniture that was falling apart? Everything looked so beautiful, but none of it was any good. Was this the world Mamma missed so much? Had it been like this even when she was young, or had things changed since those days?

The music swelled. That, at least, was beautiful. Jane had never heard such melodies before. The songs that Mamma hummed, the fiddle music that she occasionally heard in the market square in the village—none of it was like this. Jane closed her eyes and let her body sway lightly to the sound.

She was so weary. She no longer feared that someone would ask her to dance—the men were pointedly avoiding the corner where she and her sister sat in their gaudy finery. When could they go? Mamma had said that they wouldn't stay late, since it would take them so long to drive home. Not much past midnight, she had said. A clock had struck during a pause in the dancing, but Jane hadn't counted its strokes.

She sat up straighter and looked for Mamma. Maybe if Jane said she had a headache, Mamma would take pity on her and they could leave. She thought of her bed, her old comfortable clothes, a supper of broth and mushrooms and eggs—fresh eggs, not the addled ones they probably served here—and the longing for home was as sharp as the stab of a pin. *Where* was Mamma? Jane stood and turned slowly, surveying the room. Her back was to the grand stairway when silence fell yet again. She turned to look, but the suddenly motionless dancers blocked her view.

She knew that the royal family held no more princes, and the only princess had married and moved far away. The queen had been dead for many years. Then why was everyone so motionless and so hushed? The musicians had stopped in mid-note, except for one cellist, who sawed away for another measure before falling quiet. No one bowed or curtseyed, and a slight buzz of conversation hovered in the air. Jane stood on tiptoe, but still could not see. She did spy Mamma, though, and pushed through the crowd to get to her, dragging Maude with her. Mamma, like everyone else, stared in the direction of the grand staircase. "I don't believe it," Mamma said.

"What is it?" Maude asked. Mamma just shook her head.

Sound erupted behind them as a door flew open near the banquet table. Heads turned; this time Jane was positioned to see the object of their attention.

The prince, swordless now, stamped into the room from the annex where he had been gaming. "What's going on? Where is the music? I didn't tell you to—"

And then he, too, fell silent, gazing upward with his mouth open.

"What *is* it?" Jane was in agony. The crowd parted, leaving a clear passageway between the prince and the staircase. Jane, at the edge of the opening, peered up it to the landing.

And then she knew that her ill-conceived wish had been granted, and that her desire to take it back had come too late. For there, at the top of the stairs, gleaming in white satin, stood a fairy princess with sparkling slippers, jewels glinting in her hair, on her hands, around her slender neck.

It was Isabella.

23

It appeared that nobody but Jane recognized that Isabella's gown was a generation out of fashion and that her gems were merely glass and paste. Everyone else was too dazzled by the exquisite girl to examine either the style of her clothing or the quality of her jewelry. No wonder the man at the door had allowed her in even without an official invitation.

"I don't believe it," Mamma said again, still looking up the staircase. "Who brought her here? And where did she get that gown?" Jane tried to sidle away, but Mamma grabbed her shoulder. "Do you know anything about this?" Jane hung her head. Mamma said sharply, "Answer me!"

"I wanted Isabella to come to the ball." Jane was unable to meet Mamma's gaze. "I wanted the prince to fall in love with her and take her away. That's what she wanted, too. But—"

"Hush!" someone said.

Mamma stared at Jane, her mouth hanging open like the prince's at his first sight of Isabella. "How did you—" she began, and then as people turned to look at her, she seemed to recall herself and shut her mouth with a snap.

The prince approached the foot of the stairs, never taking his gaze off Isabella. His face was still rosy, and his hair, damp from the exertion of a few minutes ago, lay shining on his head. He was almost as beautiful as the girl who gazed at him from the top of the stairs, with eyes that glittered like emeralds.

As lightly as a snowflake, Isabella glided down to him. She dropped into such a deep curtsey that she seemed to melt into the floor, and she stayed there until the prince lifted her up by one hand. Then the musicians struck up again, and the pair began the complicated motions of the dance. Isabella danced so smoothly that it was impossible to believe that real legs moved under her long dress. Other couples joined them, but no matter how many people crowded the floor, Isabella and Prince Bertrand were easy to spot. It was as though a golden light shone out of them. The prince said something in Isabella's ear, and she blushed prettily as she answered him.

Maybe I was wrong, Jane thought. *Look at them—they're perfect. Perfectly beautiful and perfectly suited to each other. They'll have perfect children and a perfect palace and…* Angry tears came to her eyes, and she dashed them away, not caring if anyone saw. Let them think the stepsister was envious. It was the truth. Isabella would live in the palace and have servants to fulfill her smallest wish and a handsome husband who ruled a whole kingdom, even if he was a spoiled brat. Meanwhile, Maude would marry Hugh and work hard every day of her life without reward. As for herself—she would spend the rest of her days alone in the dairy, making butter and cheese. Nobody loved her the way Mamma had loved Papa, and nobody ever would.

"Why don't they get dizzy?" Maude was once again at her elbow, interrupting her thoughts.

"Oh, I don't know, Maudie."

"They just keep going back and forth and twirling, and back and forth and—"

"For heaven's sake, Maude," Jane snapped, "use your own brain and stop chattering at me." Maude drew back, her expression a mix of bewilderment and hurt.

The music drew to a flourish and stopped. The men bowed, and the ladies curtsied deeply. People gathered around the prince and Isabella, chattering excitedly, blocking the pair from Jane's view. Mamma frowned as she glared in their direction; evidently she couldn't see them either, even from her superior height. Jane tried to take advantage of her mother's distraction to sidle away, but Mamma stopped her with a sharp "How did you do this?"

"Oh, Mamma, what does it matter?" She didn't care that she was being insolent. Nobody could hear her but Mamma—and Maude, who was staring at Jane in amazement—and Mamma would never scold her in front of all these people. Emboldened at this realization, she went on. "The prince wanted to meet her, and she wants to leave us. If she marries him, they'll both get what they want, and we'll be rid of her, and it will just be you and me and Maude again. There will be one less mouth for me to feed—"

"For *you* to—"

"—and one less person for me to worry about. I'm tired, Mamma. I'm always tired."

Mamma's gasp was audible even above the hubbub of voices,

and Jane shrank at the sight of her eyes, which were red with rage. Mamma raised a hand to her own throat as though she was having trouble catching her breath.

"Lady Margaret."

Mamma turned her eyes from Jane to the man who had come to her side. He was tall and stood as straight as she and wore the same uniform as the man who had announced their arrival. "Lady Margaret?" This time there was a question in his tone.

"Yes," Mamma said, clearly with an effort.

The man stepped aside to show the prince, with Isabella at his side. "His Majesty."

Mamma gasped and dropped into the deepest curtsey Jane had ever seen her perform, her head bowed. Jane did the same, tugging Maude down with her. They straightened only when the prince said, "You may rise."

They did so, Maude stumbling a little as the toe of one of her shoes caught in her hem. Jane grabbed her arm to keep her from falling.

The young man seemed not to notice them and addressed Mamma again. "I have the honor of asking you to present your daughters to me."

"Certainly." Mamma sounded astonishingly calm. "My elder daughter, Jane Evangeline." Jane curtseyed again. "My younger, Maude Arianna." Maude bobbed hastily. No matter; the young man was clearly uninterested in them. "And my stepdaughter, Isabella."

Once again, Isabella's performance was flawless. The prince held out his hand and helped her to stand, although she obviously didn't need any assistance.

"Am I to understand that she has no living relatives?" the prince asked.

"None."

"No one to protect her interests?"

"I, sir, protect—"

"I meant, no man to administer her estate?"

"Her estate?"

"Her inheritance from her father." He sounded impatient. "How much have you removed from it for her upkeep?"

"Why, none. I mean to say—"

"You have papers from the bank to prove this?"

Mamma seemed tongue-tied with bewilderment. "Certainly, Your Majesty—I can show that I have taken nothing from her inheritance. But why—"

"Thank you." The prince bowed and turned to Isabella. "The music is starting again. Would you accompany me?"

Her face glowing, Isabella nodded wordlessly, and she allowed herself to be led onto the dance floor once again. She didn't cast even a glance over her shoulder at them. They danced alone, and then other couples joined them. The music went on and on without pause.

"Well." Mamma seemed to have forgotten that she was angry with Jane. "I suppose—"

Just then, one of the trumpets squeaked. The dancers stumbled, lost the rhythm, tried to regain themselves. The other musicians had been thrown off and stopped playing. The conductor raised his stick, but before he could bring it down, the prince had run up to the musicians' gallery and snatched the horn from the trumpeter's grasp.

"How dare you!" he stormed, his voice audible even to the dancers far below him. "You made me lose my step!"

"I apologize, Your Majesty." The man's voice trembled. "It has been a long night."

"You dare make excuses? Guards! Take this man away!" As the soldiers hesitated, the prince shouted, "Do as I say, at once!" and flung the trumpet over the rail.

How will that man live now, without a horn to play? Jane wondered.

She felt a tug at her sleeve. "Go away, Maudie," she said, without turning around. The tug came again. "Go *away.*" This time she glanced down. It wasn't Maude. It was Isabella, and her eyes were big and round, staring out of an ashen face.

"Oh," she said, in a voice just above a breath. "Oh—Jane—"

Jane realized that this was the first time that the girl had said her name. On an impulse she took Isabella's hand. "What is it?" She tried to sound urgent and calm at the same time.

"I can't—I can't—" It sounded like Isabella was choking.

Everyone was still distracted by the musicians, but at any minute the prince might remember Isabella and look for her. Jane pulled Isabella up the stairs, hoping that everyone's eyes would stay on the raging prince and the distraught musician. They hastened down the broad hallway and ducked into a side room that was full of sofas and chairs piled high with sweet-scented fur wraps.

Isabella turned to face Jane and clutched both the older girl's hands. "He wants to marry me."

"He does? How do you know?"

"He told me so. He said that he knew I was to be his princess the moment he saw me outside the house—remember?—the day that he came hunting. But we hadn't been properly introduced, and his father cares a great deal for doing things the proper way. He knew that if he commanded all the unmarried ladies in the land to be present at a ball, I would be sure to attend. That way he could find me again and meet me under his father's supervision, and then he could marry me honorably."

Marry a girl he had seen but once? The most Jane thought would happen was that he would begin a courtship tonight, not announce a betrothal. The marriage of princes was arranged by courtiers and diplomats and ambassadors.

"But all he's interested in is my father's money." Isabella's tears were audible. "He thinks I'm a wealthy heiress." She had the grace to blush when Jane looked hard at her. "Listen!" Isabella hissed. "Can't you hear what he's saying?"

The prince's voice rang from the ballroom, penetrating even to the small chamber where the girls were hiding. His voice boomed out, helped by his being high up in the musicians' gallery. His words were muffled, though, and Jane opened the door to hear him say, "My subjects, this is a great evening for your kingdom. The purpose of tonight's ball was for me to find a lady worthy to be my bride. And I have found her." A murmur ran through the hall.

"She is the daughter of a nobleman, now deceased, and she lives in a nearby manor with her stepmother and two stepsisters, who use her cruelly." Jane looked at Isabella again.

"Well," she said, "while we were dancing I did tell him how hard you make me work. . . ." Her voice trailed off as Jane rolled her eyes.

"We will celebrate our marriage as soon as the arrangements can be made," the prince went on. Jane closed the door. She didn't need to hear any more.

"What can I do?" Tears streamed down Isabella's face.

"What will he do to me when he finds out I don't have any money? Did you see what he did to that poor musician?"

"But I thought you *wanted* to marry the prince!"

"Not anymore." Isabella shook her head vigorously. "Not now that I've met him. I thought he would be wonderful, but he's not. He's awful. He didn't even want to learn anything about me. All he wanted to know was the size of my father's fortune and was I his sole heir, and did I have a guardian or could I get the money right away."

"And what did you tell him?"

"I told him..." The girl hesitated, and Jane saw shame on her face. "I told him that my wicked— That my stepmother had control of it." Isabella's face was almost as red as the prince's had been when he burst into the ballroom. "That was before I saw how awful he was," she added hastily.

"What else?"

"And I also told him I was sixteen."

Jane squirmed with the knowledge that it was her fault that the girl had come to the ball. If she had stayed home, the way Mamma had intended, the flighty prince would surely have found someone else whose fortune he could secure, and he would have soon forgotten all about the pretty girl in the tumble-down house in the woods.

"I have to leave," Isabella said. "I have to hide from him."

Jane looked out the tall window at the night. The long carriage drive twisted around the castle, and coachmen and stable hands stood around open fires, warming their hands and drinking and laughing. The easy thing would be just to go back into the ballroom and let Isabella sort it out for herself. But Jane knew that she was at least partially responsible for the mess that the girl was in.

"Stay here," she ordered. "I'll bring your carriage around and you must drive away as fast as you can, back home. If he comes looking for you later, we'll—" But she didn't know what they would do. "I'll think of something," she finished, hoping she sounded more certain than she felt.

Isabella nodded. "I'll wait here." A sob interrupted her words. "Hurry!"

Jane sped into the corridor, out the huge front door and down the torch-lit steps. After the heat of the stuffy ballroom filled with the smell of food—some of it tinged with the sickly odor of rot—and then the corridor that was smoky with torches, the cold air refreshed her, and she ran with renewed energy. The courtyard was choked with conveyances. Where was Isabella's carriage? Jane saw a huge red coach, noble arms painted on its side, and a gray one with elegant scrollwork on the door next to a black-and-gold carriage with heavily curtained windows.

Jane let herself into the warm stable. She passed two huge black horses and a pair of matched bays that must have cost more than the carriage they pulled. No men were in sight. Few of the company would dare offend the prince by leaving the ball so early, and the stable men would not return to their duties until their services were needed by departing guests. More tall horses crowded the stalls. She saw Saladin, his nose still in the feeding trough.

Jane finally spotted the small orange-and-white carriage against the back wall. The grooms must have drawn it inside to make more room for the larger ones in the crowded drive. "Mouse!" Jane called. "Mouse! Where are you?"

An answering whicker came from the far end of the stable. There was the pony, her eyes half-closed, her belly round.

The groom must have been sufficiently impressed by Isabella's manner to let Mouse eat her fill of oats. At least one of them had enjoyed princely food, Jane thought. She found the pony's tack—the miniature harness was easy to spot among so many large ones—and strapped it on her, and then buckled the small bridle. Her fingers trembled so that they hardly obeyed her as she fastened the harness trappings around the sleepy beast, but when it was finally done, she led Mouse out the stable door. A few grooms glanced up at her without interest and then turned back to their fellows.

She looped the reins around a ring and sped up the palace stairs. A commotion rose from the ballroom. She blessed it for occupying the attention of the prince's guests, and entered the cloakroom.

It was empty.

"Isabella!" Jane called into the dark room, as loudly as she dared. "Ella! Where are you?"

The pile of furs on the sofa convulsed, and Isabella crawled out from under them. "Oh, Jane." She clutched the older girl with trembling fingers. "He's looking for me! What shall I do? Where is my coach?"

"Outside the door. Run to it and drive away. No one will think to look for you outdoors. Go straight—"

An unfamiliar young man staggered into the cloakroom. He stopped in the doorway. "Where is she? Are you here, lovely lady? Your prince wants you, and he wants you now!" His unfocused eyes swiveled around to where the girls were standing. Isabella drew near Jane, and Jane put a protective arm around her shoulders.

"Is it one of you?" The young man reeled closer, the smell of liquor preceding him. "If it is, you have to come—if you don't come soon, the prince will lose his temper, and you don't want to see him when he's angry!"

How much worse can he get? Jane wondered, as she eased herself and Isabella toward the door. "Why, no," she said to the young man. "What lady? We've only just arrived. The prince has not met either one of us yet. You see, here we are, just leaving our wraps." The big clock in the ballroom started to strike the hour. Under cover of the clanging, Jane whispered to Isabella, "Remember, when we get to the door run straight to the carriage."

"I can't run!" Isabella whispered back. "Not in these slippers!"

"Take them off, then," Jane answered. "Take them off and run as fast as you can—now!" The girl stooped to remove her shoes, and then, faster than Jane would have believed possible, Isabella flew out the door and skimmed down the corridor and out into the night, clutching the sparkling slippers in her hand. The young man took a step in her direction, got his feet tangled with each other, and fell heavily forward.

Another figure flung itself into the room just as the clock stopped chiming. "Is she here?" It was the prince. "Is she here? Someone said she came in here!"

"There's just me, Your Majesty," Jane said, but he took no notice of her as she moved slowly and carefully to stand between him and the door.

The drunken young man spoke from the floor. "There was another one! A little one, with light hair and a white dress—she went out there!" He pointed.

The prince lunged for the door. He collided with Jane and then pushed her aside so roughly that she nearly fell, catching hold of a tapestry edge just in time. The prince ran out the door and down the stairs into the drive, Jane right behind, her heart pounding so that she could not hear anything. If Isabella was still there…

But she need not have worried. The carriage and its driver had disappeared.

"After her!" the prince cried. "After her! Don't let her get away!" The coachmen came running, but by the time any of them understood what they were to do, long minutes had passed.

Run, Mouse! Jane thought, clenching her hands into fists and willing speed to the pony's legs.

The coachmen and grooms pulled horses from stalls, fumbling with harness straps, while the prince cursed at them. "No time for carriages! To horse! To horse!" They removed the harnesses and flung them on the ground, and new grooms came running out and threw saddles on the horses' backs, tightening cinches and sliding bridles over their long faces. One, then two, then a dozen of the king's men leaped onto the saddles and tore down the dark road.

A groom led out the tall white horse. As the prince strode forward, his hand reaching for the bridle, he stumbled on something. He reached down, and when he straightened, Jane saw that he held a shoe.

A shoe that winked and twinkled, even in the torchlight. Isabella's glass-covered slipper.

24

Jane's legs gave out, and she sank to her knees on the sharp gravel of the drive. She didn't know how long she stayed there, numbly watching as the prince tucked the shoe into his shirt, mounted his white horse, and galloped off, followed by a stream of men and a pack of hounds roused from their sleep in the stable. People clattered down the palace steps asking, "What happened? Where did he go? Who was that girl?" She was shaken from her frozen state only when a hand clasping her wrist made her start.

"Where's Isabella?" It was Maude. "What happened?"

Jane told her. Maude's eyes grew wider and wider, and her mouth formed a silent O of surprise.

"He'll catch her soon," Maude whispered. "What will he do to her? Oh, Janie..."

Her words turned to sobs, but Jane had stopped paying attention. People were ordering their carriages, shouting for grooms who came running from their fires and out of the stable, many of them hurriedly pulling on boots and coats. *They must be surprised to be leaving so early,* Jane thought. Mamma had said that they would probably be the first to go at midnight, that most people would remain dancing and feasting until dawn. The drive became blocked with horses, carriages, grooms, frightened-looking ladies and gentlemen asking one another what had happened.

A tiny glimmer of hope gleamed weakly in Jane's mind. Yes, the prince knew how to get to their house, as Maude said, but he would go there by the most direct route. How had Isabella come? Did she know the shortest way? Or had she come on the road that she was familiar with, the one that ran through the village?

Still, Maude was right: Mouse was very slow. She was small and tired, and she was pulling a coach. The prince's horse was large and hadn't had to drag a carriage all the way there that evening, and he was bearing only the weight of one slender young man. If the prince went the same way that Isabella had gone, he would certainly catch her—had probably already caught her.

Jane stood and listened tensely. No triumphant cries, no terrified shrieks reached her ears. Still, it was only a matter of time before the prince or his men thought to search on the other road.

And what shelter could Halsey Hall offer, even if Isabella arrived there ahead of the prince, even if she and Maude and Mamma were there when he arrived? Mamma would never be able to see past the story she was living in to grasp the reality of what Jane had brought to pass. Only she, Jane, understood, and only she could try to fix it.

She stood up. "Find Mamma and tell her what happened." She made her voice firm, firmer than she felt, so that Maude would pay attention. "Tell her I've gone after Isabella."

"But what will you do when you find her?" Maude wailed.

Jane didn't know. She only knew that she couldn't allow the girl to flee alone into the night. "I can't just stay here," Jane said. "I have to go *now,* Maude. Tell Mamma not to worry." She evaded Maude's grasping hands and ran to where the drive met the road, squeezing between coaches, narrowly avoiding a heavy hoof that stamped the ground next to her foot, still wearing the flimsy dancing shoe. She paused when she reached the road.

More of the king's men came galloping past her in a long stream, shouting to one another and waving swords and torches. None of them paid Jane any heed, and even if anyone had noticed her, there was nothing to connect this poorly dressed, awkward girl with the lovely creature who had captivated the prince and the guests at the ball. No one had any reason to follow her. She started walking again, tripped over the flapping toe of her shoe, took another few steps, and wedged the heel in a rut. Impatiently she ripped both shoes of her feet and continued barefoot.

If the dirt road had been frozen, she would have been walking on a hard surface and not splashing through puddles and sinking in icy ooze. At first she winced as her toes turned into what felt like chunks of cold stone, but soon she lost feeling in them. Once she stopped and sat on a rock and rubbed her feet until feeling returned to them, but she was suddenly chilled, not only by the wind and the freezing mud, but by the thought of her small stepsister cowering in her orange carriage, surrounded by angry armed men and that leering prince. She took to the road again.

She allowed herself to be heartened by the absence of pursuers and even of guests leaving the palace. It would take some time for the large, grand coaches to be made ready to depart.

Jane would have given a great deal to see a farm cart or the wagon of a laborer making an early start to market or the fields. She didn't think she could walk much farther, and someone might take pity on a barefoot girl in gaudy, bedraggled finery walking alone on the cold road, and would offer her a lift. *Why did I come after her?* she thought as she stumbled on a rock that was pointing out of the mud. She knew the answer, though. She had to take care of Isabella because nobody else would. Just as nobody else would milk Baby, and nobody else would chop wood, or tell Maude to wash her face, or turn the milk into cheese if she did not.

She was too tired to go on, and her numb feet hardly supported her. A fallen tree by the side of the road would be as good a place as any to sit and wait for the sun to rise. Maybe its warmth would renew her energy. She sat down on the cold bark and hugged her knees to her chest, wrapping her feet in her dress. In the moonlight she could make out a dark stain spreading on the cloth, although whether it was mud or blood, she couldn't tell.

Jane leaned back against a branch. She closed her eyes, and against her dark eyelids, ladies in bright dresses twirled and bowed, twirled and bowed, around a small fairy princess dressed in white, with sparkling feet.

What was that? Her eyes popped open, and she sat up with a gasp. She rubbed her eyes. She couldn't believe she had fallen asleep in this piercing cold. She looked around, wondering what had woken her. She saw nothing.

Then she heard it again. A crackling sound. Someone—or something—was moving in the underbrush by the road. Her hand groped for a stick, a rock, anything to defend herself with. Nothing but mud. The crackling came again, and this time, it was nearer.

Jane couldn't keep silent. "Ella?" she called uncertainly, and instantly regretted the impulse that had led her to break the silence.

Nothing answered. Then, "Jane?" someone said in a hoarse whisper.

She squeezed her arms across her chest as she felt her heart leap. "Who is it?" she asked. She broke a branch off the tree and held it up in front of her. Whoever or whatever it was, they were not going to take her easily.

"It's me." The words were louder, and Jane's head whirled as she recognized Will's voice. His face, pale in the moonlight, peered out from the darkness along the road. He looked left, then right, and then stepped out cautiously. "The girl—that little one that lives with you, she's in our house."

"In your house? How did she get there?"

Will ignored her question. "She can't tell us how she came to be in the woods, so I came out to see if anyone was looking for her. What are you doing here?"

"I don't know." Suddenly it seemed so foolish, the way she had run after Isabella. What could she do to help her? But she knew she would do it again.

"Well, you'd best come with me." Will's voice was firm. "Father will know what to do." He strode off down the road. She stood with difficulty and took one hobbling step and then another after him. He looked around, and concern crossed his face, visible even in the moonlight. "Where are your shoes?" She didn't know how to explain, but before she could even try, he sat down and pulled the stout boots off his feet. "Put these on," he commanded.

"Oh, but you—"

"I'll be all right. I'm more used to it than you are, and we're not going far." He yanked off his thick socks. "Sit down." She sat on a rock. It was such a relief to be told what to do and not have to decide. Will picked up one of her feet, very gently, and slid the big, blessedly warm sock onto it and then the boot. He repeated the action with her other foot.

"Can you stand?" He held out his hand. She took it, and he pulled her up. "All right?" he asked huskily. He cleared his throat.

Jane saw that his eyes sparkled even in the moonlight. He looked at her with a worried frown, and she realized that she hadn't answered his question.

"Yes, it's all right," she said hurriedly, and took a tentative step. She winced.

"Do you need to rest a little more?" he asked. "I think you should warm yourself at the fire, but if you want to sit a little longer—"

"I can walk," she said.

"Good. Come with me." He moved slowly, a supporting arm around her waist, and Jane gritted her teeth and hobbled as well as she could. They were on a path strewn with pine needles, a path that Jane didn't recognize. After a short time Will stopped, his grip on her tightening to warn her from blundering on ahead. He peered warily to his right, to his left, and then nodded and stepped forward. She realized that they were crossing a road, scored with ruts in the mud, and she picked her way carefully across them, her feet sliding painfully in the too-large boots. A flash of orange caught her eye, and she saw the little coach that Isabella had been so proud of lying on its side, one of its wheels shattered against a large rock.

She realized that Will had not said if Isabella was hurt when they had found her. What if she had been injured—or even killed—when the coach overturned? She wanted to ask but was afraid of the answer.

They continued on quietly, Jane gritting her teeth, and as soon as they arrived at the other side of the road and were in the sheltering woods again, Will relaxed visibly. "It's safe to talk now. Here, sit down and rest for a moment." He helped her down onto a fallen tree and then sat next to her. The relief of getting off her feet was immediate.

The sky was lightening in the east. "They'll be wondering where you are," Jane ventured after a moment.

"Can't be helped," Will said. "You need to rest." He put his warm hand over hers. She didn't pull away, as she knew Mamma would expect her to, but after a moment dared to raise her eyes.

He looked at her intently, and as she gazed back, wondering what he saw that kept his eyes fixed on her, he leaned forward and kissed her. It felt as though that kiss was something she had been waiting for, and the warm thrill of it made her forget, for a moment at least, the pain in her feet and the worry over Isabella and the fear of the men on horseback racing over the countryside in search of her stepsister. She reached up and touched Will's cheek, the way she had at the fair, and then kissed him back.

"I'm sorry," she whispered. "I'm sorry about what I said that day at the fair. I just had to make sure those girls wouldn't tell my mother. She's…" She hesitated. *She's not well? She doesn't understand?* "Her mind—there's something wrong with her mind. I have to protect her. It's not because I was ashamed of you."

He drew her closer with his warm arm. "I think I was angry because you were saying the things I was thinking. I don't think I'm good enough for you."

"Because I'm a Montjoy? Will, that doesn't—"

"No, silly. Not because of your name. Because you're so pretty and fine, and I'm so rough." She pushed herself out of his embrace. She hadn't expected mockery, not from him, not now, but to be called pretty and fine, in her faded finery, and after the way those girls had looked at her… "What do you mean, my fine looks?" He appeared confused. "Are you trying to tell me that I look pretty like—" she forced the words out "—like Isabella?"

His lips twitched, and she started to rise, but he grabbed her arm. "No, of course not. She's pretty—of course she is, anyone with eyes can see that—but in the way a kitten is pretty, or a wildflower. But you—no, you have something different." She felt herself turn even redder as his gaze wandered over her. "You have that lovely thick hair, and your face shows who you are inside, strong and fearless. Your mouth isn't like her little pink one, true, but it's wide only because you laugh and talk. Your hands are rough because you work with them, and take care of people with them. You'll still be beautifully yourself when that pretty kitten has grown up to be a nice-enough cat and the wildflower has faded."

Jane put her fingers to her cheek as though to feel the shape of her own face. Was Will telling the truth? But before she could question him, he had wrapped his strong arms around her and kissed her, once on each cheek, and then on the mouth, where he lingered until her head swam.

With an effort she pushed herself away. "Let's go. They'll be wondering where you are."

Soon they emerged into a clearing, where a small house stood, smoke curling from its chimney. "Oh!" Jane realized where she was. She had never before approached the Foresters' house from this direction and hadn't recognized the path. She heard a familiar whicker. Tied to a tree, looking tired and bedraggled, stood Mouse. For an instant, dread chilled her even more than the cold that was making her shake. "Will—"

But he wasn't listening to her as he pushed open the door. His mother, still in her nightdress, her hair pulled back in a braid, held up her hand for silence and pointed at a little form curled up on the hearth rug. A pale brown ringlet escaped from the rough blanket around what had to be a sleeping Isabella. Jane's knees went weak with relief.

"What were you doing out there in the cold, dressed like that?" the woman asked in a low voice, and then, a little louder, "And what happened to your shoes?" Jane sank down on a stool without answering and pulled off Will's boots. Her arms were shaking so that she could hardly manage. "Keep the socks on," Mistress Forester said. "Hold your toes closer to the fire." The woman knelt in front of Jane and rubbed a foot briskly. Jane yelped and tried to jerk away as pains like hot needles jumped through her toes, but the woman held her ankle and continued. "That means the blood is flowing still." She moved to the other foot and did the same. "I don't think it's cold enough for frostbite, but it's best to make sure." She removed the socks, rubbed soothing salve on Jane's feet, wrapped them well in bandages, and then slid them into a pair of soft slippers. The relief made Jane suddenly sleepy.

A tap on her shoulder made her look up. It was Annie,

holding a steaming cup out to her. Jane took it carefully and sipped at the herb tea. Soon she stopped shivering and had to fight against the urge to fall asleep in the sudden warmth and comfort. Will sat in the shadow of the huge mantel. She ducked her head to hide a smile; she imagined he was trying to keep his face hidden in the darkness, the way she wished she could do.

"Tell us what happened, child," Annie's mother said. "We couldn't get anything sensible out of the little one."

Jane tore her eyes away from where Will sat and told them the events of that awful night, ending with "After Isabella ran away, the prince ordered his men to follow her and bring her back." Her hand flew to her mouth as she realized what that meant. She had been so caught up in worry over Isabella that she hadn't thought what would happen if the king's men couldn't find her. If they had taken all the livestock belonging to the people of the woods merely out of greed, how far would they go when urged on by the anger of that prince, who had been humiliated in front of a crowd of partygoers? Would he tell them to burn down houses, or even kill people?

"Oh—Will..." she stammered, but he ran out the door, calling to his father as he went. Jane heard the sound of a cow being urged out of its stall, and then Mouse's soft whicker. Will must have been taking them to some hiding place deep in the woods.

She shot to her feet as another thought occurred to her. The prince must even now be on his way to her own house. "I have to leave." Her voice felt thick. "I have to get home and tell Mamma. They'll be there soon—I know they will." She sat down again and pulled off the slippers.

"Wear these," the woman said, handing her a pair of stout

clogs. She didn't try to dissuade Jane from leaving, for which she was grateful.

"No." They both turned toward the hearth, where Isabella was now sitting up, her pale hair fluffy around her face.

"What do you mean, 'no'?" Jane paused.

Isabella stood, wrapping the blanket around her small form. "It's my fault they're coming." Her voice, although as high and thin as always, was resolute. "I'll go back to the prince and tell him I'll marry him. That way he'll leave everyone alone."

Jane knew that once she would have told Isabella to go ahead. She would manage to run the house without having to worry about the girl sitting in the hearth, with one less mouth to feed, one less person to pretend for. Once, Jane had wanted things to turn back the way they were before the golden-haired girl came, bringing all the change that had happened since then.

The way they were? a little voice whispered inside her. *With the house falling down, and Mamma pretending not to see it, and you and Maude working yourselves to death, and Mamma pretending not to see that either? Is that really what you want?*

She took a breath, knowing that whether she spoke or remained silent, she would regret it. Then the words slid out. "You can't do that. I won't let you. We'll go home and face him together, with Maude and Mamma."

Isabella folded the blanket without answering. She turned to Annie's mother and dropped as perfect a curtsey as the one she had performed in the ballroom the night before. "Thank you for your hospitality," she said, and before Jane could utter another word, she was out the door.

25

Jane caught up with Isabella before the first turning in the path. "Why didn't they find you on that first part of the road, before it split to the village road and the town road?" Jane asked. "The king's men, I mean. There were so many of them!"

"I hid," Isabella answered without slowing down or even glancing at her. "I drove into a barn. My carriage barely squeezed through the door. I waited there until they went past me. I don't think it occurred to them that a whole carriage could fit in a barn, and they didn't even stop. Another time, when I thought I heard horses coming, I hid in a grove of trees. I thought they would see my white dress, but they never did, just like I was invisible. I think I *was,* Jane! Then I saw them go up the hill, and I kept on toward the village, but we hit a rock or a rut or something, and the carriage wheel broke. I wasn't hurt, so I unhitched Mouse. I would have ridden her, but she was limping."

"How did you find that house—the Foresters', I mean?"

"I didn't find it by myself. A fairy led me to it."

"A *fairy?* They don't do that. They lead people *away* from safety, not to it."

"This one did," Isabella answered. "It was a fairy. It was a girl fairy, with long, curly hair. She was tall, even taller than your mother, and after my carriage wheel broke she appeared in the road, and she took Mouse's bridle and led us down a path to where there were lots of trees to hide in. We waited while the soldiers went past. I know she was a fairy," she went on, forestalling the next logical question, "because she didn't speak. Fairies don't know how to talk like people. And then she took me to the little house."

Jane ducked her head and smiled as she picked her way around a mud puddle. She wondered how Annie would like being taken for a fairy. *Not much,* she thought.

They walked more and more slowly; both were tired, and Jane suspected that Isabella's feet hurt as much as hers. The weak dawn sun barely brightened their way through the thick trees, and more than once they stumbled on a rock or a tree root.

"Why did you help me?" Isabella's voice was strained. "Back there at the palace, I mean. Why did you help me run away?"

"Why wouldn't I help you? You couldn't get away by yourself, and once I saw how awful that prince was, I knew you could never marry him."

"Yes, but you must have known that helping me would put you in danger. Why would you do that when you don't even like me?"

"But I do like you," Jane said. She felt she needed to be truthful, so she added, "I didn't at first. Not when you came, and you wouldn't do any work, and you acted so spiteful to Maude and me, and you thought you were above us—"

"Me? But it was you, not me! You thought I was stupid because I didn't know how to do the things that you do, and you know how to take care of things, and everybody likes you, and you're so pretty even with your worn-out clothes."

"I never thought you were stupid. I thought you were… Never mind. It's over now." She would have to get used to the notion that she was pretty.

They paused at the gate. Jane looked up at the drive. All appeared quiet. She saw no horses, no soldiers. Just as the thought *And no prince* formed in her mind, she caught the thud of hooves behind them. With a wild cry, Isabella fled into the barn. Forgetting her half-frozen feet, Jane grabbed the edges of her skirt and lifted the hem to her knees, and ran to the house as she had never run before, cutting across the grass, stumbling but never falling. Part of her seethed at Isabella's desertion—seethed, because she had thought that the girl had finally started to take responsibility for her own actions—even as another part of her burned with shame at her own complicity in Isabella's appearance at the ball.

She flung herself at the heavy front door, and as it grated open, Mamma and Maude burst from the South Parlor. "See, Mamma—see, I told you she'd be back," Maude babbled as Mamma enveloped Jane in her arms, still covered in slippery blue-and-white silk.

Much as she longed to relax into those arms, she knew she couldn't. "Mamma, they're coming," she said, and Mamma stepped back.

"They won't hurt you," Mamma said, and the determination in her tone made Jane stand up straighter. "No matter what happens, I won't let anyone hurt my girls." She glanced around. The cold look in her eye reminded Jane of a mother hen spreading her wings over her chicks when a hawk flies overhead. "Where's Isabella?" A trumpet blast pierced the air before Jane could tell her that she had deserted them, leaving them to clean up her mess, just like the girl she had been before and not the new Isabella that Jane had thought she had started to know.

Mamma pulled herself up straight. "Come, girls." She strode, tall and proud, cold command glittering in her eyes, to the door. Once more she was Lady Margaret Halsey, heir to a long line of proud barons and fierce soldiers, and Jane and Maude trotted to keep up with her as she threw open the huge door.

But even the newer, stronger Mamma drew back at the sight that greeted them. The prince, his face impassive, was seated on his white horse in the drive. With him were half a dozen men, one of them raising a long horn to his lips again. "There is no need," Mamma said sharply. "We heard you. We are all here."

The prince's stony blue eyes ran over them quickly. "All? Are you sure this is *all* of you?"

"I have two living daughters," Mamma said. "Jane and Maude. You see them before you."

The prince snorted, but without humor. "Do not insult me, Madam. But just to make sure you understand—" He gestured to one of the men, who dismounted and removed a box from his horse's saddlebag. The servant knelt, holding the box up to the prince, who snapped, "Don't be stupid, man! How can I reach it from horseback? Do it yourself."

The man flinched. "The prince orders—er, commands,"

he said, stumbling as though reciting a hastily learned piece, "that each unmarried lady of the land attempt to place this shoe upon her foot." He opened the box, and Isabella's glass-covered slipper glinted at them. "Each lady upon whose foot the shoe fits will be called to the palace, where the prince will choose his br— from among them his bride. Sit." He pointed at a step. "Put out your left foot," he ordered Maude. She obliged, her face a study in misery and fear. Although her foot was cleaner than usual, due to the scrubbing before the ball, there was no disguising its length or the calluses worn by going barefoot. The man looked up at the prince.

"Put it on," said the prince.

"But, Your Majesty—" the man protested.

"I said, put it on!" The prince slashed his riding crop down against the man's neck. The man winced but set his teeth in silence. He yanked the slipper over Maude's toes. It dangled far short of her heel. Her foot could no more fit in the shoe than Sal could fit in Mouse's harness.

"Why don't you cut off your heel, girl?" the prince jeered, and he pulled a dagger from his belt. "It's not too high a price to pay for marrying a prince, is it?" Maude shrank back and shook her head violently. The prince turned to Jane. "What about you? Will you cut off some of your toes?" He tossed the dagger from one hand to the other as his horse restlessly shifted its weight. Jane swallowed hard, and she, too, shook her head without speaking.

"What, nobody wants to be my bride?" The prince laughed and resheathed the dagger.

Jane was disoriented from her sleepless night, and fear battled for dominance with despair. She tried to pull herself erect, telling herself again, *You are a Halsey.* It still didn't help. Mamma gripped her shoulder, and that gave her strength.

Now the prince's expression changed from a scowl to something indefinable. *He looks like a snake,* Jane thought. *Or a fish. Something with no feelings.* "Where's the other one?" His voice was hard.

"The other one?" Mamma's tone matched his.

"You know who I mean. Your poor little abused stepdaughter."

Mamma didn't answer.

The prince narrowed his eyes. "In the house, is she? Have you imprisoned her? Or is she busy drudging?" He jumped down off his horse and tossed the reins to one of the mounted soldiers. He strode through the door, barking, "Come," at the man holding the shoe, who followed him at a trot. Jane and Maude ran after them and nearly collided with the prince in the entrance to the South Parlor. He stood as still as an oak tree, looking in and blocking the doorway. Jane and Maude exchanged glances, and then with one accord, they ran out the way they had come in. They sped to the rear of the house, through the kitchen door and then the dining room, and from there to the back entrance to the South Parlor.

What they saw was familiar enough to the two girls, but would certainly look strange to anyone else. Isabella had put on her old rags. She had poured the cooking water onto the few embers that remained in the fireplace and now sat on the hearth, running her fingers through the wet cinders. She shot Jane and Maude a warning glance, not stopping her play with the ashes. Half under her breath, she sang the melody the orchestra had played while she'd danced with the prince only a few hours before.

Isabella lifted her head and appeared to notice the men in the doorway for the first time. She jumped up and threw her arms wide. "My prince!" she exclaimed, and ran to embrace him. He shrank backward, and one of his men stepped between them with his sword drawn. Indeed, she was a disturbing sight: her bare feet were blistered and bruised, she wore soot-stained rags, her hair tumbled around her neck, and gray-and-black streaks marked her face and arms.

Isabella stopped short. "Do you not know me?" He didn't answer and looked at her warily. "But I am your princess, my lord. The lady you danced with last night. Do you not remember?" She hummed the dance tune more loudly and swayed back and forth, her arms outstretched to hold an invisible partner.

The manservant stepped forward. "Shall I try the slipper on her, Your Majesty?"

The prince looked at the man and appeared to reflect. "The slipper? Yes, I suppose so." Then to Isabella, "Have your stepmother and stepsisters done this to you?"

"Done what, my lord?" Isabella giggled and extended her small foot to the servant. The prince shook his head without answering. The shoe slid on as though it had been made for her, as of course it had. She looked even odder now with that one shoe sparkling under her torn dress. The prince looked at it and then at Isabella's soot-marked face, her red eyes, her wild hair. He hesitated.

In the silence, Jane stepped forward. "Since you were interested in my stepsister's estate," she said to the prince, "you may also be interested in this." She indicated the cedar box on the table and held her breath.

The prince gestured to one of his men, who opened the

box and pulled out the letter Mamma had received from Lady Mathilde. He glanced at it and then muttered something in the prince's ear. "Yes, yes, go ahead," the prince said impatiently.

A small noise outdoors caught Jane's attention. It sounded like—yes, it was a few notes of a song. It had to be one of the people of the woods. She wished she knew what they were saying. There it was again, closer now, and this time she recognized the voice. Will. What was he doing out there? Then she heard the sound of feet—many feet—moving over the gravel of the drive, up the broken steps, and through the outer hall. Carefully, cautiously, Jane edged to the door and allowed her eyes to swivel toward the hall.

Faces, bodies, hands holding axes, mallets, shovels, picks—people with grim expressions silently crowded the hall. Will and his father were in the front. Behind them stood Ralph next to Hannah Herb-Woman, who was gripping a sickle, her red hair tied back, her freckled face set in a stony expression. Even the old woman who had shared the Foresters' wagon the day of the fair was there, a wooden mallet in her wrinkled hand, her face set in grim determination.

And they were moving, slowly and so quietly that if there had been only one or two—or even ten—of them, Jane knew she never would have heard their footfalls. It was only the sheer number that brought their sound to her ears.

No one else in the South Parlor seemed to have noticed. All eyes except hers were on the king's man, who whispered again in the prince's ear. The prince flinched, and he hissed something at the man, who backed away hastily.

The prince turned to Isabella. "You lied to me." His eyes narrowed. "That day, when we came here hunting, you lied."

"I lied?" she asked with a gasp. "Oh, no, my prince, I would never lie to you!" Jane marveled at the lightness of her tone. Wasn't Isabella afraid? Then she saw how the girl's hands, clasped behind her back, were trembling.

The prince appeared to hear nothing. "You said—you said—" he choked.

Isabella swayed, and Jane caught a glimpse of her face. It was white, and her green eyes looked glassy. *She's about to faint,* Jane realized.

"She didn't lie," Jane broke in. "She said she was her father's only heir, as indeed she is." All eyes in the room turned to her now. The color started to return to Isabella's cheeks. Jane swallowed and went on. "She said that her father made a huge fortune, as indeed he did. You did not ask how much of it remained, but if you had she would have told you—nothing. Less than nothing. Debts."

"You—you—" The prince still couldn't speak. Jane's heart pounded as his hand strayed from his dagger to the hilt of his sword. Jane took an involuntary step forward, then stopped as Mamma's hand gripped her shoulder. What could they do, she wondered, if the prince unsheathed the weapon?

Isabella neither moved nor spoke. She stood erect, looking the prince full in the face. Jane couldn't see her expression, but something in it made the prince drop his gaze. If the prince had received the full force of those green eyes, as Jane herself had more than once, it was no wonder that he couldn't meet them.

The prince's grip on his sword loosened. *So you're just like everything in your palace,* Jane thought with an inward shock, marveling at the sight of the steady girl and the young man who looked like a dog threatened with a whip. *You're all show and no substance, and rotten underneath your fine looks. Nobody need fear you.* She glanced through the door and saw that an even larger crowd had gathered in the hall.

"What is it?" The prince was peering at her with suspicion. "What are you looking at?" He strode over to where she stood. She clung to Maude, not knowing whether she was seeking or giving comfort. The prince stood unmoving, his hand on the hilt of his sword. He seemed to have forgotten all of them, his men, Mamma, Jane and Maude, even Isabella.

"You came here to ask for my hand, Your Majesty. Do you still want it?" Jane jumped at Isabella's clear voice. She stood behind the prince, her hand outstretched to him. Jane knew that one small thumb showed a blister, and that soot and ashes were trapped under the girl's cracked fingernails.

The prince turned, looked at her hand and then at her face, and hesitated. "You may keep it," he finally said coldly. "Remove that shoe." Isabella slipped her foot out of the glass-covered slipper.

"And the other one?" Isabella drew it from her pouch. She laid it on the floor next to the first.

So swiftly that none of them guessed what he was about to do, the prince stamped on both shoes, sending brightly colored shards of glass flying. "You're living in a dream, all of you. A dream. This house…" He gestured with his riding whip. "A dream," he repeated. He faced his steward. "I am returning to the palace. There is no lady in this land who may wear that slipper. Indeed, there is no slipper. It was created to bewitch me and has since turned back to its baser element, the way the carriage and horses turned back into a pumpkin and mice at midnight. That's why I couldn't find them."

"We couldn't find them because you called off the search,"

said the steward, clearly bewildered. "You said there was no need for haste in following her, that you knew where she lived and would find—" The prince's riding crop just missed the man's face as he leaped back with the ease of long practice.

The prince ignored the interruption. "We searched all night. We were bewitched. *I* was bewitched. There was no heiress. She was an illusion, wrought by evil fairies. I promised to marry an illusion. That illusion has disappeared, releasing me from my oath. Do you understand?" He turned and strode heavily from the room, pushing his way through the crowd without waiting for an answer. The people parted without a word, all eyes on the prince's back as he mounted his horse and turned in the drive.

"Yes, Your Majesty," the steward said, still looking confused. He hesitated, glancing first at the splinters of glass on the floor and then at the four women standing silent in the middle of the room, and finally, with a start, at the people massed in the hallway. He followed the prince out the door. After a moment the sound of hoofbeats came to those standing in the parlor.

26

Mamma staggered toward the door as though to follow the prince, and nearly fell. Jane reached her first, and together, she and Maude helped her to a chair. Isabella ran for a cup of water. Jane stepped back while Maude patted their mother's face with a damp cloth and Isabella held the water to her lips.

A "psst" from the hall made her turn around. When she saw Will standing there, she glanced at Mamma, who seemed to be regaining some of her color, and slipped into the hall.

Will stood awkwardly while the rest of the people of the woods filed quietly out. His ax was slung back into his belt, and his hand rested on it as though for comfort. "What is it?" Jane asked.

Will reached for her with an expression that she couldn't resist. She gave him her hand and let him pull her to him and kiss her deeply.

"Janie?" Maude sounded tentative, as though unsure that the girl standing in the hall kissing a boy was her sister. Will sprang back, his cheeks flushed as deep a red as Jane knew her own to be. "Mamma wants to talk to us," Maude went on, glancing back and forth from one of them to the other.

"I'll—I'll be right there," Jane said weakly, and then, "Go *on,* Maude," as her sister lingered. Maude returned to the South Parlor, casting one last wondering glance at them over her shoulder. "I have to go," Jane told Will. She started to turn, but he grabbed her wrist.

"Come see me? Please? After all this is straightened out?"

She took two steps to close the distance between them and kissed him again. "I will. Now go, and tell your mother that I'll be there when I can." She watched him leave through the large front door, and returned to the South Parlor only after she had heard his light footsteps run down the stairs outside.

Mamma slumped in the big chair. "Are you feeling better?" Jane asked anxiously.

Mamma nodded, then sighed. "Oh, my girls," she said. "Whatever will we do?"

"What do you mean, Mamma?" Jane asked. "It's all right now. The prince has gone, and I don't think he'll be back." She glanced at Isabella.

"I don't mean the prince," Mamma said, and Jane waited for her to continue, *I'm worried that we have no money, that you girls work all the time, that we'll starve if we have another winter like the last one.* But Mamma said nothing more.

"We can sell the diamonds," Isabella said suddenly.

"What diamonds?" Mamma asked.

"The diamonds that a fairy left out for me so I could find the carriage and the gown." Isabella pulled a gleaming handful from her pocket. They glinted in the rosy morning light coming through the window.

"Oh, Isabella, those aren't diamonds," Jane said.

"Yes, they are," Isabella snapped, her chin raised in a hint of her old defiance.

"No, they're not." Jane picked a few out of Isabella's hand. "And no fairy left them for you. I did. They're just paste, from the costume jewelry upstairs."

"They're diamonds," Isabella insisted. For answer, Jane dropped a shining stone on the floor and ground the heel of her boot into it. She lifted her foot, but instead of the white powder she expected, the stone glinted as brightly as before.

"I thought they were false," Jane said, confused. "I thought they were false, but they're real."

"Jane," Mamma said, her voice sounding odd, "you say you left them for Isabella to find. Where did you get them from?"

"In the jewelry box in your—in the room with the rosebud wallpaper. Maude fetched them while I was harnessing Mouse."

"Maude?" Mamma demanded. Maude was trying to slip out of the room, her face a mixture of shame and fear, but Mamma's voice froze her in her tracks. She stood in the doorway, her fingers twisting around one another.

"Did you fetch the jewels from my chamber, as Jane says?"

Maude shook her head rapidly, meeting neither Jane's nor Mamma's eye.

"But I told you to—" Jane began, but Mamma gestured at her to be silent.

Maude continued twisting her fingers, and then blurted, "I didn't want to go up there by myself. I've *never* gone by myself, Janie," she appealed to her sister.

"Then where—" Jane started, but once again Mamma held up her hand.

"So I went to the henhouse," Maude went on. "There's a

box I keep there that I found under one of the nests when I was little. It has rings and pins and brooches in it, and I used to like to play with them even though they're not as big and fancy as the ones in Mamma's box upstairs. That's where I got the diamonds from. There's still a lot of other ones left, but they aren't as shiny as these, so I left them."

"Why didn't you ever tell me?" Jane asked.

"Because you would have taken them," Maude answered.

"Can you show me this box?" Mamma asked. Her voice was tight and peculiar. Maude, obviously relieved at the halt in the interrogation, ran out. Jane avoided Mamma's eye, and then Maude reappeared, holding a small casket of red-and-black painted wood in both hands. Mamma stared at it like someone in a dream.

"Where did you keep it?" Jane asked.

"Under Delilah," Maude answered. Jane smiled. Underneath the ferocious Delilah was a good place to hide something. No wonder no one else had found it.

"Aren't you going to open it?" Isabella asked.

Mamma didn't answer. After a few minutes, she said faintly, "This box," and stopped. "This box," she went on, her voice stronger, "disappeared from my room the night your father left. I've always thought he sold the jewels in it for drink." She sighed. "What was he thinking? Why did he leave it in the henhouse?" The girls glanced at one another without speaking.

"Perhaps," Mamma went on, "perhaps he took them, intending to sell them, and then repented. The jewels are mine, from my mother and father, and their families before them. Maybe at the last moment he—he had enough conscience left not to steal them from me after all, but he didn't want to come back right away, not after the way we parted."

Jane remembered the shouting, the crying, the terrible sounds that she had heard right before her father had left. No, he would not have wanted to come back. He would have sought comfort in gambling and drinking in the city, far away from Mamma. Far away from all of them. She hoped her mother was right, that her father had changed his mind about stealing from her. "He must have been planning to come home later," she ventured. "He hid them where he could find them again when he did."

"And then he never came back," Mamma finished, her voice even lower.

"*Open* it, Mamma." Maude sounded in an agony to see what was inside.

Mamma slowly lifted the lid. She poured the contents, gleaming red and blue and green, onto the table, and then held them to the light one by one. "I remember this necklace. I wore it at the masked ball at the Sutherlands' manor. And this one—" A little laugh escaped her as she picked up a brooch whose sparkling gems were arranged to look like a tiny harlequin's face. "Jane, you chewed on this when you were a baby and took off his ruby nose. Papa had a piece of red glass put in its place, see? But the rest isn't glass. It's diamonds and rubies and sapphires."

She swept the glittering pile into her hand and dropped the gems back in the box. "Did you pick up all the stones, Isabella?"

"I think so," Isabella answered. She reached into her pocket and pulled out a gleaming handful, and placed them carefully on the table, where they twinkled. "I found them after that voice called me. Jane, was that you?"

"Voice?" Jane asked. "I didn't make a voice. Truly, Mamma, I didn't."

"When did you hear it?" Mamma asked Isabella.

"About an hour after you left. It was so dark and cold, and I was sitting by the fire wishing I had gone with you. Then someone said to me— Are you sure it wasn't you?" she asked Jane again.

Jane shook her head in wonderment. "I was in the wagon by then. We were on our way to the palace."

"Well, it spoke quietly, so it was hard to tell who it was," Isabella went on. "But it said something like, 'If you would find your heart's desire, gather your courage and leave the fire. Take yourself to the prince's throne, and at the ball you will find your home.'" She looked at them apologetically. "I think that's what it said. Something like that, anyway."

"You must have been dreaming," Mamma said.

"I wasn't. I know because when I held up a candle, the light fell on the diamonds on the floor. They sparkled. So I picked them up and followed them to the stable, and there stood Mouse and the carriage, and my gown was hanging on a hook. I put it on and found my glass slippers, and then I went to the ball," she finished simply.

Mamma looked dazed.

Jane picked up one of the bracelets. It was beautiful, with green stones that caught even the faint light, but even more beautiful was the knowledge of what she could do with it. "We can buy more goats and maybe another cow, and we can hire dairymen and have a fine dairy."

"And once you have money again, surely one of your relatives will be willing to take you in," Mamma said to Isabella. The girl scuffed the ground with her toe. Jane saw that her face was turning pink, and she was biting her lip. What was the matter with her?

"Does she *have* to leave?" Maude asked suddenly.

Jane turned to her sister in surprise. "But doesn't she want— Isabella? Isabella, what do *you* want to do?" Isabella shrugged, and then made a quick gesture with her hand, indicating the messy room, the cold fireplace, the old comfortable chair pulled up in front of it. To Jane this was as clear as words. "She wants to stay, Mamma."

Mamma knelt before the girl. "Look at me," she said softly. Isabella lifted her face. Her eyes were clouded with tears, and her nose was running. "Oh, my dear." Mamma pulled a handkerchief from her sleeve and gave it to Isabella, who wiped her eyes and blew her nose.

"I do *not* want you to leave," Mamma said. "I thought *you* did. I want you to stay. This is your home. Your father would have wanted it this way." And at that, the girl began crying in earnest. Then Maude started crying, too, without seeming to know why, and Jane felt herself close to tears. So Maude made them all hot rose hip tea, and they sat and drank it while the day grew brighter around them. Maude picked up the egg basket, and Jane started for the barn. She stopped at the door and turned back.

"Eggs or barn work, Isabella?" Jane asked, and for an instant the girl hesitated, her mouth set in that familiar stubborn line. Then it softened.

"Eggs," Isabella said. Maude took her hand, and the two of them ran outside. Jane lingered in the doorway.

"Well, Jane?" Mamma asked.

It came out of her all in a rush. "Why don't we move to the

hunting lodge? There isn't enough here to repair the whole house and hire servants—"

"*Live* in the hunting lodge?" Mamma's voice was incredulous, but Jane sensed a tinge of hesitation, so she pressed her advantage.

"What you always say about being a Halsey?" Jane began. She didn't know how to put it into words, but she tried. "Being a Halsey doesn't *really* mean living in this house and not working hard, does it? Wouldn't we still be Halseys if we kept a dairy and lived in the hunting lodge, as long as we behaved honorably and treated people well?"

Mamma didn't answer for so long that Jane feared she never would. Then Mamma gave her a tremulous smile. "We'll just have to see."

Jane smiled back and looked outside, where Maude and Isabella waited for her. The first church bells were ringing, warning that services would start in an hour. *I hope they'll bring Frances for her christening*, Jane thought. *Surely they will.* Her heart lifted at the thought of seeing the baby wearing her brand-new robe in the arms of her mother, with all the rest of the family there. Especially Will.

"I'll find four eggs," Maude was saying.

"I'll find six," Isabella shot back.

"Six?" Maude's scorn was unmistakable.

"Don't quarrel!" Jane warned them through the window, but the girls ran across the yard and Jane followed them out into the sunshine, which carried the first hint of the warmth of summer to come.

epilogue

Left to itself, the house fell ever more quickly into decay. Animals crept into the pantry and the kitchen, eating the few crumbs and scraps that remained and making their dens inside the walls. Soon, owls discovered this abundant food supply, and they built heavy nests in the entry hall and the ballroom, straining the already weakened rafters. Great gaps appeared in the moldy walls.

When the cord holding a portrait to the wall rotted through, nobody was there to see if it was Great-Great-Grandmamma Esther or Great-Grandpapa Edwin who lay facedown in the dust. A few years later, heavy snow caused a great section of the roof to cave in, but even the thunder of its collapse was not loud enough to be heard in the warm little lodge at the edge of the forest. The laughter of the wedding guests and the music of the fiddles drowned it out. But the musicians' gallery in the enormous ballroom fell on an autumn day when all was quiet, startling a baby out of his sleep.

"Shhh, my darling," whispered the baby's mother, as his father went to see what the noise was.

"Just your family ghosts again, Jane," he said when he returned.

He picked up his fretful little boy. "Hush, my son—here's some of your Aunt Maude's teething syrup," and he rocked the baby back to sleep in his strong woodcutter's arms.

And when an errant bolt of lightning in a summer thunderstorm struck the decaying pile several years later, no one attempted to put out the blaze. It had been a wet spring, and there was little danger of the fire spreading, so the villagers and the people of the woods gathered with the family and watched the flames reach higher and higher. They backed away when the heat grew uncomfortable, and rats and mice fled from the ruins and ran squeaking over their feet into the trees behind them.

"Poor little things," Isabella said, holding her daughter's hand, as the little girl leaped and danced to avoid the scrabbling claws. "Don't be frightened, Serafina. They're just running from danger. They mean you no harm."

And in a few more years, the magnificent mansion with its sweeping staircase, its marble floors, its glaring portraits, was nothing more than a memory. As time went on, the history of the house and of the family that had once lived in it turned into the stuff of legend, and what was true and what was story blended until nobody could say where one ended and the other began.

*****

acknowledgments

I wrestled with this story for a long time. Reimagining a well-loved and much-retold fairy tale without losing its heart was tricky, and the creation of a new story while staying within the confines of one of the world's most familiar tales presented a set of challenges that I had never before faced in quite the same way. If I've had any success in meeting these challenges, it is largely due to the support, advice, and patience of my critique group (Shirley Amitrano, Thea Gammans, Candie Moonshower, Cheryl Mendenhall, Carole Stice, and Cheryl Zach); my perceptive and enthusiastic agent, Lara Perkins; my talented and energetic editor, Annie Stone; and always, my husband, Greg Giles.

questions for discussion

1. What does Jane think the Halsey name signifies? What about her mother? What power do you think is in a family's name and reputation, and should children feel a responsibility to live up to that ideal? Is it ever wrong to take pride in your heritage?

2. What is the difference between living up to an ideal and closing your eyes to reality? Where in the text do you find evidence of the different characters doing one or the other of these?

3. Retelling a classic fairy tale is a very popular storytelling strategy. What are some other *Cinderella* retellings in today's literature and film? What do you think makes a retelling particularly successful or interesting? Why do you think *Cinderella* is the most popular tale to retell?

4. The story of Cinderella is familiar, but Tracy Barrett brings new life to the tale by shifting the perspective from Cinder-

ella to her "evil" stepsister, Jane. What other perspectives might be interesting from a narrative standpoint? How would Maude tell the story that Jane tells in *The Stepsister's Tale?* How would Will tell it?

5. Are Jane and Maude unfairly predisposed to resent their new sister, Ella? What about vice versa? What defines a family, if not simply blood relations?

6. Mamma is too stuck in her family's past to be an effective parent, and Harry spoils Isabella. Find some examples (not always human!) of good parenting in the text that the author uses to serve as a contrast to these characters' poor parenting.

7. In *The Stepsister's Tale,* outsiders believe Ella's claim that she is a victim because she is charming and beautiful. What typical signals does a storyteller use to relay information about which characters are "good guys" versus "bad guys," and how does the author use these signals for other purposes in this retelling?

8. Why does Jane change her mind about trying to get Ella married to the prince? When do you start seeing a shift in her thinking about this?

9. Jane thinks that Will is scornful of her because their families belong to different social classes. Will thinks the same of Jane. Find places in the text that show why they think this, and where one of them has misinterpreted an action or words of the other.

10. In many Western societies of the past, people usually married for money or to improve their social standing, as Mamma and Harry do, and no one thought anything was wrong with this. Do you think these are acceptable reasons for marrying today? Does Jane? How do you know how she feels about this?

11. Do you think that a fairy godmother (or some other supernatural being) told Isabella to go to the stable and find the carriage and the ball gown, or did the suggestion come from some other person, or from Isabella's imagination? Find evidence in the text to support your opinion.

12. One theme of *The Stepsister's Tale* is the importance of the difference between appearance and reality. Find examples in the text of places where appearance and reality don't mesh.